FLASHBACK

ABOUT THE AUTHOR

Geoffrey Lewis was born in Oxford, in 1947. Educated at the City's High School, and Hatfield University (then a polytechnic), he has since followed a varied career, including spells as a research chemist, security guard, and professional photographer. After many years in the motor trade, he is currently the owner and captain of a canal-based passenger boat.

The author

Photographer, bell-ringer, and American car enthusiast, he lives in a narrowboat on the Grand Union Canal.

Flashback is the first of his D.I. David Russell novels to be published, with two more in the series to be published shortly.

TITLES TO FOLLOW FROM GEOFFREY LEWIS:

STRANGERS   The Second David Russell Novel
WINTER'S TALE   The Third David Russell Novel

And *CYCLE* - the investigation that saw the beginnings of the David Russell/Doug Rimmer partnership.

FLASHBACK

A D.I. David Russell novel

Geoffrey Lewis

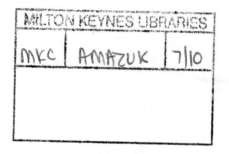

SGM
Publishing

ISBN 0-9545624-0-2

Printed in Great Britain

First published in Great Britain in 2003 by

SGM Publishing
20 Alexandra Road, Gravesend, Kent DA12 2QQ

For Sonnie & Sioux -
without whose critical encouragement,
it would never have happened.

PROLOGUE

'Malcolm Andrew Mathers, the jury last week found you guilty of two serious sexual assaults, both perpetrated upon young children. Since then, I have been deliberating deeply upon an appropriate sentence to pass which will reflect the seriousness of your crimes, but yet allow you the possibility of rehabilitation.

'Your counsel has asked that I take into consideration a further fourteen similar offences. On the face of it, this submission might be taken to show a degree of remorse on your part for the harm and suffering you have caused these children – however, I believe that I see in it an extension of the callous, calculating cynicism that has marked your attitude throughout this trial. You have sought repeatedly not only to discredit the factual evidence given against you, but also to cast into doubt the morals and truthfulness of the witnesses brought by the prosecution, in particular the two young girls who have shown the courage and fortitude to stand here and bring their accusations against you.

'I cannot commend too highly these two children, whose strength and bravery have made this trial possible. Their respective families also have shown great fortitude and resilience, providing the loving and supportive background that has held them firm in their difficult task, and helped them to recover from the horror and humiliation that your actions have heaped upon them.

'In, at this late stage, standing up and admitting to these additional offences, I am tempted to reply to you with the popular phrase, "too little, too late". Rather than an expression of your acceptance of your own guilt, I suspect this admission may be made, no doubt on the advice of your counsel, with the intention that, having been admitted and considered at this time, they cannot be brought forward at any time in future, to be held against you in any further proceedings.

'In the light of your admission, the two convictions decided against you could be considered as specimen counts. It is my view that you are at present a real danger to young girls, and therefore must be subject to a custodial sentence of some severity. However, I must take count of your admission, however late or reluctantly given.

'You are still a young man, Mr Mathers. It is to be hoped that, with the time to consider and hopefully acknowledge your guilt, you may yet become a useful and even a valuable member of society. I strongly recommend that you take advantage of the next few years to seek counselling and psychiatric help in order to rid yourself of these unnatural desires. You will go to prison for five years.'

(From the proceedings of Lewes Crown Court, October 14th 1974, Regina vs. Mathers, sentencing hearing.)

CHAPTER ONE

'I'm going round to Emily's, Mum!'

Harriet Buckland looked up from the meat she was slicing on the chopping board, and smiled at her younger child:

'All right, Han, but don't be late – dinner's at seven, I want you home for six-thirty, okay?'

'Okay!' The girls' reply was bright and carefree.

'And you be careful – it's getting dark already. Come home by the roads, right, not the footpath across the field.'

'Yes, Mum!' With a last backward glance of her blue eyes and a toss of her long black hair, the girl was gone.

Harriet brushed the hair from her forehead with the back of her hand, and cast a long look at the kitchen door where her daughter had departed. Ten years old – it didn't seem possible! Just yesterday, it seemed, Hannah had been a little bundle to be cradled in her arms, fed at her breast, rocked to sleep when she cried. And now? A skinny kid, but pretty. *So much like me at her age!* The same long thin build, the same glossy black hair; but she had her father's freckled face, and his eyes. *Those eyes!* That child could charm the devil, or enrage a saint, with one look from those eyes. One moment wide, innocent and appealing, the next they could flash with mischief, narrowing in amusement as her clear, refreshing laughter echoed around the room. No wonder she could twist her Daddy around her little finger!

The meat diced for the pie, Harriet laid the knife aside. She turned towards the door into the hallway, and called out:

'Josh! Do you two want a drink, I'm making some coffee?'

'What?' A voice echoed from above.

'Coffee, Josh?' She repeated, louder.

'Please, Mum!' She grinned and went to fill the kettle. What was he doing, closeted in his room with his mate? Playing on the computer, probably. No, certainly! The two boys didn't seem to ever do anything else these days. She sometimes worried that her son didn't go out more, didn't seem interested in much of anything unless it came on a CD-rom – but then, she shrugged, that was all that boys seemed to want these days. And he did enjoy his football, to be fair. Twelve years old, not far off being a teenager – all too soon, she and Brian would be coping with adolescent moods, worrying about girlfriends. She looked at the clock on the wall – quarter to five. Brian would be home about half past, as it was Friday; if she had the pie in the oven, they'd have time to relax together for a while before she had to put the chips on, ready for Hannah to get home, hungry and begging for her dinner.

* * *

Eager and energetic, Hannah jogged along in the gathering gloom, intermittently slowing to a quick walk. Mid-March, and the evenings were getting longer – but it was a dull grey day, and the dusk was closing in although it wasn't yet five o'clock. Emily wasn't expecting her – but she'd be in, wouldn't she? Once she'd changed out of her school dress into slacks and a sweatshirt, Hannah had found herself at a loose end. Josh had brought Harry home with him from his school, and the two boys had promptly disappeared into his room; Mum was busy getting the dinner ready, Daddy wouldn't be home for a while; and it was only a few minutes walk (or jog!) across the field to Emily's. It would take her a bit longer to get home later – she'd have to allow for that when she set off – because Daddy didn't like her walking across the field in the dark. She'd have to go along Alderley Park Avenue towards the town until she could take the road that came out in Elwood village, near the post office. From there it was only a minute or two back home along Barfield Lane to her house.

The path she was following eventually came out into the cul-de-sac which formed the very end of Alderley Park Avenue, but Hannah turned from it before its end into a narrow alley which ran along the backs of the gardens on the near side of the road. Three doors along, she went through a gate into a garden, and walked confidently up to the back door of the house as it banged to behind her. She knocked, but then opened the door and walked straight in:

'Em? It's me, Han. Where are you?'

There was no reply. She was about to call out again, but then she heard a door open and close somewhere above her, and footsteps scrambling down the stairs:

'Em?'

'No, she's out.' A boy of about fourteen appeared at the foot of the stairs, looking rather dishevelled, his brown hair awry.

'Where is she, Brad?'

'She went shopping with Mum, right after school. Was she expecting you to come?'

Hannah shook her head:

'No – I just…didn't have anything to do, so I thought… I'd better go home.' She turned to the door, but the boy stepped forward and took her arm:

'No – wait.' She looked up at him, expectantly….

* * *

That same evening, Tran Quoc Hsung pulled up outside the seedy-looking house in Bedford Road, one of the streets of terraced ex-railway workers houses off of Midland Road. He stepped out of the white Lexus, smiling as he always did at the solid-sounding 'thunk' as the door closed.

Tran had entered Britain as a small boy, with his refugee parents, in the early seventies. Applying himself diligently to his studies, he had become a star pupil at the Matthew Price School in Grancester, graduating with a number of first-class A levels. But then instead of pursuing an academic career, he had begun a small business making minor components for the electronics industry, at first in his parents' garden shed. The business had grown, slowly at the beginning, but then taking off rapidly with the development of the computer and mobile phone market. Now, Hsung Electronics was based in a smart industrial unit on the outskirts of the great Techno-city of Cambridge, and its owner was quite a wealthy man.

Somehow, along the way, he had married Martha Simpson, a slim, pretty girl with long golden-blond hair and soft blue eyes, from along the street where the Hsung family had lived. The marriage didn't last: Long after both partners had, if the truth were told, given up on the whole arrangement, Tran had left. Martha stayed in the house in Bedford Road, with their two-year-old daughter; Tran moved from a small flat in Warrenton, the poorer end of Grancester, to another terraced house, and now lived in a smart, modern house in Cherry Hinton, on the edge of Cambridge, with his new wife, a fellow Viet-namese refugee, and their two younger children. He still kept in touch with his daughter, although contact with his ex-wife remained fraught, to say the least; Martha, to put it politely, had a bit of a drink problem.

He knocked at the front door; it flew open, to reveal a slim girl of around twelve years old:

'Daddy!' Her arms were around his neck, she was kissing his cheek, making him laugh for the sheer joy of seeing her:

'Kim! It's lovely to see you, darling!'

'You too, Daddy. I've got my things ready – let's go!' He held the girl away from him:

'I should speak to your mother, Kim.' The girl's blue eyes clouded:

'She's – lying down, Daddy. I shouldn't disturb her, if I were you.' He looked into his child's eyes:

'Okay – if you say so. Is she all right?'

'Oh – the same as ever; you know!' Still, he hesitated; but then, grabbing the bag from inside the door, he smiled at her:

'Okay – come on then!'

Kim Lee Hsung was eleven, going on twelve. She loved her monthly visit to her father's house, and not just because he spoiled her rotten – it gave her such pleasure as she couldn't describe to play big sister to her two little half-brothers; and she loved her step-mother, Liu. Life, for those brief days, was so different from the routine and drudgery of Bedford Road. Tall for her age, she mostly took after her mother, at least physically; blond and blue-eyed, only her features betrayed the Oriental in her make-up, giving her that almost mystical beauty that is the best blend of Europe and Asia. Tran Quoc was proud of his little girl – she was so cute and lovely, and she was so capable, too, looking after her sad mother so well. He smiled across at her as he started the car and drove off; at least he could give her a good break from all that, even if it did pain him to have to return her to it at the end of the weekend.

* * *

'I can't offer you the price you were asking, I'm afraid' George Andrews had given the Victorian dining table and chairs a thorough examination. He had gone to the house in Alderley Park Crescent after a telephone call from Andrea Johnston, the owner, offering him the antique furniture.

'Oh, I see.' Graham, Andrea's husband, sounded disappointed.

'The problem is that the repairs to those two chairs were rather amateurish – no collector would pay top price for them. And there's the damage to the table leg, as well. I'd be lucky to get the price you're asking at retail, so you'll understand I'd have to buy them for a good deal less.'

'Yes – I can see your point, Mr Andrews. What do you suggest?'

'If you want the price, your best bet is to advertise them privately. You could well get that sort of money from a direct sale. I would make an offer, but as I said, it would be substantially lower. Do you want to think about it?'

'That might be best – what do you think, Andy?' Johnston turned to his wife.

'Maybe…' She looked around at Andrews: 'We'll be away for a month, visiting our daughter and her family in Australia – perhaps we could call you when we get back?'

'Of course. When are you going?' The woman laughed:

'Tonight! We're driving down to Heathrow shortly, staying in a hotel and catching a flight first thing in the morning.' Andrews smiled:

'I envy you! All that sunshine, when we're stuck with this cold grey weather! Doesn't seem like Spring at all yet, does it?'

'It doesn't! We are looking forward to it, I must say. Graham or I will get in touch when we're back, then?'

'That'll be fine. I'll wait to hear from you.'

'Thank you for coming over, Mr Andrews; goodbye for now.'

'You're most welcome – any time. Goodbye, Mrs Johnston.'

Graham showed the antiques dealer to the door, shook his hand as he departed. In the car, Andrews sat in thought for a moment before starting the engine; he should go straight to the hospice, Sheila would be waiting for him. But the thought of facing her illness yet again plunged him into gloom – he could use a break, a little light relief! But that wasn't going to happen. He started the car, drove off into Alderley Park Avenue, headed towards the town.

CHAPTER TWO

'Police in Grancester are becoming increasingly concerned for the safety of a ten-year-old girl who hasn't been seen since yesterday evening. Hannah Buckland left her home in Elwood village shortly after four-thirty, to walk to a friend's house in the nearby suburb of Alderley Park, but failed to arrive. The alarm was raised by her parents when she didn't return home for her evening meal – police are appealing for anyone who saw the girl, who is described as slim, with blue eyes and long black hair, wearing dark blue trousers and a grey sweat-shirt, after that time, to come forward. Meanwhile, a search of the area is continuing.'

Lunch-time television news saw the first public announcement of Hannah's disappearance. Earlier, on his arrival for duty, Detective-Inspector David Russell had been summoned into his superior's presence; as he entered the Detective-Superintendent's office in the new concrete-and-glass station, Wilson stood up from behind his desk:

'You'll have heard about our missing kiddie?' He looked up at the younger man through his black-framed spectacles, running a hand unconsciously through his balding grey hair.

'Yes, sir. Jock Buchanan told me as I came in. Do we have any idea what's happened to her?'

'Not really, Russell. She left home to visit her friend, but never got there – it's ten minutes walk, at the most, across the field path which her mother believes she took. The mother called us

17

when she didn't come home for her dinner at seven o'clock, and Uniform have been searching the area ever since.'

'No sign, I take it?'

'None.'

'Why didn't the friend alert someone when she didn't arrive?'

'She wasn't expected, apparently. Anyway, the friend was out, shopping in town with her mother – only an older brother was in, and he says no-one called.'

'So she'd been gone a couple of hours by the time we knew about it?'

'That's right. According to the family, she's not the type to wander off alone, or lose track of the time – we're assuming that the most likely thing is that she had some kind of accident. The path skirts the old woods between Elwood and Alderley Park – Uniform's boys are going through there inch by inch as we speak.'

'If not...?' Wilson's brow furrowed as if in pain:

'That's where you come in, David. I want you to begin a background investigation – if she's been abducted, we need to know pronto of any likely suspects, be they family or friends, known offenders, whatever. The Chief Super's told uniform that the ground search has got to be to the finest detail, and to cover all of the woodland, the adjoining fields, and that back alley that runs along behind the houses on the Elwood side of Alderley Park Avenue. He'll expand it further afield once that's done. You'll need to run a house-to-house, in Elwood and Alderley Park – get Doug Rimmer to handle that – and dig into anything else you think might be relevant. You know the form. We'll put out an appeal through the local radio and TV, give them a press conference this afternoon if we haven't found her by then. I'll want you in on that, David.'

'Of course, sir. I'll get started on the enquiries, and see you, what, after lunch?'

'That'll be fine. We'll face the wolf-pack about four.'

'Okay, sir.' Russell turned and left.

On the floor below, he called Detective-Sergeant Rimmer to follow him as he passed the C.I.D. room. In his own office, the tall, sandy-haired D.I. flopped into the seat behind his desk; the Sergeant, shorter, stocky and dark-haired, perched on its edge as was his regular habit:

'The missing kid?' he asked. Russell looked up at his assistant out of hazel eyes, and sighed:

'Yes, Doug. Mr Wilson wants us to start the background work, looking for reasons, suspects, what-have-you. Can you start a house-to-house, in the village where she lives, and around Alderley Park, where she was supposed to be going when she vanished? Get what help you need, the Super'll back you.'

'Are we assuming she's been abducted?'

'Covering all eventualities, really – but in point of fact, what are the possibilities? They haven't found her despite searching through the night – if she's lying hurt somewhere, you'd think she'd have heard them and called out, even if they missed her. We'll need to check, of course, but according to the family she's unlikely to have wandered off alone, and if she had any reason for running away, you'd have thought she'd have made some attempt to take at least some extra clothes with her. She was only wearing a sweater and jeans, apparently.'

'Mmm – right. I'll get teams organised for the house-to-house, and check the sex offender's register for anyone around here who might be inclined to grab a little girl. Could there be any other reason for someone to have taken her?'

'Not that I know of. I don't think the family are wealthy enough for it to be a ransom job – I'll go to see them straight away, find out if there could be anything else to look for. You'd better get in touch with her school, as well, talk to the teachers, pupils in her class, see if they can add anything.'

'Okay – I'll get started. Bang goes our quiet weekend!'

'Yeah, don't tell me – I'm supposed to be taking Daniel sailing tomorrow. He'll be disappointed if we can't make it.'

'He's a good kid, boss, he understands.'

'I know he does; but I hate letting him down.' The D.I.'s twelve-year-old son shared his father's enjoyment of building and sailing scale-model yachts, and the Sunday was to have been the maiden voyage for the boy's latest project, constructed from a kit which had been a Christmas present from his Grandparents.

* * *

Shortly before two o'clock, Russell returned to his office. The interview with Brian and Harriet Buckland had been difficult, partly because of the obvious distress of the parents of the missing child, but especially because it had been necessary for him to probe into the family background, raising, despite his best attempts to approach the subject diplomatically, the suggestion that there might be deeper, darker reasons behind their daughter's disappearance. Side by side on the settee in the comfortable living room of Ivy Cottage, Harriet Buckland, tall, slim, black-haired, her soft brown eyes shaded with worry, and her husband, shorter, well-built, the flecks of grey in his light brown hair matching those in the neatly-trimmed goatee beard, had told him everything and nothing: Everything they could, but nothing that seemed to help in his quest to find their daughter. They had provided him with all the information he asked for, been helpful in the extreme even through their fears – but the experience had left him feeling exhausted, emotionally drained. While they spoke, quiet, controlled, their fears evident but unstated, their son had come down from his room to join them, snuggling between them, his own concern for his sister plain on his face, shining in his grey eyes.

Back in his office, he sat down at his desk, leaning back and swinging his feet up onto its edge, to think through what he had learned so far about Hannah's disappearance. Moments later, Rimmer knocked and entered, perching on the edge of the desk as usual, a sheaf of papers in his hand. Russell looked up:

'What have you got, Doug?'

'Not much, yet, sir. Still nothing from the search, no sign of the kid, in the woods or the fields. Strongarm reckons they've covered the ground with a fine tooth comb, no chance they could've missed her if she was lying hurt anywhere.' Chief Inspector Clive Armstrong of the uniform branch was co-ordinating the search crews.

'Hmm. Where are they looking now?'

'They're going through all the back gardens, along that alley behind the houses in Alderley Park Avenue. And another team's searching in and around Elwood, in case she's anywhere in the village. The Super's called in all kind of help from County; I've pinched a couple of spare constables to help with the house-to-house enquiries.'

'How's that going?'

'I've got three teams out, one in the village, one covering each side of the Avenue. They've instructions to call me if anything interesting shows up. So far, the only item which has any bearing at all is a neighbour who noticed another boy going into number 197, where the Farncomes live. That's the friends family. Of course, at that time of day, in such miserable weather, not many people are about – kids are all home from school, mums are getting meals ready, dads still at work. Or any permutation thereof!'

Russell gave a thoughtful frown:

'Did the friend's brother say anything about having a mate of his own round?' Rimmer shook his head:

'Not that I recall, from what uniform have passed on. I haven't been to talk to them, I thought you'd want to be there.'

'Right. We'll do that next, Doug. Anything from the school?'

'She goes to Elwood Primary – nothing so far. We've been in touch with most of the teachers, and they've no useful information that I can see. I'll carry on contacting the families of the kids in her class over the weekend.'

'What about known customers?'

Rimmer waved the sheaf of papers:

'Just these few. And none of them look very promising. Most of them live some way away, around the county – I'll check each of them out, just to be sure, but their previous records don't really fit with the idea of abducting a kid. They're mostly cautions for inappropriate behaviour, a couple of possession of illicit material. This is the only real possibility:' He handed a sheet to his superior.

'Mmm. Kevin Olsen – I remember him. Keith Foreman put him away, what, nine years ago?'

'That's right, sir. He got six years, for raping his sister's nine-year-old. The family's moved away, up to Manchester, but he came back here after his release. He's been good since, as far as we know.'

'Yes; it was a nasty business, the father threatened to bury him if he ever went near them again – we had to warn him off. We'd better talk to him, later. The Super wants me in on a press conference at four.' He grinned; Rimmer gave a chuckle. Wilson's discomfort at facing the press was a source of mild amusement throughout the station. Russell swung his feet to the floor and stood up:

'Come on – let's go and see the – what's their names?'

'Farncome, sir. John and Carole – the daughter, Hannah Buckland's friend, is Emily, and there's the son, Bradley.'

'Right – let's go.'

The two collected Russell's Jeep Station Wagon from the station car park and headed for the classy suburb of Alderley Park, to the North-West of the town. As he drove, Rimmer asked:

'How did you get on with the Bucklands, boss?'

Russell ran a hand through his thick, sandy hair, in unconscious echo of the C.I.D. chief's habitual gesture:

'All right, I guess. Why is it things like this always seem to happen to the people who least deserve it? They come across as the nicest folk you could wish for, a happy, well-knit family, without a care in the world. The father's the manager of Barfield Antiques; the mother does the books for the business at home.

The owner is a guy called Andrews, lives in Grancester, on the Embankment; he leaves things to them most of the time, apparently. It's so difficult, with folk like them, trying to probe into the background without causing them a lot more distress.'

'Nothing to find?'

'Doesn't seem so, Doug. They're a quiet family, comfortable without being wealthy, no apparent enemies, no reason for anyone to want to get at them. Your house-to-house should give us the external picture of them – but I don't really expect it to tell us anything much different.'

'Was – is – the girl the only child?' Russell glanced across the car:

'Your slip is showing, Sergeant! Let's not jump too far ahead, even if the possibilities are narrowing down – this could all still be quite innocent, she could turn up fit and well, even now. But no, to answer your question; there's an older brother, Joshua. He's twelve, and desperately worried about his sister – he was home, playing in his room with a schoolfriend yesterday, when she left the house. The mother was preparing the evening meal; the father arrived home as expected, about five-thirty. They started to worry when she was late, and called the station when she'd missed the meal-time.'

'So, if she has been taken, we've no real ideas who or where, have we sir?'

'Not as yet, Doug. Let's see what we can learn from the friend and her family, and then get this press briefing out of the way. Once that's over, we'll compare notes and see what conclusions we can draw, all right?'

'Right, sir. I should have the house-to-house results for you; and anything else that uniform might come across in the meantime.'

Silence fell in the car. A few minutes later, Rimmer drew up outside number 197, Alderley Park Avenue.

CHAPTER THREE

The front door was opened almost immediately upon Rimmer's knock. The woman who stood there was in her forties, not unattractive in a rather buxom way, with thick curly brown hair and dark eyes, casually but not inexpensively dressed.

'Hello?' The two men flashed their I.D.s:

'Sergeant Rimmer, Grancester police; this is Inspector Russell. Mrs Farncome?'

'That's right, Sergeant. This will be about little Hannah?'

'Yes, Ma'am. Can we come in and talk to you?'

'Of course – follow me.' She led them inside, into a comfortably-furnished sitting room, and waved her hand for them to take a seat. The two officers took the two arm chairs; Mrs Farncome sat on the settee facing them:

'You haven't found her, I take it?'

'I'm afraid not, Mrs Farncome. We're still searching, of course, but there's no sign of her as yet.'

'Do you think…someone's taken her?' Russell sighed:

'We don't know. It has to be a possibility, of course – and we're running short of other ideas. That's why the Sergeant and I are here, to see if you can give us any suggestions about what might have happened to her. After all, you know the child and her family?'

The woman released a heavy breath through her lips:

'We know Hannah pretty well, of course, she's been Emily's

24

best friend most of the way through school. But I wouldn't say we know her family that well. Brian and Harriet seem like really nice people – they more or less run the antique shop in Barfield, you know – but we only know them through their daughter, we don't really socialise with them directly.'

'Is there any reason for that?' Rimmer took up the questions. She shook her head:

'No reason – it's just that they have their circle of friends, the same as we do. We meet them at school functions, and things like that, and get on very well – They're very good to Emily, taking her out with Hannah quite a lot. They even let the two girls help in the shop, sometimes, and I know Emily loves that!'

'You know Joshua Buckland?'

'Hannah's brother? Of course! He's a nice boy. Oh, he fights with his sister occasionally, but that's nothing. He loves his little sister, really – you can see it in the way he treats her a lot of the time. John and I have taken him along a few times, when we've been taking the girls somewhere and Brian and Harriet have been busy.'

'He's not a friend of your son's? She laughed:

'Oh no! Bradley's fourteen – to be caught playing with a younger boy at that age? Totally unacceptable!' Rimmer smiled:

'So you're not aware of any problems, any tension, in her family?'

'No, far from it. They always seem to be as happy and relaxed a family as you could wish for. You want tension, you should look at us, Sergeant!'

'Oh?' She smiled at him:

'It's not that bad, really! Brad's had some trouble at school, and it's caused some stress between him and his father. Oh, he's not a difficult kid, not like some; but it seems he's got under the influence of one or two unpleasant types, older boys in his class. He's been involved in one or two incidents, his teacher thinks because they've intimidated him into going along with them. But that's our problem; It can hardly have anything to do with Hannah, can it?'

'I doubt it!'

'Is your husband home, Mrs Farncome?' Russell roused himself.

'John's in the garden – he's got Emily out there, helping him, trying to keep her mind off Hannah. Do you want to talk to them?'

'Briefly, if we may. And I'll need to talk to Bradley, as well.'

'Of course, Inspector. Brad's upstairs, I'll call him in a minute; Come with me.'

She rose, and led the two officers through a well-appointed kitchen into the back garden. As they left the house, Russell asked:

'I understand that Hannah is in the habit of coming in this way when she comes to see Emily?' The woman glanced back:

'That's right, if she's walked across the field. It's quicker than going round into the road, to the front door. She knows she's always welcome, if we're in, so she comes to the back door.'

'She would come into the garden?'

'Oh yes! She's left notes on the kitchen door once or twice, when she's called and we've been out.'

Part of the way down the long garden, sloping gently to the fence and the pathway behind, they found John Farncome, a short stocky figure, looking younger than his almost fifty years but prematurely white-haired. Kneeling beside him, her dungarees muddy-kneed, trowel in hand, was a slightly dumpy child of about ten.

'John – this is Inspector Russell, and Sergeant…I'm sorry?'

'Rimmer, Mrs Farncome!'

'Sergeant Rimmer. I'm so sorry, I'm hopeless with names! They'd like to talk to you about Hannah.'

The man brushed the dirt from his hands as he turned soft blue eyes on the officers; the little girl leapt to her feet, showering earth from the trowel over Russell's polished shoes:

'Have you found her? Oh, sorry!' She looked at the mud

spattering the shiny black leather. Russell smiled as he squatted down, to bring his eyes to her level:

'We're still looking for her, Emily. And we won't stop until we have found her.'

The child, so much a smaller version of her mother, regarded him gravely out of big brown eyes, and nodded, making her thick wavy hair dance in the spring sunshine.

'Can you tell me about Hannah?' She nodded again.

'Can you think of any reason why she might have decided to go away?' The girl looked puzzled, wrinkling her pert nose at him:

'What, on her *own?*' It was Russell's turn to nod:

'No! She wouldn't want to do that! Where would she *go?*'

'I don't know, Emily. I wondered if there was somewhere, maybe a secret place in the woods, she might have gone if she was upset, or anything?' The child shook her head; then she looked at Russell out of wide eyes:

'Not in the woods – but we've got our den, by the river. We go there sometimes, when I go to Hannah's to play. It's just outside Elwood, not far from her house. She *might* go there on her own, I suppose – but she wouldn't stay there *all night!*'

'No, I don't suppose she would; but we'll have a look there, just in case! Thank you, Emily.' The girl returned his smile, as he asked:

'You know Hannah's brother, Joshua?'

'Josh? Of course!'

'Do you like him?' She smiled, and nodded:

'Yes; he's all right. We don't have a lot to do with him.'

'Oh? Why not?' The girl looked puzzled by the question:

''Cos he's a *boy,* of course!'

'Ah – right. Did he get on with Hannah? I mean, did they argue much, or anything like that?' She shook her head:

'Not much. Sometimes.' She shrugged her shoulders.

'You don't think they might have had a row, and she's gone off to be on her own somewhere?'

'No!' The girl's expression was scornful: 'Hannah wouldn't go and hide like that, she'd give him what for!' Russell laughed gently:

'Okay, Emily! Thank you for talking to me – you've been very helpful.'

'I'm sorry about getting mud on your shoes' she said as he rose to his feet; he smiled down at her:

'Don't worry about it – I get much muddier in this job, sometimes.'

He turned to John Farncome, who had been standing watching his exchange with the child:

'Could you spare me a minute, as well, Mr Farncome?'

'Of course, Inspector. Go inside with Mummy, Em, and get yourself washed, I'll be in in a minute.' He watched his wife and daughter head for the house, and then turned to the two officers:

'What can I do for you gentlemen?' Rimmer responded:

'Your wife has already told us what she can about the Buckland family, and of course we have the statements you all gave to the officers last night, about your own movements. The Inspector and I are trying to get an overall picture, trying to find out what might have happened to Hannah after she left home to come here.' The white head nodded:

'Yes, of course. Tell me, do you think she's been abducted?'

'We don't know, sir. It has to be considered, of course, but we're following all possible avenues at the moment.'

'Hence your questions to Emily?'

'Exactly, sir.' Russell concurred. Rimmer went on:

'You yourself didn't get home until quite late, sir?'

'No. I usually work late on Fridays, Sergeant. I was home around seven-thirty last night, which is about normal.'

'Where do you work, sir?'

'I'm the Parts Manager at Frost's Ford. My department stays open until seven on Fridays; I generally stay to catch up with the paperwork then, as it's quiet with the workshops closed. I had two staff there with me, they can vouch for me!'

'I'm sure that isn't necessary, sir!'

'Come on, Sergeant – I know the child, for all you know I could be some kind of pervert, so don't tell me you won't check! I'd rather think you were being too cautious, than not enough!'

'Er – yes, sir. Anyway, you arrived home to find the hue and cry already under way?'

'That's right. Brian had called to see if Hannah was still here – Carole had only just got in then. And then your officers arrived shortly before I did, looking for her. I went to help, for a while, as I know the paths around here quite well – I used to take our dog out around the fields.'

'Not any more, sir?' Farncome smiled sadly:

'No. Buster died last year – he was the same age as Brad – that's our son – and he was so upset that he said he didn't want another dog. Not yet, anyhow.'

'All right, sir, thank you. Could we speak to your son now?'

'Yes, of course. Come inside.'

He led them through the kitchen once more, where Emily was helping her mother baking a cake. The little girl looked up and smiled at Russell as they passed; Rimmer leant towards him and whispered:

'I think you've got a fan there, sir!'

'Get away with you!'

Farncome led them into the lounge, and waved for them to be seated:

'Wait here, I'll get Brad for you.' He went into the hallway, and they heard him call as he went up the stairs:

'Brad? Can you go downstairs a minute, there's some people to see you.' A door closed above them, and heavy footsteps rattled down the stairs; the door opened to admit a youth as stocky as his father, but with his mother's brown eyes and dark wavy hair. Shirtless, he wore scuffed denim jeans, and expensive but well-worn trainers; he looked at the two men suspiciously for a moment:

'Yeah? Who're you?' Rimmer stood up, and waved at the settee:

'Sit down, Bradley, please. I'm Detective-Sergeant Rimmer; this is D.I. Russell. We're trying to find out what has happened to your sister's friend, Hannah Buckland.'

'Oh – yeah, right.' He sat down expectantly; Rimmer went on:

'You were here alone, last night, I believe?'

'Yeah – that's right. Mum took Em shopping in town – I didn't fancy dragging round the shops with them, so I stayed here.'

'What did you do?'

'I stayed up in my room, listening to CD's.'

'You didn't hear Hannah arrive, knock at the door, or anything?'

'Nah. I had my headphones on – Mum worries that my music would disturb the neighbours! I didn't hear a thing 'til they got home.'

'Which is your room, Bradley?'

'I've got the bedroom at the back – It's the next biggest after Mum and Dad's. And for heaven's sake call me Brad; I hate that Bradley thing!' The boy's grin was quite disarming after his earlier antagonism.

'That looks out over the garden?'

'Yeah.'

'So if Hannah had come that way, she'd have seen the light on in your room?'

'Nah! I didn't bother putting it on, just lay there listening in the dark. Saving energy, you know!' The boy's expression made it clear his comment was thoroughly tongue-in-cheek.

'So she could have come into the garden, knocked at the door, and gone away again, without you knowing?'

'Yeah, sure!'

'And equally, she wouldn't have known you were there, either?'

'No, I guess not.'

'Okay, Brad. There's not much else you can tell us, I imagine?' The boy shook his head. Russell intervened:

'How well do you know Hannah, Brad?'

'Quite well, I suppose – she's round here a lot, playing with Em.'

'You like her?' He shrugged his shoulders:

'She's okay, I guess. She's…livelier, than Em, always dashing around. And cheeky – she takes the mickey out of me as well, sometimes.'

'You don't mind that?'

'Nah! She's harmless – all I have to do is grab her and tickle her if she gets too cheeky.'

'Pretty girl, is she?' The boy's brow furrowed as he considered the idea:

'Never thought about it. No, not really, she's a skinny sort of kid. She's got nice eyes, though…' he went on, thoughtfully 'real bright blue, you know?'

'Yes – we've got some pictures that her parents have given us. Do you have anything else to ask Brad, Sergeant?'

'I don't think so, sir.' Rimmer turned to the boy again:

'Will it be all right if we come and see you again? If we need to, that is?'

'Yeah – I guess so.' Russell closed the interview:

'Okay – we'll get back to the station, then, Sergeant.'

The two men stood up; the boy followed suit, and stood watching as his mother, who had been keeping an eye on their exchanges from the kitchen doorway, stepped forward to show them out.

CHAPTER FOUR

As the two detectives got into the Jeep, Rimmer looked quizzically at his superior:

'Very formal in there, boss?' Russell raised his eyebrows and smiled:

'Is that boy telling the truth, Doug?'

'He seemed relaxed enough, didn't you think?'

'Hmm, yes. But you told me the house-to-house had brought up a mention of another boy going to that house, didn't you? I just thought I'd play it a bit heavy, put a little bit of pressure on him. If he's not telling us everything, it might make him think.'

'Yes – you're right about that report, but I'm not sure of the details off-hand. Could be a friend who called round, and couldn't make himself heard any more than Hannah did.'

'Maybe – we'll check later. Right now, I'd better get back, the Super'll be getting in a stew about the press.'

'Right!'

As the two entered the station, Wilson appeared down the stairs and accosted the Inspector:

'Where have you been, Russell? The press are waiting.'

'Sorry, sir. We've been to see the missing girl's friend and her family, and she gave us a possible location the kid might have gone; we came back via the search area to get someone to check it out.'

'Any luck?'

'Don't know yet, sir – it's in an area they've already covered, but Mr Armstrong's sending a couple of constables to take another look.'

'Oh – right. Well, come along man, don't let's keep the reporters waiting!'

He hurried the Inspector along to the press room, where the media, both local and national, were waiting. Wilson's reluctance to deal with the press alone was not entirely due to a natural reticence – he was well aware that his short, rotund, balding and bespectacled figure wasn't what the great British public expected of its law-enforcement officers. He genuinely felt it was better for public morale if he was accompanied by a senior officer out of the preferred mould; and Russell, tall, handsome and blond, filled the bill nicely.

The press conference passed off pretty well as expected, given that they had little of any real consequence to impart. The known details of Hannah's movements were reiterated, with the added possibility that she could have begun a return trip from Alderley Park after getting no reply at the Farncomes' house; Wilson handed out copies of the girl's latest school photograph, and a recent snapshot taken by her father in their garden, and appealed again for anyone with any knowledge of the child's movements to come forward.

Russell returned to his office, to find Rimmer sitting at his desk, going through the information from the day's enquiries. He looked up and grinned as his superior took his own usual place perched on the desk's edge:

'Sent the wolves away hungry, sir?'

'Yes, pretty well!' Keith Foreman, Russell's predecessor as senior C.I.D. Inspector at Grancester, had always referred to the press as the wolf-pack, and the epithet had stuck after his retirement some years before.

'So what do we know, Doug?'

'Not as much as we'd like, boss. You want to go through it?'

'Yeah. Let's start with Hannah – what do we know, and what can we surmise?'

'Well, all we know for sure is that she left home about four thirty-five on Friday, in dark blue trousers and a grey top, and trainers. Her mother took it for granted that she would go by the field path, Southwards along the edge of the woodland, and then by the back-alley to Emily's house – we've no reason to suppose otherwise. We haven't had anyone come forward who saw her, on the path or elsewhere, after that time – it was a mucky evening, and it's not really the time of day for dog-walkers to be about, so that's perhaps not surprising. After our talk with Brad Farncome, it has to be possible that she did get there, but got no reply at the house. The only sensible assumption then would be that she set out to return home, I suppose?'

'Probably – we'll check with her family, there might perhaps have been another friend she would have gone on to, but I would have thought they'd have mentioned it themselves if there had been. The search has found no trace of her?'

'Nothing. There are some footprints that might be hers, on the path – but most of it is hard-surfaced, and the odd soft spots have been so trampled by the people looking for her that they can't say for sure. The ones that might be her are all heading towards Alderley Park, not back the other way. They've found no other trace, no clothing, anything like that.'

'So she's just vanished into thin air?' Rimmer shrugged:

'Looks like it.'

'Damn! The kid's got be *somewhere!* She hadn't arranged to visit Emily, had she? So, if she has been taken, it can't have been premeditated, can it?'

'No, sir. A chance encounter?'

'It would have to be, Doug. I take it there's no other footprints on the path that might be meaningful?' The Sergeant shook his head:

'Not that uniform can identify. And you can't get a vehicle

along that way, as you know. The nearest she could have been put in a car would be either in the village where she started, or Alderley Park Avenue, so that seems kind of unlikely – someone would have had to have seen them, wouldn't they?'

'You'd think so, Doug. But we'd better add that idea to the next appeal, ask if anyone saw someone getting into a car with a little girl in either place, around that time.' He paused: 'There's nothing untoward in anything we've learnt about the families, is there? No reason to even suspect that any of them could be involved in her disappearance. The only jarring note is that possible discrepancy with Brad Farncome, isn't it?'

'That's right. I checked that report from the house-to-house – a neighbour claims to have seen another local kid, from across the street, going into the Farncomes front garden, around four thirty. She didn't see him go into the house, or watch to see if the door was answered even. So he could well have got no reply and gone home, which would leave Brad's story unchallenged.'

'Okay. Do we have a name for this kid?'

'Yes. Charles Gidding – he's about Brad's age, the lady thinks they go to school together. He's known as a bit of a hard case – or likes to think he is! – calls himself Spike. The Giddings live the other side of the Avenue, and a few doors towards the town end. We'd better talk to him?'

'Yes – tomorrow will do, I think, it's all probably irrelevant. Although – Mrs Farncome said the boy had had some trouble at school, didn't she? I wonder if this Spike is one of the kids behind it? If that's the case, and Brad's afraid of him, it might explain why he wouldn't want to admit he'd been there. But even so, I can't see how it has anything to do with Hannah.'

'Nor me, sir. I'll go talk to the boy in the morning, if you like?'

'Thanks, Doug. I'll go and see the Bucklands again, I think, try to find out if Hannah might have gone off anywhere else if she found Emily out rather than going straight home. There's nothing else from the house-to-house of any significance?'

'There's one house, in Alderley Park Crescent, where no-one's home. According to the neighbours, the owners, a Mr & Mrs Johnston, are in Australia, visiting their daughter and son-in-law; left on Friday, apparently, so I doubt if they could tell us anything useful.'

'Probably not, Doug.'

Rimmer looked up at his superior for a moment:

'What about Olsen, sir? Should we pull him in, do you think?'

'Hmm. How likely is it that he could have the girl?' Rimmer shuffled through the papers on the desk, found the one he was looking for:

'Difficult to say, boss. He got out four and a half years ago, and he seems to have kept his nose clean since. Lives in his old house in the Warren, still.'

'The sister and her family used to live there too, didn't they?'

'That's right, in the next street. Uncle Kevin was the regular babysitter, until the little girl finally told someone what had been going on. Seems he'd been touching her up for quite a while, and finally got carried away and raped her one night when he put her to bed. Forensic evidence nailed him, primarily. DNA match, all that. The sister moved to Manchester right after the trial, to try and give the kid a fresh start.'

'Does he have a car? If he has got Hannah, he can hardly have taken a kidnap victim across town on the bus.'

'Yes – a little Fiat.'

'Mmm.' Russell stood up, paced the room for a minute or so, then turned to the Sergeant:

'We'll have to go and see him. We don't have anything to connect him with Hannah, so we'll have to go softly with him – we don't want to be accused of harassment. But we'd be failing the Bucklands if we don't check, and it turns out he's got their kid.'

'Now, sir?'

'I think so – sorry it's making a late night for you, Doug.'

'I'll just call Julie, tell her to hold dinner for a while!'
'Okay – tell her I'm sorry!'

* * *

At the moment Russell and his deputy were leaving the police station, George Andrews walked into his wife's room, and greeted her with a bright smile. A short, plumpish man with curly brown hair and a matching full beard, he was, as always, dapper in appearance, cravat at his throat, an expensive shirt beneath his plum-coloured jacket. Sheila looked up, her pleasure at seeing him clear on her thin face, and reached one hand to him:

'Hello, Mac darling.'

He took her hand in both of his own:

'Hello, Sheila. I'm sorry I'm later than I meant to be; but I had to stop in on Brian and Harriet, you understand?'

'Of course! Is there any sign of little Hannah?' He shook his head, sadly:

'Not so far. What on earth can have happened to her?' His wife looked up, her pale green eyes full of her concern for the missing child:

'I hope she's all right – it must be terrible for Brian and Harrie, not knowing where she is....' Andrews nodded:

'I'm sure they'll find her, very soon.' He smiled down at her, his expression hiding his concern – she seemed to have lost weight again, even in the time since he'd last seen her, late the previous evening:

'What about you, my love? How are you feeling today?'

* * *

A little later, the Jeep pulled up outside number 27, Newtown Road, in the district of Grancester known as the Warren. Warrenton on the official maps, it had been for many years the poorer part of the town, mostly consisting of run-down ex-council housing, on the East side close to what had been the railway marshalling yards in years gone by.

The door opened to Rimmer's knock, and a thin, weaselly face looked out:

'Oh. I bin expectin' you – you're the old bill, ain't yer?' Russell couldn't hide his amusement at the man's tone of resignation:

'Well spotted, Mr Olsen! D.I. Russell – this is my assistant, Sergeant Rimmer. Can we come in?'

'Spose so.' The man stood back to let them in, and followed them into the kitchen, which faced out onto the road as was common in the local council housing of that period. He waved the two officers to seats at the kitchen table, and sat down to join them. Kevin Olsen was a small, skinny man in his mid-thirties, roughly dressed, with a thin face, pale eyes and short, bristly reddish hair:

'This'll be about the missing kiddie, I 'spose?'

'That's right, Mr Olsen.'

'Yeah, thought so. When I 'eard it on the news, I thought you'd be round. Can't leave me alone, can yer?' His tone was resigned rather than aggressive.

'We have to check anyone who might be implicated in a case like this, as I'm sure you'll understand – we'd be failing in our duty to the child's family, otherwise.'

'Yeah, yeah, okay. Just 'cos I made fool of meself once – well, you can go through the 'ouse, if yer want, I've nothin' to hide. She ain't 'ere.'

'We'll perhaps take a quick look around in a minute, since you offer, Mr Olsen. But first – can you tell me where you were yesterday evening, from four thirty until about seven o'clock?' The man gave a deep sigh:

'I finish work at five, Fridays. I come straight home, got here about quarter past – got changed, sat down for a bit, then got me tea. 'Fore you ask, no, no-one can vouch for me, unless one of the neighbours saw me come in. I went out later, 'bout nine, down to the Railway for a coupl'a beers – a few folks saw me there, but I guess that's not much help, is it?'

'Where do you work, Mr Olsen?' Rimmer asked; the man turned to him:

'Frost's. I'm a mechanic there, 'ave bin since I come out of jail. He's bin good to me, old Mr Frost. Taken on one or two other ex-cons, as well, 'e 'as.'

'Do the other men there know about your record?'

'Nah – don't be daft! They know I've bin inside, that's all.'

'So you can't account for your time last night, Mr Olsen?' Russell took up the questions again:

'Only what I've tol' yer! If I'd known a kiddie was going to choose then to go missin' I'd have made sure to have me an alibi, wouldn' I?'

'I suppose so.' Russell smiled at him: 'Now, how about showing the Sergeant and I around?' Olsen stood up:

'Come on then!'

Accompanied by the scruffy mechanic, the detectives went through the house quickly, their eyes alert for any sign of the presence of a child. Finding nothing, he took them also to check the garden shed. Satisfied, they returned to the house and went to take their leave. As he opened the door for them, Olsen asked:

'Mr Russell – you were with Mr Foreman when… last time, weren't you?'

'I was, Mr Olsen.'

'Yeah. Thought I remembered yer. 'Ow is Mr Foreman – 'e still on the force?'

'No – he retired a couple of years ago. You've got me to deal with now, I'm afraid!'

'Oh, right.' He hesitated: 'Well – good luck to yer, Mr Russell, if someone's got that kiddie, I 'ope yer catch the bugger. I'm really sorry for what I did, all those years back, yer know. Even if you don't believe me, I am.'

Russell paused, catching a look of genuine sadness in the man's eyes:

'Thank you for your help, Mr Olsen. Come on, Doug.'

In the car on the way back to the station, Rimmer asked:

'What did you make of him, sir?' Russell thought before replying:

'I don't know, Doug. On the face of it, he has no alibi, and his record was for an attack on a little girl of just about Hannah's age, so we can hardly rule him out. But – what would he have been doing around Elwood, or Alderley Park? He'd have had to have driven there right after leaving work, so why?'

'Yeah, I see what you mean. He doesn't seem likely to have friends in that neighbourhood, does he? And even if he was giving in to his old urges, it's hardly the place you'd go with the idea of picking up a little girl, is it? You'd head for one of the bigger estates – or even prowl the Warren, wouldn't you?'

'That's how I feel. He could fit the bill of our theoretical abductor with his record, but it all seems unlikely, somehow. And what's he done with the kid? There's no trace of her ever having been at his house, at least from our quick look around. Did you make a note of his car?' Rimmer grinned:

'Yes, boss! I assume that elderly Uno outside was his – I'll check the number with vehicle registrations in the morning. And I'll go through what we've got so far, see if there's any mention of a car like his anywhere around the village or the Avenue last night.'

'Okay, Doug. I think that's all we can do for tonight – I'll drop you off at the station for your car, and then I'm going home for my dinner!'

CHAPTER FIVE

At the breakfast table the next morning, Russell studied his son quietly. The boy sat with his head bowed over his eggs and bacon, the quiff of sandy hair obscuring his face, munching contentedly - his little sister Sarah had at last ceased her incessant chatter, and a momentary silence had fallen. Daniel looked up and grinned at his father out of hazel eyes that matched his own:

'Quiet, isn't it?'

'Makes a change, doesn't it?'

The little girl looked at her father quizzically, not realising that they were having a gentle dig at her; then she saw their expressions:

'*Daddy!*'

'It's all right, sweetheart, Daddy's only pulling your leg!' Tracy Russell looked on, smiling at the exchange. Russell turned to the boy again:

'I'm ever so sorry about our sailing today, Daniel. But…' His son pulled a face and shrugged his shoulders:

'I know, Dad. You can't help it, you've got to find that little girl. But still…' he shrugged again.

'It's disappointing, I know. But we'll do it next week, okay? The club's back at the quarry, then.' Daniel smiled:

'Yeah – that'll be good.' The old quarry, only a mile from the village where they lived, had been turned into a country park in recent years, and it was one of the boy's favourite places to go. He went on:

'Will it be okay if I go to see Jacko, after breakfast?'

'Yes, of course – but…'

'I know – be careful on the roads!' The boy interrupted his father, grinning; Russell grinned back.

The meal over, Russell took his leave of his family as Tracy began to load the dishwasher. Daniel had already leapt on his bike to cycle the two villages down the old road to visit his friend; Sarah was playing, quiet and content, in the living room. The weather had improved considerably, the dank greyness of Friday lifting over the course of the last thirty-six hours until Sunday morning was bright and clear.

* * *

At about the same moment, Brad Farncome was slipping out of the front door of his home into the sunshine.

'Where are you off to, Brad?' His mother called, catching sight of him.

'Just want some fresh air – I won't be long.' He closed the door behind him. He crossed the street, and began walking towards the town; as he passed a house a few doors along, another boy joined him, and fell into step. Charlie Gidding was six months older, several inches taller, and a lot heavier than Brad – square of build and square of face, his white-blond hair was cropped into an almost startling crew-cut.

'Hello, Bradley!' Brad glanced at the older boy:

''Lo, Spike.' His greeting was less than enthusiastic. The other boy had called him on his mobile a few minutes before, telling him to come out to meet him – and it wasn't advisable not to do what Spike told you.

'Had the fuzz round, then?'

'Course.'

'What'd you tell them?'

'Nothing!'

'You sure?'

'What d'you think I'm going to say? I told them I was on my own, listening to music in my room all the time.'

'They believe you?'

'Why wouldn't they?' Spike grabbed him by the shoulders, turned him and forced him back against the brick wall they were passing. He leant close:

'They'd better! You breathe a word of what happened – or – the other things we had planned… You know what to expect!'

Brad felt a surge of amusement and pride at the sight of the other's bruised and split lip; but he kept his expression carefully obsequious. Laughing at Spike was something else you didn't do.

'Yeah, I know! Don't worry – I don't want trouble any more than you do.'

The bully held him still, looking close into his eyes, for a long moment, the tension almost sparking through the air between them. Then he stood back, giving the younger boy a hard push against the bricks as he released him:

'I should beat you to a pulp, the way you dared to hit me – but I'll let you off, this time. You dare try it again….' He let the threat hang in the air

As his tormentor turned and stomped off, Brad stood away from the wall, and brushed his denim jacket down. Despite the threats, he was smiling to himself – he'd caught the look of reluctant respect in Spike's eyes behind his last words. Boy, it had felt *great,* to punch that bastard in the mouth! And, somehow, he'd got away with it – probably only because Spike knew that if he told, the older boy would be in such deep shit he'd never climb out! Still smiling, he walked on along the Avenue a little further, before turning into a side street and going around the block on his way back home.

* * *

In his office, Russell found Doug Rimmer already sitting in front of a mug of coffee. The Sergeant leapt to his feet as his superior entered:

'Boss! I wanted to catch you before I go to see the Gidding kid.'

'Why didn't you call me at home, Doug?' The shorter man shrugged:

'Didn't want to disturb you and the family too early – it's probably not that important. But it occurred to me, there's a connection between Hannah and Olsen, even if it's pretty distant.'

'Yeah, I'd spotted that! But, as you say, it's pretty tenuous. All right, he and Farncome have to know each other, working for the same garage – but I'd hardly imagine they're on the same social level, would you? I can't see Carole Farncome welcoming that scruffy little rat into her home, can you?' Rimmer chuckled:

'Hardly, boss. But still, we should check it out, don't you think?'

'Oh, of course. I was going to suggest that you stop in and talk to the Farncomes today; you're going to be over the road from them to see the other boy anyway.'

'That's what I thought. I'll find out how well Farncome knows him, if there might be any reason for him to go to the Avenue on Friday night.'

'Okay, Doug. Nothing new from the search, I suppose?'

'Nope. They're extending it out wider around Elwood, and into the country further afield from the woods and the path today. I thought I'd send the house-to-house teams into the side streets off the Avenue.'

'Sounds fine. Have their enquiries shown anything unexpected at all, so far?'

'No, sir. The picture they've been getting of the Bucklands is just what we expected – a happy, close-knit family, with no problems that anyone was aware of. Much the same goes for the Farncomes, although some of the neighbours knew about the boy's trouble at school. No-one seems to have seen or heard anything unusual on Friday – just the mention of the Gidding boy going to the Farncome house, the occasional passing car, heard rather than seen, and none of them stopping in that vicinity. Seems like no-one much was about at that time.'

'Well, it was a mucky sort of evening, wasn't it? Damp and grey, not the weather to be out in unless you had to. You can hardly blame people for staying in doors, even if it doesn't help us much!'

'I guess not. Anyway, I'll get off to Alderley Park. See you later, sir?'

'Yes – I'll go and talk to the Bucklands again, see if they've anything more they can add to what we know, if there might have been anywhere else the girl might have gone when she found Emily out. I'll be back in the office in a while.'

* * *

Charles Gidding senior was very much his son's father. Tall and thick-set, with the same white-blond hair and little, pale blue eyes, the owner of Sweeney's night club was a self-made man; an ex-bouncer for other establishments, he'd taken the lease on what had once been the town's police station in Midland Road, and turned it into the place that all of the local youth wanted to be seen in. From time to time, drug dealers had tried to move in – but the local police had dealt with the ones he hadn't been able to frighten off himself. Gidding prided himself that his place was clean, whatever else might go on there.

He answered Rimmer's knock at the door:

'Morning?'

'Mr Gidding? I'm Detective-Sergeant Rimmer, Grancester C.I.D.'

'Oh? You'd better come in, Sergeant.' The man stood aside, his expression saying that he didn't appreciate having his Sunday morning disturbed. In the hallway, Rimmer turned to him:

'Is your son home, sir?'

'Charlie? What do you want with him?' A defensive tone had crept into his voice.

'Nothing serious, sir – I just need to ask him about his whereabouts on Friday.'

'Oh?'

'Can I speak to him, sir? I'll explain then.'

'I suppose you'd better, then.' He turned and bellowed up the stairs:

'Charlie! Get down here!'

'What is it?' An answering bellow echoed from above.

'Policeman wants to talk to you!' Rimmer's expression reflected his annoyance at this warning, intended or not.

'Oh, okay!' A door slammed, and Spike slouched down the stairs, making his lack of haste deliberate and obvious. He stopped, leaning on the newel post.

'Charlie Gidding?' Rimmer confirmed.

'Yeah?'

'Can you tell me where you were on Friday evening?'

'Why d'you want to know?' Rimmer kept his temper:

'You'll have heard about the little girl who's missing?'

'Yeah – so?'

'I gather you know her best friend's brother, Bradley Farncome?'

'Yeah – we're at school together.'

'We believe she came to see Emily Farncome the night she disappeared. Did you go to the house, to see Bradley, by any chance?' The boy shook his head:

'No – does he say I did?'

'He doesn't. But one of your neighbours says she saw you go into their front garden about half past four that evening.'

The boy stood silent, his eyes shrouded, his mouth open – Rimmer felt he could almost hear the gearwheels of his mind turning. Then, his expression cleared:

'Oh, yeah – that's right. I went over, to ask if he could help me with some of my homework. But there was no-one in, so I came home again.'

'Straight away?'

'Yeah, that's right.'

Rimmer looked at the boy thoughtfully for a moment:

'Okay, Charlie. That's all, at least for now – thank you for your help. We have to check everyone's movements over the time when Hannah disappeared, I'm sure you understand, sir?' He addressed his question to the boy's father. Gidding nodded:

'Of course, Sergeant. Anything we can do, just ask. Is there any sign of the poor kiddie?'

'Not so far, sir. We're still searching, of course.' The man nodded again. As he turned to leave, Rimmer cast a last question at the boy:

'How did you hurt your lip, Charlie?' The boy put on a rueful expression:

'Walked into a door at school! Not looking where I was going, I suppose.'

'Right! Thanks again.'

Across the street, he knocked at the door of number 197. Emily opened it to him:

'Hello! You're the policeman, aren't you?' Rimmer smiled down at the child:

'That's right, Emily! Is your Daddy in?' The girl led him inside:

'He's in the garden, I'll get him for you.' In the living room, she turned to him, a worried look on her pretty face:

'You still haven't found Han?' Rimmer shook his head:

'No – I'm sorry, Emily. But we're still looking, don't you worry. We'll find her soon, I'm sure.' She gazed at him, her eyes full of fear for her friend, before responding:

'Okay. I'll get Daddy.'

A few minutes later, John Farncome entered the room, again brushing the dirt from his hands:

'Good morning, Sergeant. What can I do for you today?'

'We've no news of Hannah, I'm afraid, sir.'

'No – Emily told me. She's so worried about her friend, as you can imagine.'

'I'm sure she is, sir. We all are, come to that.' Farncome nodded gravely.

'Do you know a man called Kevin Olsen, sir?' The man frowned:

'Kev? Of course – he's a mechanic at Frost's, where I work.'

'You know him well, sir?'

'No – I wouldn't say so, not really. I only see him at work; he's just one of the eighteen men in the workshop. Why are you interested in him, of all people?'

'We're just looking into anyone who might have a connection with Hannah, sir.'

'What? You're not going through every casual acquaintance of mine, I'm sure, Sergeant. Why is Kevin so special?' Rimmer took a deep breath before he replied:

'Are you aware of Mr Olsen's background, sir?'

'I know he's been to prison, if that's what you mean, yes. So have a couple of our other men – one of my own staff in the parts department, even. Are you looking at them, too?'

'Er – not yet, sir.'

'So why Kevin?'

'I'd really rather not say, if you don't mind, sir.' Farncome looked hard at him for a moment:

'Okay – I'm sure you have your reasons, Sergeant.'

Just then, footsteps thundered down the stairs, and Brad stopped short in the doorway when he saw the detective standing there with his father. Rimmer caught a flash of concern, almost panic, in the boy's eyes, before he took hold of himself:

'Hello again, Brad.'

'Hello – Sergeant Rimmer, isn't it?'

'Right!'

'Did you want to see me again?'

'No – I needed to talk to your father. But since you're here – you didn't have a visitor on Friday evening, did you?' The boy shook his head:

'No – I told you and the Inspector.'

'You didn't hear someone knock at the front door, about half past four?'

'No – did someone call?'

'Charlie Gidding from across the road – he says he came over to ask you to help with his homework. But he thought you were all out, and went home again.'

'Oh! Yeah, well, like I told you, I had the CD on upstairs, I suppose I just didn't hear him.' Relief flashed in the boy's expression before he could hide it.

'Okay – thanks, Brad. It just ties up the loose ends, you understand.'

'Yeah – right!'

'And thank you again, Mr Farncome. I'll leave you all to your Sunday now.'

As the man showed him to the door, Rimmer was ruminating upon the changes of expression he'd caught in the boy's eyes – and the way his questions had seemed to throw the Gidding boy, as well. Hmmm….

CHAPTER SIX

As Rimmer was talking to Spike Gidding in Alderley Park Avenue, David Russell's Jeep pulled up outside Ivy Cottage, on Barfield Lane in the village of Elwood. Elwood still retained much of its little village feel – an independent community for a thousand years or more, it had only in the last ten years become an adjunct of Grancester, with the almost nervous approach of modern housing to its Eastern bounds. The estate of Elwood Farm now filled the space between village and town, but had yet to dare to spread its limbs around and engulf it entirely, with the result that the Western edge of the village still straggled vaguely into open countryside. The cottages of Barfield Lane petered out into woodland and fields before taking the traveller the three miles to Barfield itself, another quiet hamlet with little claim to fame unless it was the reputed quality of the goods sold by Barfield Antiques in Church Street.

Russell stepped reluctantly from the car. Even after twenty years in the police force, he still found it difficult to remain detached from people's suffering; and any case involving a child was particularly difficult. As a father himself – a father who's own son had been in jeopardy at the hands of child-killer only the previous year – his sympathy with the Bucklands' plight was as deep as it was understandable. A missing child could be worse in some ways than a dead child, he reflected as he walked up the path to the door – you could grieve for a death, but not to *know*....

To spend your time wondering if your child is well or suffering, dead or alive, what kind of anguish they may be going through....

He rang the bell; moments later, the slim black-haired figure of Harriet Buckland opened it to him, her brown eyes red-rimmed:

'Oh, hello, Inspector. Come in, please.' She stood back to allow him in. In the simple, comfortable living room she waved him to a chair alongside her husband. Brian Buckland looked up, smiling weakly:

'Good morning, Mr Russell.'

'Good morning, sir. How are you?'

'We're coping, Mr Russell. But it's so difficult....' Harriet's voice trailed off; the Inspector nodded sympathetically:

'I do understand, Mrs Buckland. I – we all – want to make this as easy for you as we can; and to get you your daughter back as quickly as possible, of course.'

'Thank you. I know you're all doing everything you can – but it's still so hard, just waiting.'

'That's the worst.' Brian agreed: 'If someone's holding her – I'd like to get hold of *him!* I'd like to tear him apart...' He buried his face in his hands for a moment, then looked up at Russell, tears in his eyes:

'Sorry, Inspector – but it's my little girl, you understand.'

'Of course, sir.' He allowed silence to reign for a minute or two. As he was about to speak again, the living room door burst open, and a grey-eyed boy rushed in:

'Have you found her?' Russell looked at the lad, the same age as his own Daniel, and felt a lump rise in his throat at the eager hope in his face:

'No, not yet – I'm sorry, Josh. We're still looking, as hard as we can; we'll find her for you, don't worry.' The boy's face fell at his words; he stood silent for a moment, obviously fighting back his tears, and then nodded and turned away, going to sit beside his mother on the settee. Russell turned his attention to Harriet Buckland:

'Mrs Buckland – we're not sure if Hannah might have got to the Farncome's house on Friday after all. It turns out that the son, Bradley, was playing music in his room, wearing headphones, and with the lights off, so he wouldn't have heard her if she did knock; and she wouldn't have known he was there. So she might have gone away again, thinking the house was empty. Could there be anywhere else she might have gone, another friend perhaps, if that happened?'

Harriet thought, slowly shaking her head:

'No, Mr Russell. We don't know anyone else in Alderley Park, not that Hannah would have gone to. Her only other close friend is Briony James, and they live on Glebe Farm, right across the town – she wouldn't have tried to go there on her own, it's too far.'

'She would have just come straight home, then?'

'Yes – I can't think what else she might have done. If it was still quite light, she'd have come straight back across the field, I imagine; she might have come back around the road way, of course, just for the walk.'

'That would take her up the Avenue, into Turner's Lane to Elwood and back here past the post office?'

'That's right, Inspector.' Brian confirmed. Russell nodded:

'Okay. We have checked all that area already – but we'll go over it again, talk to people again, if it looks like she might have set off home by that route.' He smiled at them, trying to look encouraging:

'That's all I wanted to talk to you about – I'm sorry to have disturbed your Sunday morning. Are the liaison people looking after you all right?'

'Yes, thank you, Mr Russell.' Harriet replied: 'Amanda – Sergeant Mills – is coming over in little while, again. She's been so good; everyone's being so nice….'

'Would you be prepared to join me in a press conference? Appeal for help in finding Hannah?'

'Of course we would, Inspector! Amanda had suggested we

should, already, and we told her we'd be more than willing, if it would help.' Russell smiled:

'Thank you! I'll set it up – would later this afternoon be possible?'

'Whenever you want, Mr Russell! Just tell us, we'll be there.' Brian confirmed.

'Thank you again.' A thought struck Russell as he rose.

'You drive a Ford, don't you, Mr Buckland?' Brian looked up in surprise:

'Yes – It belongs to the business, really, of course. I've got a Mondeo Estate; Harrie's got one of those little sports jobs, a Puma.'

'Both new?'

'Yes – relatively. Mine's eighteen months old, Harrie bought hers last autumn some time.'

'That's right' his wife agreed: 'Is it important, Mr Russell?'

'It might be, Mrs Buckland. I imagine you got them from Frost's, in the town?'

'Yes – both of them.'

'And you take them back there for servicing, and so on?'

'Of course – they're both still under warranty.' Thinking hard, Russell sat down again:

'Have you ever had contact with anyone in the actual workshop there, for any reason?'

'No – we just drop the cars of with the receptionist, and collect them when they're done. I haven't met any of the actual mechanics, if that's what you mean.' Brian replied; but Harriet Buckland was looking thoughtful:

'I have, Brian – you remember that rattle I had on the Puma? Last time I took it in to complain, one of the men came out in it with me, to listen. Once he'd heard it for himself, he managed to fix it.' Russell's mind was working overtime, now:

'Can you describe the man, Mrs Buckland?'

'Oh, now! A little man, very thin – wiry, I suppose you'd call him. Thin faced – reddish hair. That's all I can remember.'

'Mrs Buckland – ' *The sixty-four thousand dollar question!* 'I don't suppose you had Hannah with you that day, did you?'

'Yes, I did! How did you guess that? It was at the end of the Christmas holiday, before the schools went back – I was annoyed because I'd had to live with that rattle all over the holiday, when they were supposed to have fixed it already. She came with me for the ride – where were you, Josh?' The boy looked up:

'Harry's, I expect, Mum.' She smiled down at him:

'Yes, I expect so. I know you were out somewhere. Brian was at work, of course.'

'So this man, the mechanic, met Hannah?'

'Yes, of course! I remember he smiled at her, made a fuss of her as we went out to the car. And he gave her a sweet – he came out to tell me he'd fixed the rattle, when we went to collect it, later, and he gave her a barley-sugar from his pocket.'

'Is all this significant, Mr Russell?' Brian had clearly been thinking, too.

'It could be, Mr Buckland. If you don't mind, I'd prefer not to explain exactly how, but it might fit in with another line of enquiry we've been following. If anything comes of it, I'll let you know straight away, of course. But for now, I need to do some more checking. I'll leave you now, get straight onto it – thank you for your help and your patience.'

As he drove back to Grancester Police Station, Russell felt a surge of hope – perhaps they were getting somewhere! So Olsen had actually met their missing girl! He couldn't imagine Frost's having two mechanics who would fit that description. And it sounded as if he'd been quite taken with the child. So? Would he have known where she lived? Could have found out from the garage service records, probably. By his own admission, no-one could confirm that he'd gone straight home, and stayed there, on Friday night after work; he could have been around Elwood, or the Avenue. Had he gone there, for some reason? And spotted Hannah, walking alone, offered her a lift, maybe… But then, where *was* she? He and Rimmer had seen no trace of her at his house, the previous evening.

His hope suddenly crumbled into despair. If Olsen had grabbed the kid, but he hadn't taken her home... Unless he had some other hideaway, the only likely scenario was that he'd assaulted her, and disposed of her somewhere. Could she still be alive? The only flicker of hope came from the fact that they'd not found her body. *Oh God, please, let her be alive!*

In the station car park, he met Rimmer returning from Alderley Park. The two detectives adjourned to Russell's office to compare results; the Inspector quickly filled his subordinate in about Harriet Buckland's revelation:

'So Olsen had actually met the kid, sir?'

'Seems so, Doug. But we still can't place him in the right locality to have picked her up on Friday. We need something, a sighting of his car, anything, to put him there at the right time.'

'We can't just sit back and wait, though, can we?'

'All we can do, I reckon, is to bring him in for questioning. Put the pressure on, as much as we dare, hope he'll tell us – if it *was* him! It's far from certain, still, Doug.'

'I know, sir - but it's a hell of a coincidence, isn't it? A known child rapist, and a missing little girl?'

'Yes, but – we can't jump to conclusions. It could be just coincidence; strange things do happen. Who'd have reckoned on Daniel, of all people, befriending that bastard Evans, last year?'

'I suppose so, sir. Shall we go and bring him in?' Russell looked at his watch:

'In a while, Doug. In the meantime, what did you find out in Alderley Park?'

'Ah, right! Well, those two boys aren't telling us everything, sir. But I don't know how significant it is.'

'Oh?' Rimmer paused, to put his thoughts in order:

'The Gidding boy: He's not the brightest scholar on the block, if you see what I mean. A penny or two short a full till. When I confronted him with the fact that he'd been seen going to the Farncomes, he had to think about it before he could answer me.

He says he went over to ask Bradley for help with his homework, but thought no-one was in, so he went home again.'

'You don't believe him, Doug?'

'Not really. Why hadn't he told anyone before – he must have known how important it was to us. And like I say, I got the feeling he was making it up as he went along. And what he did say, if you think about it, fits with what Brad himself told us, that he would have been unable to hear the doorbell – as if he knew what the other boy had said. And, at the Farncomes, Brad came downstairs while I was talking to his father – he looked worried, almost frightened, to see me there. I asked him about the Gidding boy coming over, and he had a kind of desperate look in his eyes for a moment until he realised what the other kid had said about finding no-one in. There's something going on between those two, but I've no idea what, not yet. Or even if it's important.'

'No – could be something of no significance to Hannah, but that they don't want their parents to know about. But we need to know, just to be sure. We'll go and see those two again, lean on them very gently – if it is something irrelevant, no doubt they'll tell us if we just push a little bit. After we've collected Mr Olsen. What did John Farncome say about him?'

'I doubt if it matters, after what you found out from Harriet Buckland, does it, sir? He said that he knows Olsen, of course; but only as one of the mechanics. I got the feeling he doesn't like him very much – I certainly can't see him being invited to visit the house!'

'No, like you say, Doug, it's the contact with Mrs Buckland that's likely to be important, I think. Come on – let's go and surprise him!'

Friday 4.30pm.
Bradley Farncome heard the knock at the door as he was going up to his room. Dad was still at work, of course; his mother and

Emily had left ten minutes before to go shopping. He put the plate with his sandwich and glass of cola on the stairs, and went to answer it.

'Oh – Spike.' He sounded as unenthusiastic as he felt to see the boy from across the street, one of his tormentors from school, who had been responsible for getting him into trouble more than once.

'Well, Bradley – aren't you going to invite me in?'

'I guess so.' Charlie Gidding pushed past him, into the hallway; Brad closed the door.

'Well?' Brad hesitated; reluctantly, he offered:

'Come up to my room.'

'Right!'

He led the way; Spike looked meaningfully at the drink he picked up:

'Do you want something?'

'Why not, since you ask?'

'Coke?'

'Yeah, that'll do.'

He went back to the kitchen, filled another glass from the bottle in the fridge, and took it to the boy waiting in the hall. They trooped up the stairs, and into Brad's room; he sat on the edge of his bed as Spike took the chair in front of his desk.

'What do you want?' he asked.

'You don't sound very pleased to see me?' The bigger boy responded.

'You surprised?' Spike laughed, and shook his head:

'Maybe not!'

'Well?'

'What are you doing tomorrow morning?' Brad shrugged his shoulders:

'Not a lot, I guess.'

'Good! Tig and I have a job for you.' Peter (Tig) Radstock was Spike's chief crony, another big-built bruiser of a teenager,

but with an even lower mental capacity than his mentor.

'What's that?'

'We want you to come into town with us.'

'Why?'

'I need some new CD's; and Tig fancies that new martial arts programme for his playstation. We might even get a CD or two for you – you like music, don't you?'

'Where d'you get that sort of money from?' Brad was suspicious.

'Oh, we're not going to pay for them! That's where you come in – we need someone to keep a lookout.'

'You want me to help you steal them? You've got to be kidding!'

'Oh, now, stealing isn't a very nice word, is it? Let's say we're going to liberate them, shall we?' It was a term he'd heard his father use for items he'd gained not entirely legitimately

'No way! I'm not getting involved in shop-lifting!'

Spike looked at him, eyes narrowed, in what he fancied was a threatening way:

'It could get...difficult, at school next week' he suggested. Brad just stared at the bully, frantically trying to think of a way to get himself out this without getting a beating in the playground as a result. He was still searching for the answer when they heard the garden gate bang to. He got up from the bed, and looked out of the window, to see Hannah Buckland, his little sister's friend, walking up the path to the back door. He turned to Spike:

'It's Hannah, Emily's mate.' The older boy got up, and looked over his shoulder:

'Cute little girl, isn't she?' He sounded surprised.

'Yeah – guess so. I'll go down, get rid of her.' A knock sounded at the kitchen door.

'Okay – no, wait!' Brad turned back; Spike went on:

'Let's have a bit of fun! Bring her up here.'

'What are you going to do?' Bradley felt afraid for the girl, knowing his companion's vicious sense of humour.

'Oh, nothing much! Just fetch her, all right?'

CHAPTER SEVEN

Kevin Olsen was about to put his pork chop under the grill when the knock came at the door. Muttering under his breath, he went to answer it:

'Oh – Mr Russell!'

'Morning, Kevin. Can we come in?'

'I suppose so.'

The two detectives entered, and stood in the hallway as Olsen, clad only in a dirty singlet and grease-stained jeans, closed the door:

'What do you want now? I told you all I could yesterday.'

'We'd like you to come to the station with us, Mr Olsen.' Rimmer answered him.

'What? Why?'

'We need to ask you some more questions, and it would be easier there, if you don't mind.'

'About the little girl? Like I said, I've told you everything!'

'We just want to make sure, Mr Olsen. If you'll come with us now, maybe we can get this all cleared up quickly.'

The skinny little mechanic hesitated; then he nodded, and agreed reluctantly:

''Kay, then. I don't suppose I got much choice, 'ave I? Just let me put me shirt on.'

He disappeared up to the bedroom, returning a minute or so later looking a little more respectable. He picked up a grubby overcoat as Rimmer opened the door for him, and the three left the house and got into the C.I.D. car waiting outside.

* * *

At twelve thirty, George Andrews pulled up outside St Mungo's Hospice. The hospice, attractively set in its own well-tended grounds, secluded from the surrounding suburb of the town, had been home to his wife for the last two months. The cost of keeping her there was considerable; but all that mattered to him was that she was well cared for, and that he was able to be with her as much as he could. He was about to join her for Sunday dinner, as he did every week.

Locking the crimson Mercedes convertible, he went up the steps to the front door. A man of only medium height, he nevertheless had an air about him, a kind of presence that belied his relatively ordinary appearance, which had no doubt helped him enormously in building up the business. Sheila it was who had first taken over the empty green-grocer's shop in Barfield, with a loan from her parents, and started to buy and sell antiques; he had joined her, as soon as he could; and over the next few years, it had become a thriving establishment. There was that about Andrews which seemed to inspire trust – an important factor, if you were in a business which had a reputation for its vague shadiness. The smile on his mobile lips, matched by the one in his bright brown eyes, put potential buyers at their ease, parted them from their money, as it seemed, effortlessly.

They had been there for more than twenty years now – at first living over the shop, then moving to a house in Grancester when they decided to convert the upper floors into more showroom space. A few years ago, they had fulfilled an ambition in buying the big town house on the Embankment, looking out across the road and the wide grassed bank to the slow-flowing water beyond. And they had spent more and more time together, as Brian Buckland had taken on more and more of the responsibility of running Barfield Antiques, with the two regular staff supporting him; Andrews own involvement had reduced until his main contribution was in travelling to inspect possible purchases, visiting both auctions and private homes around the area, negotiating and buying the items he felt would sell well in his market.

But then, last year, Sheila had been diagnosed with cancer. It had begun with her stomach; they'd operated, but in no time, it seemed, the disease was back. It had invaded her lymphatic system, the body's internal drainage network; and now, there was no stopping it. She was going downhill – slowly, but inevitably – and he could do nothing but watch, supporting, encouraging, trying to keep her happy and smiling while inside he felt as if his world was coming to an end. She wouldn't see the summer. The thought of that made him cry, at night, in the big house, all alone, remembering the happy times over the last few years, strolling in the sunshine along 'their' riverbank.

Carefully adjusting the cheerful smile on his face, he strolled into her ground-floor room, bent to kiss her pale cheek when he found her dozing. She awoke, looked up, her face reflecting her pleasure in his presence, as he took his seat beside the bed, holding her hand.

* * *

At the station, Russell and Rimmer deposited their guest in a cell temporarily, and repaired to Russell's office to confer over their line of questioning. As they were talking, a uniformed P.C. put his head around the door:

'Mr Russell? Sergeant Buchanan said to tell you that Mr Wilson's arranged the press conference for four o'clock, sir.'

'Okay, thanks, Dorman. Is someone picking the Bucklands up?'

'Yes, sir. That's all in hand.' He withdrew quietly.

Their thoughts in order, Inspector and Sergeant collected Olsen from his cell, and took him to an interview room. The preliminaries over, Russell got the man to repeat his story, as he'd told it to them the evening before; he gave them the same tale, in different words, which was no more than they had expected. Then Russell bowled their new back-spinner at him:

'You didn't tell us that you know Mrs Buckland, and her daughter, did you, Kevin?' The little man gaped at him:

'I don't! What are you on about?'

'She tells us that you've met Hannah – and that you made quite a fuss of her.'

'What? When? I dunno what you're talkin' about!'

'She took her car into Frost's, a little while ago, and you went out in it with her, to listen for a noise. Hannah was there, and Mrs Buckland tells us you were quite taken with the child.'

'Oh God – I don't remember! I see quite a few o' the customers – I do most o' the warranty work, and you get all kinds o' things like that. When was it? What sort o' car?'

'About the beginning of January. A new Puma, with a rattle under the floor.'

'Oh, 'ell, let me think.' Olsen sat with his face in his hands for a moment, then raised his eyes to Russell's:

'Yeah, I know now. She'd come in several times wi' the same trouble, and we'd gone all over it. I went out in it with 'er – turned out to be a loose fixing on one o' the back seat belts. Dark green puma.'

'That's the one. You remember the little girl?' Olsen was starting to look scared; but he nodded:

'Yeah, I do. Cute little thing, all big blue eyes and long black hair. Real nice kid, 'ad a kind of sparkle about 'er, you know what I mean?'

'Yes, indeed. It's a shame her family are missing her so much, isn't it?'

'Oh come on, Mr Russell! I 'ad nothing to do wi' that, you

gotta believe me!'

'But you did take a liking to the kiddie, didn't you?'

'All right! Yeah, like I said, she was a crackin' little girl. But I wouldn't… *do* anything to her! You gotta understand, I wouldn't do things… like that, again!' He leant forward on the table, his eyes desperate:

'When I was in Bedford, I 'ad therapy. You know, to stop me… feelin' like that. It worked, sort of – I still… like to *see* pretty little girls, and talk to them; but I wouldn't *hurt* another one, not now! I still 'ave nightmares, 'bout what I did to little Angie. I couldn't do that again! You gotta believe me, Mr Russell!'

Russell sat back in his chair, looking at the disreputable little man across from him:

'Our priority, Kevin, is to find that little girl, and get her back to her family. You're telling us that you don't know anything about that, where she is, what's happened to her?'

'That's right, Mr Russell! I don't know nothin' 'bout that! Okay, so I met 'er, that once – but I didn't even know it was 'er as was missing, I swear I didn't!'

Russell thought for a moment:

'Okay, Kevin, we'll hold it there for the time being. Mr Rimmer and I'll probably want to talk to you again, though.'

Olsen sat, elbows on the table, his face in his hands; he looked up:

'Can I go 'ome, now, Mr Russell?'

'Not just yet, Kevin.'

'Listen! Ol' Mr Frost – like I told you, 'e's been ever so good to me, givin' me the job, sending me on courses, so's I could make a career for meself. If I don't turn up for work tomorrer, 'cos you've got me in 'ere, what's 'e goin' ter think?'

'I understand, Kevin. Let's hope we can get this all straightened out soon, eh?'

'Yeah – right!' Olsen didn't sound convinced.

Shortly after returning their suspect to his cell, Russell joined the Superintendent in the press room. Wilson was looking as uncomfortable at the prospect as always; just before four o'clock, Amanda Mills, the family liaison officer, brought the Bucklands through from the briefing room. Brian and Harriet took two of the chairs behind the table, the microphones ranged in front of them, flanked by Wilson and Russell; Josh had accompanied his parents, and stood behind them, his small, stocky figure looking somehow lost as he gazed around him, slightly awed by his surroundings, his light brown hair catching the lights. Amanda Mills stood by his side, her hand comfortingly on his shoulder.

The massed reporters were allowed in; Wilson began the conference, passing quickly over to Russell to bring the press up to date, including the news that they were questioning a local man in connection with Hannah's disappearance. Then Brian Buckland made his appeal for information that might help to find his daughter, mostly reading from a prepared script on the table before him. He went on to address his daughter, through the medium of the cameras, telling her to be strong, that they'd soon have her home and safe again. Questions followed; all was going smoothly, even if Brian's distress was becoming more apparent as time went by. Harriet sat silent but supportive by his side.

Then one reporter looked up at Josh, asked him how he was feeling. The boy looked at the woman, his dark grey eyes wide:

'I – miss my sister.' He swallowed, and went on: 'It's – all wrong, without Hannah there, I want her home, with me.' Following his father's example, he spoke to his sister through the cameras, his words unrehearsed, unprepared:

'Hannah – I miss you – and I'm so sorry, for all the times I shouted at you. I promise I'll never tell you off again, ever! Just please come home to me!'

Total silence held the room; the tears began to run down the boy's cheeks as he turned and threw his arms around the startled liaison officer's waist, sobbing into her tunic. At a nod from Wilson, she gently eased him from the room. Coughs and snuffles sounded from all around, as the conference wound up with a few more desultory questions.

In the briefing room, as Josh was tearfully reunited with his parents, Russell took Wilson aside:

'This fellow Olsen, sir, the one we're holding at the moment? I don't see how we can hang on to him; I'm not sure if we need to, to be honest.'

'Oh?'

'Well, we've nothing to connect him with the girl's disappearance, really. He met her once, at the garage when Mrs Buckland took her car in – we've only that, with his record, of course. And I'm not convinced he's our man, at all. He seems too scared, if you know what I mean?'

'If he has got the kid, and we're closing in on him, he *would* be scared, surely?'

'Yes, but – it doesn't *feel* right, somehow. He's no alibi for the time she went missing, and he's done time for child rape, but as I said, we can't place him anywhere near Elwood or Alderley Park, there's no indication that she's been in his house. We've no evidence to hold him on, have we, sir?'

'You've had the house searched?'

'Of course. Uniform have been there this afternoon, but they've found nothing.'

'You don't think he's got anything to tell us?' Russell shook his head:

'I'm beginning to think not. Sergeant Rimmer and I will talk to him again, this evening, but if we can get nothing from him, I think I'll let him go, if you agree, sir.'

'Yes – I think you'll have to, David. Do you have any other leads?'

'Not really, sir. There's something odd, between Bradley

Farncome, the friend's older brother, and one of his mates; the two of them are keeping something from us – but I doubt if it has anything to do with Hannah, to be honest.'

'All right, David – keep me informed.'

'Yes, sir.'

* * *

Late that afternoon, as the dusk closed in outside the window, George Andrews rose from his wife's bedside. She looked up:

'Are you going, Mac?' He nodded gently:

'I think I should, darling. You're getting tired; and I ought to get home – I haven't done the housework yet!' She smiled; his hopelessness with keeping house had always been a standing joke between them.

'You'll come tomorrow?'

'Of course! In the evening – I'll have to go to the shop, you understand? I can't expect poor Brian to just carry on as if nothing's happened. I've told him to stay home with Harrie; I can look after things for a while, with Pete and Steph. But I'll try to be here in time for tea, all right?'

'Yes – give my love to Brian and Harrie, won't you? Tell them I'm praying for them, and for little Hannah.'

'I will, my love. See you tomorrow.' He bent to kiss her, and turned to leave the room, pausing at the door to give her a last lingering smile; She lifted a hand from the bedspread, waved weakly as he stepped out.

Walking out to the car, Andrews grief at his wife's condition gave way to a surge of elation. He had a treat waiting for him at home, something he'd been enjoying for the last couple of days, something which had, for brief periods, taken his mind entirely off of his sorrow. He'd said nothing to Sheila, of course. Not only did he not want to admit to feeling such pleasure while she lay there dying, but if she knew what he'd been up to…. Having Sheila by his side was what had kept him faithful, kept him on the straight and narrow, for all these years. But now, as he was about to lose her, the urge to stray was there – even then, he could have put it aside, if circumstance hadn't conspired against him, put temptation right under his feet…. It couldn't go on, of course. Tonight, he'd have to finish it. After….

* * *

Martha Simpson got unsteadily to her feet as she heard the car draw up outside, She had long ago reverted to using her maiden name, tired of the raised eyebrows, and irritated by the need to explain every time she gave her name or filled in a form anywhere.

She peered under the curtain covering the grubby window. The passenger door swung open; under the interior light, she saw her daughter lean across, her arm around her father's neck, and kiss him soundly on the cheek.

''Bye, Daddy – thank you for a lovely weekend!' Tran Quoc gazed into the girl's denim-blue eyes, smiled lovingly at her:

'I wish it could be all the time, Kim.' Her expression turned serious, her head tipped slightly to one side in the way that intrigued him so:

'So do I Daddy – but you know I can't! Who'd look after Mum? I can't just leave her all alone to…' Her voice trailed off. They both knew that without her child's presence and support, Martha would drink herself to death, sooner or later. He nodded:

'I know, Darling. If only she would get some help – then maybe you could be with us more…' His voice sounded wistful; the girl smiled at him:

'Give my love to Liu – and Kai, and little Tran. I'll see you all again next month.' She kissed him again, and turned to step out of the car. As she did so, the front door of the house opened, her mother appearing in the doorway, leaning on the jamb:

'You're bloody late, Hsung! Where've you been with my

daughter?' Kim stepped quickly to the woman's side, shushed her:

'It's all right, Mum. It's my fault – we took the boys to Wimpole Hall – you know, the farm there?- and I was enjoying it so much we forgot the time. Don't blame Daddy – come on inside, I'll make you a cup of tea, all right?'

'Don' want a cuppa tea. Want my girl home.'

'I'm here now, Mum! Come on in the warm.' She turned, gestured for her father to go. He leant across, pulled the far door shut, gave his daughter a last wave, and drove away. The girl led her mother back into the house, deposited her into a chair and went through to the kitchen to put the kettle on.

CHAPTER EIGHT

Monday saw little progress in the search for Hannah Buckland. Russell and his deputy had interrogated Olsen once again the previous night, but achieved nothing unless it was to reduce the man almost to tears of frustration as he tried to convince the detectives that he'd had nothing to do with the girl's disappearance; they'd sent him home in a police car around seven o'clock.

The search on the ground was beginning to wind down, with nowhere sensible left to look. Rimmer's house-to-house teams had been laid off, after making a second sweep of Hannah's possible route home via the Avenue and Turner's Lane; and they seemed to be no closer to finding the missing girl. With nothing more significant to turn their attention to, Russell suggested they should try to settle the anomaly over the two boys, Brad Farncome and Charlie Gidding.

They arrived in Alderley Park Avenue just after three thirty, thinking to catch the boys as they got home from school:

'We'll split up, Doug – you go and see the Gidding boy, I'll take young Brad.'

Rimmer looked across at his superior, a twinkle in his eye:

'Going to see your girlfriend, as well, boss?'

'What?'

'Little Emily – she seemed quite disappointed it was me, not you, who turned up yesterday!'

'You could always go back to the beat, Sergeant!'

'Yes, sir!' The two men exchanged grins across the car, then got out and went to their respective destinations.

As he approached the front door of number 188, Rimmer was passed by a small BMW which pulled onto the drive beside him. A short, mousy woman got out, locked the door, and spoke to him:

'Hello – can I help you?'

'Mrs Gidding?'

'That's right.'

'I'm Detective-Sergeant Rimmer, Grancester C.I.D. I spoke to your husband, yesterday, and Charlie.'

'Oh, yes – Chuck told me. What can I do for you?'

'Is your son home, Mrs Gidding?' She shook her head:

'Not yet, Sergeant. He plays football on Mondays, he won't be home for a while. Would you like to come in?'

'Okay; thank you.'

She opened the front door and led him inside, showing him to a seat in the living room. Slipping off her coat, she took a seat facing him:

'What's it all about, Sergeant?'

'It's in connection with that little girl who's missing, Mrs Gidding.'

'Oh? What's that got to do with Charlie?' Rimmer smiled:

'Nothing, probably! It's just that your son went across to see Brad Farncome – his sister Emily is Hannah's best friend – at just about the time she went missing; and we need to be sure of everyone's movements. I'm sure you understand?'

'Yes, of course. That's right, I remember Charlie went over there, around half past four?'

'That's what he told us, yes.'

'Oh well, that's fine, then! He was out about an hour, I suppose – when he came home, he'd cut his lip – I expect you saw – and told me he'd walked into a door! *I* think the two of them had a fight – Charlie's a bit prone to getting into fights, I'm afraid – but he wouldn't want to tell me that, of course!' Rimmer's ears had perked up:

'He was out about an hour, you said?'

'Yes, about that. More or less – he was in by the time Chuck came home for dinner, around six.'

'I see. Thank you, Mrs Gidding; I wonder, what time do you expect Charlie home today?'

'Oh, he'll be in around five, I should think. Would you like to come back later? You're welcome to wait, if you prefer?'

'Thank you – I think I'll call back in a while. Mrs Gidding – I know it's asking a lot, but I'd prefer if you didn't mention that I've been here?' The woman looked a little surprised, but she nodded her head:

'All right, if you wish, Sergeant.' She got up to show him to the door. Her husband's relations with the police could be a little strained, at times, and she had no problem with not telling him that she'd been entertaining a Detective-Sergeant in his absence.

Rimmer dashed across the road, and knocked at the door of number 197. Carole Farncome let him in, and took him through to the lounge, where Russell was talking to Bradley; Emily was in her room, despatched by her mother to leave their coast clear. The D.I. had so far kept to going over the boy's story as they had it, that he had been incommunicado in his room, and hadn't heard anyone at either door; he looked up as Rimmer beckoned him aside, and rose to his feet. The two conferred in the hall before returning to the room; Russell resumed his seat, facing the boy:

'All right, Brad. I've listened to what you want to tell me – now I need the truth. What really happened on Friday?' His mother went to get up, her face angry, but Rimmer gestured her to stay where she was. Brad looked at the Inspector, his eyes wide:

'I've told you!'

'No, you haven't. We *know* that Charlie Gidding was out of his house for an hour, that he came over here to see you, and that he went home with a cut lip. I need to know what went on, Brad – I understand that it might have nothing to do with Hannah, but I can't have loose ends, *any* loose ends, when a little girl's life might be at stake. You're sensible enough to know that.'

The boy looked across at his mother, his brown eyes wide and appealing. She looked back, smiling lovingly at her son:

'If you haven't told the Inspector everything, you must, Bradley. Your Dad and I won't punish you, I promise – that boy's been bullying you, hasn't he?' She smiled again: 'We're not stupid, you know.' He smiled back:

'I know, Mum – I'm sorry.' He took a deep breath, and turned to Russell:

'All right, Inspector. Spike – Charlie – did come here; he caught me as I was going up to my room. I let him in; he came up with me. He… he wanted me to go into town with him, the next morning, him and Tig. That's Pete Radstock, he's Spike's mate – he's the ugly bastard…'

'Brad!' His mother interjected; the boy grinned apologetically at her, and went on:

'He's the one who enforces Spike's orders at school. He's not very bright, but he's all muscle, you know? Anyway, they wanted me to go along with them, keep a lookout while they pinched things.'

'Shop-lifting, you mean?' Russell asked; the boy nodded:

'Yeah. I told him to get lost.'

'I should hope so!' He smiled at his mother:

'Don't worry, Mum, I'm not *that* stupid, myself! I've let him push me around at school, I know; and got into trouble for him, as well. But not any more! I smacked him in the mouth, Friday!' He sounded really proud of himself.

'That's how he got his split lip, then?' Russell couldn't help the amusement in his voice.

'Yeah, right! I've wanted to do that for, oh, so long, you can't believe it! I half expected to get a good beating from Tig, today, for it, but nothing's happened. Not yet, anyway.'

'So what happened, after you'd hit him?'

'Not much – I think it really shook him, that I'd finally stood up to him. He told me I'd better watch out, that I was in real trouble – but then, he just got up and left.'

'He went home?'

'I suppose so – I don't know.'

'And that's everything, Brad? There's nothing else you want to tell me?'

The boy sighed, and shook his head.

'Okay. Thank you, Brad. I know it maybe doesn't seem important to you, as it was nothing to do with Hannah; but I had to know for sure.' Big brown eyes looked up at him as he rose to his feet:

'What will you do now? About Spike, I mean?'

'Go and talk to his father, I imagine. I doubt if he'll be too impressed to find out his son was planning to go shop-lifting; I don't think *we'll* need to do any more! Do you want me to have a word with your headmaster, tell him what's been going on?'

The boy thought for a moment:

'Would you? It might get through to him, if you talk to him. Some of the teachers are pretty good, but Beattie doesn't seem to want to know about bullying.'

'Okay, I will. That's Matthew Price School, isn't it? Over in Glebe Farm?'

'Yeah, that's right.'

'We put Brad up for The Priors, but he didn't get in, I'm afraid.' Carole Farncome explained. Russell nodded understandingly, keeping to himself with a swell of pride that his own twelve-year-old had got in with no difficulty.

'All right – thank you, Mrs Farncome; and thank you again, Brad. I'm glad we've got that all cleared up now. We'll leave you to your evening in peace.'

She showed them to the door, leaving her son slumped in the settee, looking exhausted but relieved. As she heard the movements below, Emily appeared at the top of the stairs, smiling down shyly as the Inspector caught sight of her, gave her a quick wave. Outside, Rimmer asked his superior:

'Well, sir? What about the Gidding kid? He should be home by now.'

'I think we'll leave it until the father is home too, Doug. I want him to hear what I've got to say. Wait in the car, I'll just check with Mrs Gidding.'

'Okay, boss.'

Rimmer climbed into the driving seat of the Jeep. Russell often had his assistant do the driving, even when they were using his own car, a situation which Rimmer relished; he enjoyed the surging power of the big six-cylinder engine, the massive feel of the four-wheel-drive vehicle.

Russell knocked at the door of number 188; Mrs Gidding opened it to him.

'Mrs Gidding? Detective-Inspector Russell. My Sergeant spoke to you a little while ago?'

'Oh, yes, Inspector. Charlie's home now; do you want to see him?'

'That's your son?'

'That's right; shall I call him?'

'No, it's all right, Mrs Gidding. Can you tell me what time your husband will be home?'

'Oh, Chuck'll be in soon, I expect. The club's closed at the moment, I expect you know that – they're redecorating inside, and Chuck likes to be there , to make sure it's all done properly – he'll be home in time for dinner, I'm sure. It makes a nice change, him not having to rush off to get there for the evening opening.'

'I'm sure it does.' Russell could imagine the man's response if any of the work was not to his satisfaction, too, but refrained from commenting.

'I'll drop by a bit later, after you've eaten. I only need a moment of their time; we've resolved our little problem, I'm pleased to say. I just need to confirm the details with Charlie, and I'd rather do that when his father's here.'

'All right, Inspector. We'll see you later, then – should I tell Chuck you'll be calling?'

Russell thought, then replied:

'You can if you wish - it's not important. I'll see you later on. Thank you, Mrs Gidding.'

'Good evening, Inspector.'

* * *

George Andrews arrived too late for tea with his wife. He entered her room, smiling apologetically:

'Sorry I'm late, darling. We were busy, in the shop, and I couldn't leave Steph on her own.' Sheila smiled up at him, a twinkle in her faded eyes:

'I think you're enjoying being back in the front line, Mac! It's ages since you've been at the sharp end, dealing with the customers.' He grinned:

'You could be right! But you know I wouldn't be late for you, if I could possibly help it.'

'I know, my love,' she squeezed his hand 'even if you were late on Friday, too!'

'Friday? We had tea together on Friday, don't you remember? Cheese sandwiches and swiss roll! It was Saturday I was late.'

'Yes – you'd been to see Brian. But wasn't it Friday you went to look at those chairs, in Alderley Park, that you told me about?' He smiled:

'No, love! That was on Wednesday!' She shook her head:

'I don't know, I must be losing my grip! With all the drugs

they keep pumping into me, I suppose it's hardly surprising if I lose track of the days, is it?' Andrews' smile was fondly sympathetic:

'Don't let it worry you, sweetheart. Every day must seem so much like all the rest, stuck in here. Maybe soon the weather will get a bit warmer, and we'll be able to go out into the garden sometimes.'

'That'll be nice, won't it?'

The love shone in their eyes as they exchanged smiles, neither voicing the thought that she might not live to enjoy the sunshine, if it failed to materialise soon.

CHAPTER NINE

Tuesday was as frustrating for David Russell as Monday had been. Still no word or sign of the whereabouts of little Hannah Buckland; and no real leads in the search for her either. National appeals had elicited a good response; but every reported sighting of the child had proved to be a false alarm; locally, Olsen's involvement still seemed like a long shot, and nothing new had come to light.

The previous evening, Russell had stopped at 188 Alderley Park Avenue on his way home, after consulting again with the Detective-Superintendent. He'd confronted Spike with Brad's changed story, and taken a kind of guilty satisfaction both from the bully's obvious discomfiture, and the furious reaction of his father. He had left the boy in no doubt that the police would be keeping an eye on him for the next little while, at least. The only thing which came back to worry him slightly as he drove home to Bevington village was that there had been a hint of something else in the teenager's eyes as his father had been berating him about shop-lifting; relief? That's what it had felt like to the watching policeman. He dismissed his doubts: *You're getting too suspicious, Davey-boy!*

He returned to his family in time for dinner that Tuesday night, no closer to knowing what had happened to the little girl. Another day gone by; another day of fear and anxiety for the Buckland family. Josh was staying home from school, naturally enough, to be with his parents, and Amanda Mills was there for much of the time, lending what support she could; although there was little enough that anyone could do to relieve their suffering, in truth. Russell had driven out to see them briefly, more to show his face and just be with them than for any other reason.

Once he'd talked over with them the progress, or lack of it, in the search for their daughter, he asked who was looking after the antiques shop, more by way of making conversation than for any other reason.

'Mr Andrews is there today, with our other staff; he's said he'll look after things for us, while…' Brian Buckland shrugged his shoulders.

'It's very good of him, really' Harriet added: 'He's got so much trouble of his own, after all.'

'Oh?'

'Yes – didn't you know? His wife's seriously ill, she's in St Mungo's, you know, the hospice on the edge of the Greenland Estate. She's got cancer – they don't expect her to last very long.'

'Oh yes, I think I saw it in reports. We've interviewed so many people! One of D.S. Rimmer's teams spoke to Mr Andrews, when we were checking with all your friends the day after Hannah disappeared. You've known each other a long time?'

'Yes – I've worked for George for fourteen years now' Brian replied. He went on: 'Harriet has been doing the books for him for nearly as long – she trained as an accountant before Josh came along. I don't know how poor George will manage when Sheila's gone – she was always the strong one. He seems confident and assured, I know, but she was the one who really kept it together.'

'You're good friends?'

'Well, not that close, perhaps. Not in and out of each other's homes, or anything; I suppose we see too much of each other in the shop! Or we did, before he began to leave so much to me. But we've always got on very well; we used to go for dinner as a foursome, but when the children appeared, that kind of fizzled out.'

'Does Mr Andrews have any children?' Harriet Buckland shook her head:

'No, Mr Russell. Sheila…can't, I don't know why. They know Josh and Hannah, of course, buy them presents for their birthdays, and Christmas. But I think they're happy not have any of their own, somehow.' Mention of her missing daughter brought the brightness of tears into her eyes:

'Where's my baby, Inspector? What's happened to her? Is she all right – is she…is she *alive?*' Russell sighed:

'I wish I knew the answer to that, Mrs Buckland. You mustn't give up hope; she's out there somewhere, and we're going to find her.'

* * *

Over dinner, his wife, Tracy, had sympathised with his feelings, noting how quiet and distracted he was. His son had looked across the table at him, puzzled:

'How can a little girl just *vanish,* Dad?'

'I wish I knew, Daniel!'

'Do you think someone's kidnapped her?' Russell sighed:

'I don't know – It's beginning to look like the most probable thing that can have happened to her.'

'But *why,* Dad? Have they asked for money, or anything?'

'Not so far – and her parents aren't what you'd call wealthy, anyway. If she's been taken, it was most likely for… other reasons.' The boy hesitated to ask the next question, glancing at his mother before opening his mouth:

'You mean, for *sex* reasons?' His voice was hushed.

'Daniel! Not in front of your sister!' Tracy objected; Sarah, not yet four, looked up questioningly, having understood nothing of her brother's question, or her mother's reaction. Russell grinned conspiratorially at his son:

'Don't upset your mother! But yes, you're probably right. I can't think why else, at least at the moment.' Daniel hesitated again, then asked:

'Do you think she's still alive, Dad?'

'I wish I knew – I hope and pray that she is, but the longer she's missing….' He let the inference hang in the air. Daniel looked at him for a moment, and then nodded, a look of sorrow in his hazel eyes.

* * *

Harvey Goldman was a quietly happy man. He had a wonderful family, a successful business, a comfortable life – what more could a man ask? Jeweller by trade, he had recently taken over the family business in the centre of Grancester, at the end of the High Street. Steiner and Goldman had been in the same premises for two previous generations; founded by Harvey's grandfather, and old Mr Steiner, it had passed to his father, the Steiner's having no children, and now to him. His father had decided to take early retirement in the autumn, and to go and visit Israel with his wife and her elderly mother. Now, they'd taken the plunge, and opted to settle there; Harvey was planning to take Tarah and little Taylor to visit next summer.

They lived in Alderley Park Avenue – number 139, a few doors from the junction with Turner's Lane, the old road which led to Elwood Village. That Tuesday, they were talking about the missing child over dinner; Harvey felt great sympathy for the Bucklands, he could imagine how he'd be feeling if it was his little girl who'd disappeared like that. Tarah was saying how surprising it was that no-one had seen the girl after she left home:

'Well, it was a miserable evening, remember – I expect everyone was in doors, keeping warm and dry.'

'Yes, I suppose so. They're saying she might have got to her friend's house, found no-one at home, and started out to walk back, did you know?'

'I'd heard. She might even have come past here, down Turner's Lane, that way to Elwood. And still no-one saw her!'

The little girl, sitting opposite her father, looked up, a frown on her chubby face:

'What day was that, Daddy?' Harvey smiled at the six-year-old:

'Friday, darling. Five days ago, now.'

'Oh.' The frown stayed in place: 'That was the day you were late home?'

'Yes, that's right!' He was surprised and pleased at the accuracy of his daughter's memory.

'Oh.' The frown gave way to a look of satisfaction: '*I* saw her!'

'Taylor! What do you mean?' Tarah, caught totally by surprise, sounded sharper than she had intended. Harvey reached out, took his wife's hand; he addressed his daughter gently:

'What do you mean, Tay? You saw *a* girl, that evening?'

'Mm-hm. I bet it was *her,* wasn't it, Daddy?' His grip on his wife's hand tightening, he spoke quietly again:

'What did she look like, Tay?' The little girl cocked her head on one side, thinking:

'Bigger'n me. She had long hair, I saw that…' she tailed off, shrugging her shoulders. Tarah was staring at the child – she lifted frightened eyes to meet her husbands'. Harvey smiled at her, gesturing with his free hand for her to leave this to him, and turned back to his daughter:

'Anything else you can remember, Tay?' Taylor's face screwed into a frown again; then she brightened up:

'I think she was crying – but it's all right, her Daddy picked her up!' A feeling almost of dread was growing in Harvey's midriff – what had his child seen?

'How do you know it was her Daddy, darling?'

'Must've been, mustn't it? He came along in his car, and she got in, and they went away.' Tarah flashed a look of pure horror at her husband; he squeezed her hand again in reassurance:

'Do you remember what sort of car it was, sweetheart?'

'*I* don't know, Daddy!' The child's voice was scornful, but she went on: 'It was quite big – and it didn't have a sticky-outy bit at the back, like ours.'

'What colour was it, Tay?'

'Don't be silly, Daddy! You know how funny the lights make everything look!' Harvey nodded – the sodium street lights in the Avenue made colour almost indistinguishable. But the girl went on:

'I think it was silvery – it looked the same colour as Esther's Daddy's car, when he comes to pick me up for dancing.' Esther Rosenberg's father drove a silver Volvo saloon. There was one last question Harvey had to ask:

'What time was this, Tay? Before I came home?'

'Of course, Daddy! I was looking out for you, from the front room.'

'You were in the kitchen?' Harvey addressed his wife for the first time; she nodded, her eyes wide, scared.

'Was it a long time before I came home?' The child's head tilted to the side again, a habit she adopted when thinking hard; then she shook it:

'Not long. I remember I was still wondering who the little girl was when you came, and I forgot all about her. 'Til now.'

Harvey sat back in his chair, the meal forgotten in front of him. He passed a hand across his brow, and then pushed his chair back. Taylor looked shocked as he rose to his feet:

'You haven't finished, Daddy!' Leaving the table with a meal unfinished was taboo in the Goldman household. Harvey smiled down at the child:

'It's okay, darling – I've got to make an important telephone call. I'll be right back.'

In the hall, he wiped his brow again before picking up the receiver. His fingers were shaking as he dialled the police station.

CHAPTER TEN

David Russell was relaxing in front of the television, watching a repeat of Inspector Morse, when the telephone rang. He stirred, but Daniel leapt up and beat him to it:

'Hello, the Russell residence?'

'Oh, right.' He looked around, hand over the mouthpiece: 'It's for you, Dad.'

Russell got up and took the phone from his son's hand:

'Russell.'

The girl at the other end, trying hard to sound calm and professional, failed to keep the excitement from her voice:

'Sir! We've just had a call from a Mr Goldman. He lives in Alderley Park Avenue, number 139 – and he says he's pretty sure his little girl saw Hannah Buckland on Friday evening, getting into a car!'

'Right! Number 139?'

'Yes, sir.'

'I'm on my way. Can you call D.S. Rimmer, ask him to meet me there, ASAP? I take it the Goldmans will be expecting me?'

'I said someone would be there, yes, sir. I'll call the Sergeant right away.'

'Okay – thank you, Penny.'

* * *

Harvey Goldman put the telephone down, and returned to the dinner table. Tarah was still gazing at him, her knife and fork poised but unmoving; Taylor, blissfully unaware of the stir her tale had caused, had finished her dinner and was quietly waiting for the sweet. He sat down, and went back to eating as if nothing had happened, gesturing for his wife to do likewise. When they had finished, she got up to remove the dishes; he followed her into the kitchen, pulling the door to behind him. Tarah turned to him, her eyes wide:

'Harvey! Do you think she really saw…?' He nodded, gravely:

'Our little girl doesn't make things up, does she, darling? I'm certain she saw what she says she saw. It might not have been the girl who's missing; but equally, it might – she had long hair, didn't she?'

'I…I think so, yes. Oh, Harv! Did Tay really see her…being taken, do you think?' He took her by the shoulders, looking into her eyes:

'I should know? The way she tells it, the girl wasn't struggling or anything – maybe it's all innocent, maybe it wasn't her at all.' He leant forward, kissed her quickly on the lips:

'I want you to get her into bed, as soon as you can. A policeman will be here soon, to talk to us. If she asks for her story, tell her I've got something to do, I'll be up as soon as I can. Okay?' She nodded, the frightened look easing in her black eyes.

* * *

Russell got out of the Jeep as he saw Rimmer's Astra pull up behind him. The Detective-Sergeant hurried up to him; they walked side by side up the garden path:

'Penny told you about the call?'

'Yes, sir. Could be the break we need.'

'I hope so, Doug.' He rang the doorbell; a man of medium height, heavily built but looking plump in his middle-age, opened it to them:

'Mr Goldman?'

'Yes – you'll be the police?'

'Detective-Inspector Russell, sir – this is my assistant, D.S Rimmer.'

'Come in, Gentlemen.' He ushered them into a well-furnished living room, and waved them to two of the soft leather armchairs:

'Can I offer you a drink?'

'Not right now, thank you, sir. We need to know exactly what it is your daughter saw last Friday – can we speak to her?' Goldman hesitated:

'Can I repeat what she told her mother and myself over dinner, first? Taylor is only just six, and I don't want to frighten her. Her mother is putting her to bed right now – maybe you could talk to her in a while, if she's still awake?'

'All right, sir – we don't want to upset the child, either. I will need to see her, ask her more about it; but perhaps we could do that in the morning, if you can give us the bare bones of it, now.'

'Of course, Inspector.'

Goldman drew a deep breath, and repeated to the officers everything his daughter had said, word for word as far as he could remember it. They listened in silence; at the end, Rimmer glanced at his superior, his hope evident in his eyes. Russell hadn't taken his own eyes from Goldman:

'Thank you, sir. Can you give us some idea of just when this would have been?'

'I was a little late that night, Inspector, I usually try to be home in good time on Fridays as it's the beginning of our Sabbath – we're Jewish, you understand? I got here around, oh, a quarter to six. If Taylor says it was just before then, I'd put it at maybe twenty or twenty-five to, at the earliest – you know what a little child's attention span is like!'

'Your wife saw none of this?'

'No. She was in the kitchen, preparing the meal. Taylor was

impatient for me to get home, I guess, so she was looking out of the front room, past the curtains, waiting for me.'

'The car she saw – you've no idea whose it might be?' Goldman shook his head:

'None. When she says about the sticky-outy bit' he grinned broadly at the child's choice of phrase 'I think she means it didn't have a boot; like a hatch-back maybe. Not like our car – you saw my Jaguar on the drive, I expect?'

'Yes, sir.' Russell hesitated, then asked:

'Could I talk to her, sir? Just for a moment, there's one thing I'd like to ask her, to try to confirm if it was Hannah she saw.' Goldman nodded:

'Just a moment, Inspector – I'll ask my wife if she's still awake.' He rose and left the room; Rimmer turned to his superior:

'This could be it, sir – the break we need!'

'Yes, Doug. Even the description of the car as it stands gives us somewhere to start; and maybe she'll remember more about it, with a little gentle prompting.'

Goldman returned to the room, beckoned Russell to come with him. He rose, waving Rimmer to stay where he was:

'Wait there, Doug. We don't want to scare the kiddie, all piling into her room.' He followed the man up the stairs, and into the child's bedroom:

'Tay? You still awake, darling? This is Mr Russell – he's interested in the little girl you saw on Friday. Can you talk to him about her?'

The six-year-old turned wide, dark brown eyes on Russell; she wriggled up in the bed, to sit with her back against the headboard, and nodded:

'All right, Daddy.' Russell perched on the edge of her bed:

'Hello, Taylor. The little girl you saw – she was older than you, do you think?' The child nodded:

'Mm-hm. She was bigger'n me.'

'She had long hair?'

'Mm-hm.'

'Could you see what colour it was?' She giggled:

'Not in those funny lights! They make colours go all queer!'

'Was it dark? Or light?'

'Her hair?'

'Yes.'

'Dark.'

'Do you think it might have been black?' Russell was treated to a tilt of the child's head, a thoughtful look:

'Mm-hm – might've been.'

'That's good, Taylor, thank you. Now, you remember the car, the one she got into?'

'Mm-hm.'

'Was it big? Or small?' Another tilt of the head, a thoughtful pause:

'Sort of, biggish. Not's big as *ours!*'

'And it was a silvery colour?'

'Mm-hm. Like Esther's daddy's car.'

Goldman whispered in the Inspector's ear:

'Mervyn Rosenberg has a silver Volvo saloon.' Russell nodded, his eyes still on the little girl.

'You didn't recognise it? Had you seen it before?' She shook her head:

'Uh-uh.'

'Thank you, Taylor. You've been a great help. Can I come and see you again, maybe?'

'Okay – if Daddy says so.'

Russell got to his feet, smiling down at the child. Goldman saw him out of the room, then bent to kiss his daughter's cheek before following him back downstairs. Rimmer came out to join them in the hallway:

'All right, sir?'

'Yes, Doug. Thanks to that little girl, we might be getting somewhere.' He turned to Goldman:

'She's a remarkable child, Mr Goldman. We can take all she said at face value?'

'I'm sure you can, Inspector. We've brought her up to always tell the truth, and while she's as imaginative as any child, I'm certain she's not making this up. She does have an unusually good memory, too, for her age.'

'Thank you, sir. I probably will need to talk to her again, at some stage – but you can be sure we'll try to make it all as painless as possible for her.'

'Thank you, Inspector. We'll do whatever we can, anytime. You can reach me at the store, during the day; Tarah is usually here, and I try to be home for dinner by seven, except for Fridays, of course. And I don't work Saturdays.' He paused:

'Do you think it was little Hannah that she saw?'

'I'm pretty certain it was, sir. If we can trace that car, maybe we can find the girl.'

'I hope you do, Inspector. And I hope she's all right, when you do.'

'So do we all. Thank you again, Mr Goldman - good evening.'

'Good evening, Inspector – Sergeant.'

'Good night, sir.'

The two left the house, and both got into Russell's car. Rimmer's eagerness was evident:

'So we're looking for a biggish, silver car, probably a hatchback, sir?'

'Right, Doug. I tried to get a bit more from the kiddie – she says it was quite big, but not as big as theirs – the Jag there on the drive. And the silver colour seems quite definite. No boot – could be an estate car, perhaps.'

'Mr Buckland drives an estate, doesn't he?'

'Yes – a Mondeo. But it's dark blue, rules him out. Do we have any silver estate cars in the offing, Doug?'

'No, sir. But…' A light came into the Sergeant's eyes:

'What?'

'Olsen! That Fiat of his – the Uno's a hatchback, and his is not far off being silver. Metallic grey, really, but under those sodium lights?'

'Could be, Doug. But an Uno's hardly a big car.'

'No, sir – but his is the four-door model, and to a child, from the other end of her front garden? It might be, sir!'

'Mmm. But little Taylor says the girl she saw got into the car quite willingly. Or at least, I think she'd remember if she was struggling, resisting in any way – that kid's got a remarkable memory for her age. Would Hannah have got into a car with Olsen? She'd only seen him once, as far as we know – would she even remember him?'

'Yeah, I see what you mean. But she could have remembered him, how friendly he was to her at the garage. And if he had taken a liking to her, maybe he's been making opportunities to see her, without her parents knowing?'

'Grooming her, you mean? I suppose it's possible, Doug.'

'Shall we go and pick him up?'

Russell sat back, deep in thought. It all could fit together, the man's record, the car, the fact that he'd met the girl – but? What was he doing in Alderley Park Avenue – he couldn't have been there to meet Hannah, she hadn't known herself that she'd be there. And it didn't feel right, somehow. The man's obvious fear of being blamed for her disappearance, his reaction to their previous questioning – was the grubby little mechanic that good an actor? They'd found no trace of the girl at his house – so where was she? He drew a deep breath, let it out slowly:

'I think we should. There're things that don't fit, Doug, I'm not convinced it was him. But we'll have to talk to him again, come what may; and at the station, under a bit of pressure, he might just cave in, tell us all about it. If he did take her. Come on – I'll drop you back here for your car, later.'

He started the engine, and drove off in the direction of Warrenton. The Sergeant picked up the radio microphone, and called in to warn the station that they'd be arriving shortly with a prisoner. As he drove, Russell glanced across at his subordinate:

'There's another problem, Doug.'

'Sir?'

'Where was she? If Goldman's timings are right, little Taylor saw her getting into the car after half past five – and we know she had to be at the Farncome house by around quarter to. So where was she, for forty-five minutes? And why was she crying?'

'Yeah – I see what you mean.'

'The Bucklands say they don't know anyone else around here. So – was she wandering the streets? And what had upset her? Even kids don't like to show their emotions in public, not if my two are anything to go by! So she had to be seriously scared, or something. If she'd been walking around, bawling her eyes out, for very long, surely *someone* would have seen her, or heard her?'

With no explanation to offer, Rimmer kept quiet. Silence reigned in the car for a few minutes; then Russell spoke again, thoughtfully:

'I wonder? Do we know if the Farncome's back door was locked, Doug?'

'I don't know, sir. It'll be in their statement, I expect.'

'Hmmm – when young Jack Carter comes to see my Daniel, if he knows we're in he'll knock at the front door, and then come on inside without waiting for someone to open it. I wonder – might Hannah have done the same? She was in and out of the house all the time, according to both families.'

'You think she might have just walked in?'

'It's possible, Doug. Maybe she overheard the two boys talking about Spike's intended shop-lifting exploits?'

'They were up in the Farncome boy's room, surely?'

'According to their story, yes – but if they're still holding out on us, if they don't want us to know Hannah was there, they'd say that, so that we'd assume they hadn't heard her knock. Suppose they were actually downstairs somewhere, in the kitchen even, and she walked right in on them?'

'And they put the fear of God into her, to keep her quiet?'

'Maybe, Doug. I doubt if Brad Farncome would want to hurt her, I get the feeling he's essentially a decent kid – but that Gidding boy is quite a nasty piece of work. I wouldn't put anything past him.'

'Nor me, sir.'

'Hmmm. I think we'll go and see those two again, in the morning. In the meantime, let's see what Olsen wants to tell us.'

Friday, 4.45pm

As the boy took her by the arm, Hannah looked up at him, puzzled. She wasn't concerned – Brad was Em's brother, she knew him well, and would happily have trusted him, had it even occurred to her to think about it.

'Come upstairs with me – just for a minute.'

'What for?'

'Oh – I've got something to show you. Come on!'

'All right, just for a minute, then.'

He led the way upstairs, then threw the door of his room open, and waved for her to precede him inside. Hannah stepped into the room; Brad followed, and closed the door at his back. She was startled to see another boy there, a bigger boy, with piggy little eyes and short-cropped blond hair – she took an instant dislike to him:

'Who're you?'

'That's Spike' Brad told her, still standing behind her.

'What's he want?' She knew instinctively that it had been this boy who'd wanted to see her. He got up from the chair in front of Brad's desk, and grinned at her – a grin which she didn't like the look of:

'I want to do a trade with you, Hannah. I'll show you something, if you'll show me something.'

'What?' she was immediately suspicious.

'I'll let you see my dick, if you'll show me your cunt.'

'What! No! Don't be horrible – I'm going home!'

'Oh no you're not. Not til I've seen your cunt. Stay where you are, Bradley.'

'No! I won't let you!'

'You won't stop me.' The boy took a step towards her; Hannah cringed away from him, felt Bradley behind her, blocking her escape. The big boy reached for her, undid her belt, unfastened the waistband of her slacks. He slid down the zip; Hannah stood petrified, tears of shock beginning to run down her face. He pushed her trousers down, then slipped his hands onto her waist, and eased her knickers down after them. She stood still, terrified of the bully, scared by Brad's apparent support for what he was doing, as he pushed his hand between her legs. His touch was repulsive to her, his fingers stroking her vagina, poking roughly at her, hurting the sensitive skin of her crotch. All the time, the little piggy eyes leered at her, the boy's mouth partly open, his tongue running around his lips. He went on feeling her for what seemed like ages, but was probably only a minute or so; then he stood back, dropping his hand from her sex organs.

Hannah dared to breathe again, hoping her ordeal was over. But the brute addressed her:

'That was nice, wasn't it?' She just looked at him.

'How about something even nicer? Would you like to play with my dick?'

Even more frightened, Hannah nevertheless dared to shake her head.

'No!'

'Oh, come on, Hannah!' He paused, then asked: 'Have you got any brothers?' She nodded.

'How old?'

'Josh? He's twelve.'

'Oh! I bet you've seen his dick, haven't you? Does he let you *play with it?'*

She didn't reply, horrified at what the boy was suggesting. He persisted:

'Come on, Hannah! I bet you like feeling his dick, don't you? Does he get you to suck it for him, too?' The little girl stood there, shaking her head, her blue eyes wide with terror.

'Tell you what, just one thing, and you can go home. You suck us off, and I'll let you go – how about it? I'll even let Bradley go first. Go on, Bradley, get your dick out for Hannah!'

All through the exchange so far, Bradley had been becoming more and more horrified at what Spike was doing to the girl. At the last suggestion, he pushed her to one side, and stepped around her:

'Stop it, Spike! Can't you see she's scared? That's enough!'

'Well well! What's up, Bradley? Don't you want your cock sucked by a pretty girl? Why not? You're not a queer, are you? Or are you? Are you a bum-jumper, Bradley? Would you rather have a little boy *do it for you? Do you want a little boy's willy to play with?'*

That was when Bradley Farncome stepped forward and punched the bully in the mouth. Later, he would pride himself that he'd done it, at least in part, to protect little Hannah; but if he was really honest with himself, it was the sheer blind anger, the accumulated shame and fury at his own treatment at the bigger boy's hands over a long period which put the power behind his fist. Spike staggered back, one hand to his mouth, blood beginning to seep between the fingers, a look of stunned surprise on his fat face. He caught his foot on the chair in front of the desk, and lost his balance; he fell, failed to save himself, and landed heavily on his back, his head striking the carpeted floor with a dull thud. He lay still - looking down, amazed at his own action, Brad wondered almost idly if he'd killed him; but then he gave a groan, and began to stir. Brad turned to the girl, who still stood petrified, her trousers and pants around her knees:

'*Han! Get out of here!*' *She didn't respond, too shocked to move. He took her by the shoulders, feeling the slender fragility of her between his hands, and shook her gently:*

'*Hannah! Come on, kid – pull your knickers up, and get moving. He'll come round any time – get out, before he does!*' *She looked into his eyes, blinked as if coming round herself; she nodded, jerkily:*

'*Okay – thank you, Brad.*' *She reached down, pulled up her trousers. He turned her to the door, gave her a gentle push:*

'*Go on, Han – and – I'm sorry, I should have stopped him sooner. I hope he didn't hurt you too much?*' *the girl shook her head; she smiled up at the boy. His heart lurched at the tears in her big blue eyes as she opened the door and fled from the room. He turned back, to look down at where Spike was raising himself onto one elbow, a look of fury in his piggy little eyes.* Oh, shit! I'm in trouble now, *he thought.*

CHAPTER ELEVEN

It was almost nine o'clock when the Jeep pulled up outside number 27, Newtown Road. A group of youths, sitting on a garden wall opposite, glanced across indifferently as Russell and Rimmer got out, and walked to the door.

Olsen answered the bell, as before in a dirty singlet and scruffy jeans:

'Oh no – not you two!'

'Hello, Kevin.' Russell greeted him.

'What d'you want now? I've told yer, I don't know nothing about that kiddie!'

'We need to talk to you again, Kevin.'

'Get inside, then – I don'want me neighbours seein' you on me doorstep, do I?'

'Where were you on Friday evening, Kevin?'

'I tole yer! Fer Chrise'sake! 'Ow many more times – I come 'ome 'ere straight from work!'

'But you can't prove that, can you?'

'No! Course I can't! But it's true, all the same! Listen – if it was me as grabbed that kid – where the 'ell is she, eh? You've looked 'round 'ere; you 'ad the bloody boys in blue 'ere all day, when I was in the nick wi'you. What d'yer think I done with 'er? Waved a bloody magic wand 'n made 'er disappear?'

'That's what we want to know, Kevin. Perhaps we should check with the Magic Circle?'

'Oh, fer Chrise'sake! 'Ow can I convince the two o'yer I 'ad nothin' to do with it?'

'Maybe by coming to the station with us for a while, Kevin. We want to go over your story again.'

'Oh bloody 'ell! I know you buggers – I ain't gonna make it to work in the mornin', am I? What am I goin' ter tell 'em, eh? You're gonna lose me me bloody job, 'fore you're done!'

Rimmer took him by the arm, a look of disgust apparent on his face. The man shrugged him off:

'Let me get me bloody shirt on, at least!'

'Okay, Kevin' Russell gestured to the Sergeant to let him go: 'Tell you what – I'll talk to Frosts, in the morning, tell them you're just helping us, voluntarily, all right? If you're telling us the truth, I'll square it with them. If you're not....' He let the thought hang in the air. The man looked at him for a moment, then turned and went upstairs, to return after a minute or so, wearing a slightly grubby shirt, a jacket over his arm:

'Come on, then! Let's get it over with!'

The youths across the road took a little more interest as they saw the two men lead Olsen from the house to the big station wagon. Darren Morgan turned to his mates:

'Those two Old Bill, you reckon?'

'Could be.' Al Barton agreed.

'What's Kinky Kev been up to, d'you think?' asked Will Christie. The other two just shrugged; the three returned to their illicit cans of Stella, and talk of girls and motorbikes.

In Grancester Police Station, Russell and his cohort once again left Olsen with the Custody Sergeant. They went up to the office; on the way, Rimmer asked his superior:

'Do you want to question him tonight, sir?' Russell shook his head:

'I don't think so, Doug. He's more likely to cave in if we let him spend a night in the cells first, don't you think? Right now, he'll be as stubborn as he was at the house, we won't learn anything, I'm sure.'

'Yeah, I guess so, boss.' He paused:

'If it was him that took Hannah, she's got to be dead, hasn't she?'

'I'd imagine so. He's not keeping her at the house, we know that – so if it was him, I'd assume he's dumped her somewhere, somewhere we haven't looked yet.'

They turned into Russell's office; he sat behind the desk, Rimmer perched on the edge as always:

'That's one of the things that worries me, Doug. Olsen may have got carried away once before, and raped his sister's kid – but that was a case of opportunity under his nose, wasn't it? And he didn't kill her. This case is just so different, a kiddie grabbed off the street, we assume for sex, and maybe murdered? I'm not sure I can see that scared little runt doing it, for all his record.' He stretched his back in the chair, rose to his feet again. The Sergeant looked up from his perch:

'I'm not so sure, sir. These perverts don't often change their ways – I think he's probably our man – I mean, this time, he'd *have* to kill her if he wanted to get away with it, wouldn't he?'

'Maybe, Doug, maybe. Anyway, I'm off home. We'll let him cool his heels 'til the morning, see if he tells us anything new then.'

'Right. I'll see you then, boss.'

'Okay – 'night, Doug.'

'Good night, sir.' Russell left; Rimmer stopped long enough to check over a couple of details in the file on the desk, and then followed his Inspector's example.

* * *

Late that Tuesday night, George Andrews made his way down to the garage in the ground floor of the house. Some years before they had bought it, a previous owner had got around the lack of local parking by converting the old kitchen and dining room at the back of the ground floor into a big double garage; a drive led in from the rear service road down one side of the long garden. That had been one reason why they had opted for Sheila to move into St Mungo's; as her illness progressed, as she grew weaker, having to mount the stairs all the time to get to the living accommodation on the first floor would soon have become too much for her.

In the garage, he opened the big chest freezer, and lifted out the wire-basket trays in the top. From below, he hauled out, with some difficulty, a long bundle, tied into black plastic refuse sacks, and deposited it on the floor. He replaced the baskets, closed the lid, and stood contemplating the bundle. He had been agonising for the last two days about it, where to dispose of it – it could hardly go out with the rubbish! He would have to get rid of it, somewhere as far away as was practicable, somewhere where this evidence of his pleasure and his shame wouldn't come back to haunt him, where it might lead the investigation off in other directions. After much thought, and poring over maps, he knew where.

He turned; which car? Not the convertible! Sheila had been the one who'd always wanted a soft-top; he'd bought it for her, really, although he did love driving it, and to use it for this job was anathema to him. He took the estate car keys from their hook on the wall, and opened the tail-gate. Heaving the bundle into the back, he covered it with the old blanket which lay there to protect the carpet from sharp edges when he used the car to carry pieces of furniture, and closed the lid on it.

In the driving seat, he pressed the remote control to open the garage door, and started the engine. On the drive, he pressed the button to close the door again, and drove out into the road.

He left Grancester, heading towards Northampton, where he took the ring road. Following the dual carriageway to the West, he bypassed Towcester; approaching the village of Silverstone, he took the left turn onto the Buckingham road. Through Whittlebury; past one of the back entrances to the world-famous motor racing circuit; yes, there it was, the turning he remembered! Swinging left again, he drove about a mile along the narrow country road and pulled into a farm gate just at the edge of an area of woodland.

Checking to be sure no-one was in sight, he got out of the car and opened the tail-gate. He hauled his bundle out, and dropped it over the gate onto the track beyond; looking around once more, he climbed over, and lifted it onto his shoulder. For his fifty-six years, Andrews was a fit man. He had always enjoyed walking; latterly, with more time on their hands, he and Sheila had taken walking holidays two or three times a year, around the U.K. and abroad. The bundle was pretty heavy, for sure – but he could get a long way from the road before dumping it.

He followed the bridleway for the best part of a mile, along the edge of the woods. Feeling the strain, the weight beginning to drag at his shoulder, he finally dropped it beside him. He rested for a minute or so; then lifted it in his arms, and carried it into the woods a little way. Setting it down, he carefully removed the plastic bin-bags, and laid the contents flat on the ground. He spent some time collecting fallen detritus – leaves, twigs, even small branches – and covered it as best he could. Then he walked slowly, thoughtfully, back to the car, taking the bags with him.

At the gate, he was startled by the approach of lights on the road. Ducking down so as not to be seen, he swore under his breath – he'd hoped the car wouldn't be spotted while he was away from it. But then, the other driver would probably assume it was lovers out for an illicit romp in the woods – it was a pleasant night, cloudy for sure, but not too cold – and think no more of it. It passed; he rose, and quickly hopped over the gate, got in, and drove off before anyone else could come by.

Friday 5.25pm.
Hannah ran down the stairs, and out of the front door. She didn't think about where she was going – it was the quickest way out of the house, rather than go through the kitchen to the back door. And anyway, long conditioning made her opt for going home by the roads after dark.

She stopped by the gate, leaning on it, still terrified by what that brute had done, unaware of the tears streaming down her face. She looked around behind her – was he chasing her? No – Brad wouldn't let him, would he? Despite her own distress, she spared a thought for her friend's brother – was he all right? Would that horrible boy hurt him, for letting her go? Should she go back, try to help him? But no – he'd told her to go, to get away before he woke up.

She raised her head, brushing away the tears with the back of her hand, and looked around. There was no-one in sight, no-one to help her; but in a strange kind of way, she didn't mind, she didn't really want to see anyone, to have to tell them what had happened to her. She felt dirty, ashamed – she wanted to be home; and yet, she didn't, somehow. She wanted to be alone for a while, to think things out, to let herself calm down. Straightening her back, she opened the gate and went out onto the pavement. She'd walk home, by the road – that would give her time!

She set off, along the Avenue, towards the town, trying to sort out her thoughts. The memory of that horrible boy's hand between her legs kept returning, his ugly, leering face; despite her best efforts, the tears kept coming. She went on, passing no-one. Not even a car came by – little traffic came this way, because the road only went as far as the cul-de-sac at the end; only people who lived here would drive by, and none happened to in the time it took her to approach the turning for the lane which would take her back to Elwood.

But as she was almost there, she heard a car behind her. She ignored it, not even looking up; but even so, it stopped next to her. She walked on, but the passenger door was pushed open; a voice called to her:

'Hannah?' At the sound of her name, she looked round, too polite to ignore the man who'd spoken it.

'Hannah? Are you all right?' The car door open, she saw him under the interior light, recognised him:

'Oh, hello! I'm fine, thanks.'

'It's a horrible evening – let me give you a lift. Are you on your way home?' She nodded, but told him: 'It's okay – I like walking.'

'Come on, don't be silly! You'll catch your death, you with no coat, even! Get in here in the warm!' Reluctantly, she turned and walked up to the car. The man inside beckoned to her; she got in, and clipped her seatbelt on, pulling the door closed.

CHAPTER TWELVE

Seven forty-five a.m., Wednesday morning, David Russell emerged from the bedroom, slipping on his suit jacket. Turning toward the stairs, he collided with a bleary-eyed twelve-year-old:

'Oh! Morning, Dad!' Russell grinned at his dishevelled son; shirtless, his pyjama trousers askew, sandy hair tousled from his pillow, the boy blinked up at him:

'Morning, Daniel!'

'You're early, Dad?'

'Yeah – I've got a man I need to question about Hannah Buckland, and I want to make an early start.'

'Right - catch him before he's really awake, see if he'll confess?'

'Something like that!' Russell laughed at the boy's precocity.

'Do you think he did it, Dad?'

'Did what? We don't know what's happened to Hannah, yet.'

'You know what I mean! Did he…take her away?'

'I'm not sure, Dan. He might.'

'You haven't arrested him?'

'No – we're just holding him for questioning, at the moment.'

'Is he a… you know, a sex pervert?'

'Don't let your mother hear you talking about things like that, you'll get me in trouble as well! And anyway, you know I'm not allowed to tell you.'

'Yeah, I know.' The boy's hazel eyes reflected the tone of

102

disappointed, excited curiosity in his voice. Russell took pity on him:

'He's been in prison before, for – something like this.' He took his son by the shoulders: 'And if you repeat that to anyone, I'll have your hide! Even Jacko – or your mother!'

'Sure, Dad!' Daniel grinned up at his father. The occasional secret shared was part of the bond between the two of them; and, despite his words, Russell knew the boy could be trusted. A voice sounded from below:

'David! Your breakfast's getting cold!'

'Sounds like you're in trouble already, Dad!' Russell made a grimace, and nodded:

'I'd better get down there! Get yourself washed and dressed – have a good day at school.' He turned and hurried downstairs.

By the time Daniel got down for his own breakfast, his father had left for the police station. As soon as he arrived, he collected Doug Rimmer, and the two went down to question Olsen once more. The session proved fraught and frustrating; the little man's story was unshakeable, and the news that a car similar to his own had been seen to pick up the missing girl only served to send him into even more desperate denials of any involvement. When Rimmer suggested that he might have been seeing the girl, since their casual meeting in January, he broke down completely, sobbing into his folded arms as he lay forward on the table, still vehemently protesting his innocence.

They returned him to his cell; in Russell's office, they sat to confer, Rimmer as always perched on the edge of the desk.

'I'm still not sure I can see him as our kidnapper, Doug.'

'If we could get a positive identification of his car, it would clinch it, wouldn't it?'

'Yes – but the only one who saw it was little Taylor Goldman. Even if she *did* ID it as his, can you see it standing up in court? Any defence lawyer would soon make mincemeat of her testimony. The kid's only six, after all. And it could still be another

Fiat, same model, same colour – they're quite common.'

'I know, sir. I just can't accept that it's all coincidence – he's at least met the girl, he's done time for raping a kid her age, we've got a car that could be his picking her up. It's got to be him, surely?' Russell sighed:

'I don't know. Look at him, just now – he's scared shitless.'

'Of course he is! He thinks we're about to nail him for it!'

'I'm not so sure. There's something about his fear, a quality to it that makes me think what he's scared of is being put away for something he *hasn't* done. And through it all, he hasn't changed his story in the slightest, has he?'

'No, I know.'

'Anyway – let's leave him to cool his heels for a while. We need to talk to the Farncomes, find out if young Brad can shed any light on where Hannah was between getting to their house and Taylor seeing her three-quarters of an hour later. I guess we'd best leave that until the lad's home from school – I should go and see the Bucklands, bring them up to date. Can you take a forensic team over to Olsen's house, go through it thoroughly; and bring his car in, go through that too? I'll talk to the Goldmans, ask if we could maybe take the car over there tonight, after dark, see what little Taylor makes of it.'

'Right, sir. I'll let you know straight away if we find anything.'

Leaving his Sergeant to make a start on the searches, Russell took the Jeep and drove out to Elwood village. Parking outside Ivy Cottage, he walked up the pretty garden and knocked at the door; it opened, to reveal the missing girl's brother, hope shining in his dark grey eyes:

'Have you found Hannah?' It wrenched Russell's heart to have to dispel that excited anticipation – he shook his head:

'I'm sorry, Josh.' The boy turned away, his shoulders slumping, his face averted; then he turned back to look up at the policeman, the tears glistening on his cheeks:

'Mr Russell....' His voice failed. Russell took him gently by the shoulders, the gesture itself bringing into sharp focus for him the similarity with his own son, the pain the boy had to be suffering:

'Josh – I want so much to bring your sister home for you. We really are doing everything we can, believe me – there are a lot of policemen, not only here but all round the country, all trying to find her. I believe we will, too; and I need you to believe it, as well, so that you can be strong, and help your Mum and Dad, okay?'

The boy nodded, brushing his tears away with the back of his hand:

'Okay. I'll try. But – it's so *lonely,* without Han.'

'I know. Now – are your Mum and Dad home?' The boy looked up, gave him a sad smile, nodded:

'Yeah – they're in the living room. Come in.' he led the way.

Brian Buckland got up from his seat on the settee as Russell entered the room. Amanda Mills, the police liaison officer, looked around, and jumped up also:

'Mr Russell! Is there any news, sir?'

'We've still no trace of Hannah, I'm afraid. Mr Buckland – how are you?'

'Not so bad, Inspector, considering. Harriet's laying down – the doctor's been this morning, given her some tablets. She's been getting very depressed, you understand.'

'I can imagine, sir. You're – managing all right, yourself?' The man snorted:

'Most of the time! I can't tell you how much I'm missing my little girl. My children are all the world to me, Mr Russell.' He put an arm around his son's shoulders: 'Josh here has been terrific, looking after his mother – and me! Without him, I doubt if either of us would have the strength to carry on.' He smiled proudly at the boy, who turned equally proud and affectionate eyes on his father.

'Mr Andrews is looking after the business, I assume?'

'Yes – our staff have been great, keeping things going without me, and he's been going in regularly. He tries to visit his wife every day, as well, you understand.'

'Of course. Now, can I take up a little of your time, Mr Buckland?'

'Certainly! Sit down, please.' He waved at the easy chairs, and returned to his seat on the settee, the boy snuggling against his side. Amanda took her seat; Russell sank into the one remaining armchair:

'I have some news for you. We've found a witness, who saw Hannah get into a car on Friday...' Both Buckland and his son sat forward, their faces eager:

'You have?' 'Who's car?' Young and old voices intermingled.

'We don't know, as yet. Our witness is a little girl; she was watching from their front room window for her father to get home from work, about half past five. She saw a girl – I'm pretty sure it *was* Hannah – walk along Alderley Park Avenue. A car pulled up, and she got in. The details are a bit sketchy, I'm afraid – the kiddie's only six. It's remarkable that she's given us as much as she has, really.'

'Hannah got into the car? Just like that?'

'It would seem so.'

'Then it must have been someone she knew, Mr Russell! We've always impressed it on both of them, never to talk to strangers – Hannah could be a bit forward, sometimes, with people, but she would never have got into a stranger's car, I'm certain of that!'

'That's my feeling, too, sir. Can you think of anyone she would know, who has a silver car, either a hatchback or an estate car?' Buckland sat back, his face creased into a frown of concentration; then he looked up, his expression perplexed:

'The only one I can think of is George, George Andrews. He's got a silver Mercedes Benz estate – but if George had picked her up, he'd have brought her home, surely?'

'No he hasn't, dear!' Harriet Buckland's voice sounded from

the doorway. Brian jumped up, went to her and took her arm:

'How are you feeling, darling? Come and sit down. Josh, move up, there's a good lad, make room for your mother.' The boy hotched along on the settee; his parents sat beside him, Brian's arm comfortingly about his wife. She turned to him:

'George swapped the estate for that red convertible, you remember!' She smiled sadly: 'Poor Sheila – she'd always wanted an open-top car. And then, when they get one, she finds out she's got cancer.'

'Harrie's quite right, Mr Russell. I'm afraid I'm…not thinking as well as usual, at the moment.' Brian confirmed. Harriet looked at Russell:

'They'd only had it a few weeks. She was so pleased, so proud of it! And now look at her, poor dear.' He nodded his sympathy:

'Mr Andrews traded in the estate car, you think?'

'I'm sure he did – or he might have sold it privately, perhaps. They didn't really need it any more, since Brian was more or less running the business by then, and he's got the Mondeo. If they have bigger pieces to collect or deliver, we use Braggins, in the town – they've got big vans as a well as the articulated lorries.'

'You can't think of anyone else, someone Hannah would have got into a car with, who's got a silver estate car – or a hatchback?' Harriet shook her head:

'No, Mr Russell. I don't know anyone with a car like that.' The Inspector sat back in the chair, disappointed – he'd hoped for a useful lead. He'd check out Andrews, of course, see if he just might still have the estate as well as the soft-top. For the moment, he changed tack:

'There seems to be a discrepancy about the times – Hannah must have got to Emily's house by a quarter to five, we're assuming, and yet this little girl didn't see her until almost an hour later, no more than five minutes walk away. We will be trying to find out where she was in that time, of course. Tell me – this is just idle supposition on my part – if Hannah had found the back door of their house unlocked, is it likely she would have walked straight in? Or would she wait until someone came and opened it to her?' Harriet glanced at her husband, looked back at the Inspector:

'I can't be sure – she might well have done. Emily often will, when she calls here, especially if she knows we're in, if the car's outside. And John and Carole are always pleased to see Hannah, I can't imagine them being upset if she did. But if they were out, perhaps the door was locked, anyway?'

'Possibly. We'll check with the Farncomes, of course – young Brad was in, remember, it might be that they hadn't bothered to lock up, with him there.'

'Maybe, Mr Russell. But why would Hannah stay there for so long? She got on well enough with Brad, to be sure, but I doubt if she'd spend time with him if Emily was out.'

'You're probably right – I expect I'm chasing red herrings, Mrs Buckland! There is one other thing, though: The little girl who saw her says she thinks Hannah was crying – can you think of any possible reason for that?'

Brian and Harriet exchanged mystified glances; both shook their heads:

'No idea, Inspector' Brian replied. 'She's not the sort of girl to be upset very easily – there's a bit of the tomboy about our daughter! She certainly wouldn't give way to tears for nothing – and especially not if she might be seen! It would have to be something pretty serious, I'd imagine.' His face reflected his concern for his child; Harriet's brown eyes were wide with worry, as well:

'My poor baby! If she was so upset, and we weren't there for her... Oh Brian! What's happened to her? Where *is* she, Mr Russell?' Russell's heart went out to the woman, but all he could do was shake his head:

'I wish I could tell you, Mrs Buckland. We *will* find out, I promise you. And bring her back, safe and sound, if it's humanly possible.' The brown eyes held his; he was also aware of a pair of bright blue eyes, and a pair of dark grey ones, hanging on his words as she said, dully:

'She's dead, isn't she? Our baby's not going to come back.' The Inspector drew a deep breath, let it out slowly:

'We have to accept the possibility, of course. But – remember – we haven't found her. If someone has killed her, they would want to get rid of...of her body; and the chances are that we *would* have found her by now, if that had happened. So please, don't give up, not yet. I won't, not until I know *all* of the truth about what has happened to her.' The eyes continued to hold his; but then, the woman nodded:

'Of course – thank you, Mr Russell. We've got to hang on, for Hannah's sake, I know that. It's just so hard...not *knowing!*'

Russell paused, and then went on:

'I should tell you, we are questioning a man about Hannah. I can't tell you too much at this stage, you'll understand – it's the same man we brought in a few days ago. There is a possibility – I can't be any more positive than that – that it might have been his car the little girl saw.'

'Who is he, Mr Russell?'

'I can't tell you that, Mrs Buckland - I'm sure you understand. I can tell you, in confidence, of course, that he has a previous conviction that might be relevant, and that we know he has met Hannah at least once. Not in suspicious circumstances, I assure you! I don't know if he has anything to do with her disappearance, to be truthful, but we're trying to find out.'

'It's that man at the garage, isn't it? That's why you were so interested in him, when I told you about taking the Puma in!' Now the brown eyes sparked with anger which supplanted Harriet's despair. Russell held his hands up, palms outwards;

'I can't tell you, really! When my Sergeant and I have finished questioning him, I'll try to tell you more. I promise!'

'All right, Mr Russell. I understand. But please tell us what you can, it helps us to cope if we know what's happening.' She paused: '*Is* our little girl all right, Inspector? *Are* we going to see her again?' Tears were beginning to glisten in her eyes; again, Russell felt their pain as his own:

'I wish I knew the answer, Mrs Buckland. My hope is that she is being held somewhere, that one of the leads we are following will take us to her very soon. But until it does, it would be dishonest of me to make any promises.' She nodded, gripping her husband's hand tightly:

'Of course, Mr Russell. We understand. But please – bring us our baby back, soon?' She held his eyes for a moment; then, as the tears started to come, turned and buried her face in her husband's shirt. Russell rose to his feet, took the hand that Brian Buckland proffered:

'I must go. I'll keep in touch, of course – and as soon as I know anything positive, I promise you'll know it too.' Brian nodded; Amanda stood up:

'I'll show you out, sir.'

Friday 5.40pm
The man drove away, with a reassuring smile at Hannah. They turned the corner into Turner's Lane; he glanced across again, aware of the little girl's distress, the tears glistening on her cheeks. She sat hunched down, snuggled into the soft black leather seat, not looking at him. He pulled the car into the kerb again, just past the last house, and turned to her:

'What's wrong, Hannah? Why are you crying?' The girl shook her head:

'It's okay, it's nothing.'

'No, come on – a girl like you doesn't cry for nothing, especially in public. What is it?'

She looked up at last; he could see more tears coming, but she just sat in silence, her big blue eyes red-rimmed.

Hannah didn't want to talk about it. Or did she? She couldn't have told her mother or father, even Josh, what that brute of a boy had done to her, she'd have been too ashamed. But this was someone beyond her family, someone outside; and someone she trusted. Someone, maybe, that she could talk to without feeling so embarrassed, so upset....

Suddenly, it was all coming out. She poured out the whole tale, tears running unrestrained down her cheeks as she told him of the bully's taunts, the horrible things he'd done, of Brad's eventual efforts to protect her. As he listened, as she told of the boy pulling down her knickers and molesting her, the man felt the stirring of urges, of desires, long suppressed. He fought them down; but they raised their fiery eyes to his again, begging, expecting, to be recognised, to be acknowledged. The girl had finished speaking; he tried to collect his thoughts:

'It must have been awful, Hannah.' She just nodded, tearfully.

'Do you want me to take you home?'

'I don't know – I don't...want to see Mummy and Daddy, just yet, I need to...to think, a bit.'

'Tell you what, why don't you come home with me for a little while? You can have a nice wash – have a shower, if you like – get all brushed and polished! You'll feel much better; and I'll run you home when you're ready. What do you say?'

'I...I don't know. I shouldn't. And I don't want to be a nuisance....'

'You won't be! And I think there's some ice-cream in the fridge?'

'Won't your wife mind?'

'She's away at the moment. Come on, Hannah – It would be nice company for me, too, if only for a bit.'

'Oh – All right. As long as you're sure?'

'I'm sure! Just let me see a smile, Okay?' She gave the man a rather tentative smile; he put the car in gear again, and drove on, turning from the Lane into a road which would take them into the town.

CHAPTER THIRTEEN

At the house in Newtown Road, Rimmer led the forensic team in through the front door. Already briefed on the task in hand, the experts promptly set about their examination of each room; others went on through to the garden and its shed.

Watching their efficient procedures, Rimmer felt rather surplus to requirements. He left them to it, returning to the station by way of Elwood Primary School, where he was informed in response to his questions that no-one had seen a suspicious silver car hanging around in recent weeks. In the office, he went back over the relevant statements, ending up only the more convinced that Olsen had to be Hannah's abductor.

* * *

Andrew Dorman had only been a fully-qualified Police Constable since the middle of the previous year. It had been a long-time ambition of his to join the force, since his older brother had been murdered when Andrew was only seven years old; he had achieved his ambition, with the support of the now-retired D.I. Keith Foreman, Russell's predecessor. He had taken to the job with quiet efficiency, earning praise from his superiors on a number of occasions already.

That Wednesday, he was stood outside Olsen's front door on what those engaged upon it called sentry duty. He felt slightly self-conscious, standing there at ease in his freshly-pressed uniform – three youths, probably bunking off school if his assessment of their ages was correct, were sat on the low front garden wall of the house almost directly opposite. They had kept glancing in the direction of Olsen's house, obviously curious about the goings-on there, joking amongst themselves, laughing at private jests he could not hear. But eventually they lost interest; their conversation appeared to take a fresh turn, and they no longer looked across, unsettling Andrew with their frank gazes.

Just after lunchtime, a couple of the forensic team came out of the house in their protective clothing, placing bagged samples in the van parked outside. They returned inside; the three lads, their interest restored by the activity, watched them go in and close the door. They exchanged a few words, and then heaved themselves lazily to their feet. They sauntered across, to halt in front of Andrew; one, the apparent ringleader, asked him:

'What's goin' on, then?' Andrew looked at the youth for a moment, unsure how much to say:

'We're just checking over the house.'

'Oh yeah? What's Kinky Kev been up to, then?' Andrew smiled and shrugged his shoulders, trying to get the lads on his side:

'I wouldn't know – I'm just a lowly P.C.!'

'Bin screwing kids again, 'as 'e?'

'Like I said, I don't know. Is that why you called him Kinky Kev, then? You reckon he has sex with children?'

'Did before, din't 'e? That's what my Dad says. Went to jail for it.'

'That's right – we lived 'ere then, I remember it!' A second youth concurred.

'You do?'

'Yeah! Didn't know what was goin' on, o'course, I was only about four or five. But I remember all the fuss, 'n my folks bein' all pestered when they found out we'd 'ad a prervert livin' just across the street all that time.'

'S'right. Ever since 'e came back, we've kinda kept an eye 'im, just in case, like. Will 'ere's got a little sister, so we've bin on the lookout for 'im getting' up to 'is old tricks.'

'I see. Well, I hate to disappoint you, but as I said, I don't know what's happening – I've just been told to stand guard outside!'

The boys' leader grinned at him:

'Yeah – I know! Poor bloody troops, just do what you're told, never mind why, eh?' Andrew nodded:

'That's about the measure of it!'

'Okay, mate – good luck!' The youths turned away, at the same time taking their leave of each other, separating to find their respective lunches, agreeing to meet again later.

* * *

As Andrew Dorman was being approached by the youths outside Olsen's house, Russell returned to his office. Rimmer brought him up to date with progress on the search, telling him excitedly that the officer in charge of the forensic team had just called to tell him that they'd found some black hairs on a chair in the living room, and had taken them for analysis. But so far, there was no other evidence of Hannah's presence in the house or garden. The discovery of the hairs had served to bolster Rimmer's conviction that Olsen was their man:

'It *must* have been him, boss! If those are her hairs on the chair, we've got him!'

'*If* they are, Doug! Let's wait for the analysis, eh?' Rimmer gazed at his superior, feeling somewhat annoyed by the D.I.'s reluctance to accept what he saw as the inevitable truth. All right, if he was right, the down side was that the next thing they'd come across should be the kiddie's body, probably in the garden somewhere – and he would be the first to rejoice if she could yet be found alive; but how likely was that?

'Come on, Doug – let's go and find some lunch, then we'll go and talk to Brad Farncome again, see if we can fill in Hannah's time on Friday. The Black Horse?'

'Yeah – good idea, sir!'

The two went down to the car park at the back of the station, and took Russell's Jeep to drive out to Bevington village for a meal and a pint (shandy for Rimmer, who had the car keys, of course!).

* * *

Over a relaxed lunch, the two detectives talked over the details of the case once more. And again, Doug Rimmer found himself becoming impatient with his superior – Russell's refusal to accept that Olsen had to be the culprit was getting under his skin. The Detective-Sergeant had a great deal of respect, and even affection, for the more experienced Inspector, but he did on occasion find his insistence upon taking a wide-ranging view of the evidence in a case almost frustrating. Russell, for his part, accepted his Sergeant's tendency to follow the most obvious path with a kind of amused tolerance; when the two differed, neither took things personally – the mark of a good, efficient team. And so far, the honours were about even – sometimes the obvious solution was the correct one, but on a number of occasions Russell's insistence upon keeping options open had paid off when a less than apparent truth had proved to be actual one.

As he went to pay for their lunches, Russell told the Sergeant that he had spoken to Harvey Goldman, and had permission to take Olsen's car around to the house at five-thirty, to see if little Taylor could identify it. They went out to the Jeep, and Rimmer drove to Alderley Park Avenue, arriving before Brad Farncome had got home from school; Emily, just in from Elwood Primary with her mother, opened the door to them; Rimmer smiled at the way her face lit up when she saw the D.I:

'Hello! Come in!' She turned and called out: 'Mummy! It's the policemen!'

The little girl led them through into the living room as her mother hurried in from the kitchen:

'Inspector – Sergeant; good to see you. Is there any news of Hannah?' She waved them to be seated, and herself sat in one of the easy chairs. Rimmer took the other, leaving Russell the settee; he gave his superior a broad grin as Emily sat next to the Inspector, slipping her arm through his. The D.I. smiled down at the child:

'I'm afraid not, nothing definite. We are questioning a man, who might have something to do with her disappearance, but it's too early to say yet. There are other leads we're following.' He settled himself more comfortably, and glanced down at Emily again:

'We'll find your friend for you, Emily, you wait and see!' The little girl nodded her curly head, her face solemn. Russell turned to her mother again:

'We do at last have a sighting of Hannah on Friday night. A little girl along the street saw her get into a car, as she was looking out for her father to come home, so we do have some firm information to go on, now.' He paused, and went on:

'I have a question for you, Mrs Farncome – when Hannah calls to see Emily, when she comes in the back way, would she knock at the door, and wait? Or, if it was unlocked, would she come on inside anyway?' The woman frowned, thinking:

'If we're here, she'd just walk in, more often than not. I imagine she would knock, then try the door; if it wasn't locked, she'd assume we were in.'

'That's right, Mummy' Emily concurred: 'She usually comes in, and calls out if she doesn't see me right away.' Russell nodded:

'Just like my son's friend, when he comes to see Daniel! I thought as much! Now – can you remember, when you and Emily went shopping on Friday, did you lock the back door when you went out?'

'Oh! Heavens, I don't know, now. Let me think – Brad had come in, and gone up to his room to change; Em was already out of her school things, and I was in a bit of a hurry because there was a lot I wanted to do…. I don't remember locking it; and with Brad in, I wouldn't necessarily make a point of it. I think it was probably open, but I can't be sure – so much happened later, I don't remember whether I unlocked it again during the evening or not. It was open then, when John went to help look for her.'

'Right – thank you, Mrs Farncome. When do you expect Brad home?'

'Any moment. Do you want to talk to him again?'

'Yes, I do. You see, the little girl who saw Hannah up the road saw her at around five forty; she must have got here from Elwood by about four forty-five. So where was she, in between?'

'You think she might have been here? But Brad says they didn't hear her knock… Oh! If she'd walked on in…? But why would she stay, if Emily wasn't here? She's quite fond of Brad, I think – but she wouldn't stop with him, I don't imagine. And if that other horrible boy was here, I expect she'd leave straight away.'

'That's what I think, Mrs Farncome. But you see, it begs the question, if she did walk in, why hasn't Brad told us that?' She nodded, her face troubled:

'Yes, I see….'

Just then they heard the front door open:

'I'm home, Mum!' The boy's voice sounded from the hallway.

'Come in here a moment, Brad!' She called out; the door opened, to reveal the fourteen-year-old, looking like any other teenage boy at the end of the school day: Jacket draped over one arm, tie askew, one tail of his shirt hanging out, shoes scuffed and dirty. The look on his face when he saw the two detectives was one of carefully controlled interest; but both had caught the flash of concern which preceded it:

'Oh, hello! Have you found Hannah yet?'

'Not yet, I'm afraid. I'm wondering if you can help us a bit more, Brad?'

'Me? How?' His mother cut in:

'The back door was unlocked on Friday, Brad, when Em and I went out. So – when Hannah called, she would have walked on in, wouldn't she? Thinking we were here?' The boy looked worried, now:

'But she didn't, Mum! We'd have heard her, wouldn't we?' His mother turned her attention to the little girl:

'Emily – go up and get changed now, there's a good girl.'

'Oh – must I?'

'Yes, please. You can come down again when I tell you.'

'Oh – all right.' The disappointment was clear in her voice as she let go of Russell's arm and left the room. Gently, he took over the questioning as the boy dropped his school bag on the floor and sat on an upright chair beside the bureau:

'Brad – we've found a witness, who saw Hannah after she left here, on Friday.'

'Oh – well, that's good, isn't it?'

'Yes – but: She saw her, just along the street, no more than five minutes from here, almost an hour *after* she would have come to your back door. So – where was she, all that time? Do you know?'

'Me? How should I?'

'You would – if she was here, Brad.'

'Here? Don't be daft! Why would she stay here, with me, and that brute Spike? That's the last thing she'd want to do!'

'That's what I thought. But – the other thing our witness says is that she was crying, as she walked along the road. Why would she be doing that, do you think?'

'I – I've no idea, why should I have?' The boy was beginning to sound desperate, now.

'Well, now. Let me throw an idea at you, Brad: Suppose she had come here, knocked on your back door, found it unlocked, and walked straight in? And suppose she'd overheard you and Spike talking about his plans to go shop-lifting the next day? I imagine that Spike wouldn't want her talking about that to anyone, now would he? Did he try to frighten her into keeping quiet? Put the fear of God into the poor kid, to save his own skin? Is that what happened, Brad? Is that where she was, all that time, before she was seen along the road here, crying her eyes out?'

'No! It wasn't – she – oh, Jesus Christ!' He buried his face in his hands. No-one spoke, but his mother got up, went to him, and put her arm around his shoulders. He looked up at her:

'I'm sorry, Mum! I know you and Dad are disappointed in me, and I don't want to make it worse, but...' He heaved a deep sigh, and turned to the Inspector:

'All right. I'll tell you everything – but it's much worse than you think! It's...horrible!' Russell smiled gently at the distraught youth:

'Come on, lad, get it off your chest, you'll feel better. It can't be that bad, surely?' The boy nodded:

'Oh yes, it can!' He drew a breath, and began to talk. And this time, he gave the whole, unvarnished truth, of how Spike had told him to bring the little girl up to the room, how the bully had pulled her trousers down and molested her, of how at last he'd given in to his anger and hit the bigger boy, telling Hannah to get away while he was down. He knew nothing of where she'd gone, after that. And this time, he was believed; by the time he'd finished, his distress was so obvious, the tears streaming down his face, that Russell felt he had the truth at last. When the boy stopped talking, the Inspector sat back in the settee, absorbing his story, wondering just where this took them in the search for Hannah. He looked up, to see the boy gazing at him, his eyes full of trepidation:

'Are you going to arrest me?' Russell smiled:

'No! What for?'

'Well – it's…assault, isn't it? What Spike did? And I was there, so I'm a – what do you call it – accessory, aren't I?' Russell shook his head:

'Maybe, technically, you're right. But I'm sure you've told us the truth, now, Brad, and that's what's important to me. And you did stop him, you did protect her, even if it was – a bit late, perhaps. I may not be so lenient on Spike, though!' That got a smile from the boy:

'Good! Can't you lock him up? That's what that bastard needs!' Russell grinned at him:

'Maybe we will, at that! Thank you, Brad. I wish you'd told us this in the first place, mind, it would have narrowed the times down for us if nothing else; and it may just be that Hannah's state of mind affected what happened to her later. She was seen to get into a car, after she left here – all we have to do now is find it!' He rose to his feet, beckoning Rimmer, who had sat in silence throughout, mildly shocked by the boy's revelations. As they went to depart, Brad spoke, almost tentatively:

'Mr Russell?' The Inspector turned; he was surprised to see a look of fear and distress on the boy's face:

'Yes, Brad?'

'There's something – I need to ask you?'

'What is it?'

'Is – I mean, do you think – Hannah's… still alive?'

'I don't know, Brad. I *hope* she is, of course. But I don't know.' The boy nodded, then said:

'Do you think, maybe – after what Spike did to her, she might've – I mean, She was really upset, and frightened, and… You don't think, she's – jumped in the river, or something?' Realising the train of the boy's thoughts, Russell went over to him; he stood up as the policeman approached, tears glistening in his eyes again. Russell took him by the shoulders, shook him gently:

'No, Brad, I don't! I've learnt a lot about little Hannah in the last few days, and I'm quite sure that, however upset she was, she'd have got over it. She's – too strong, too full of life, to just give in and do something like that! You know that, too – so don't go scaring yourself with ideas that Spike's brutality might have driven her to kill herself; it didn't happen, you hear me?' The youth nodded, smiling through his tears:

'O – Okay! Thank you. And – thank you for – understanding. I'm just so sorry, for everything….'

'It's all right. It's all over – I know what I need to know. I might ask you to make a statement, about what Spike did to Hannah – would you do that for me?'

'Y – Yes, of course!'

'Okay, then! Relax, have your tea, and leave the worrying about Hannah to us, all right?' The boy nodded again; Russell gave him a last reassuring smile as he turned and left.

CHAPTER FOURTEEN

As the two detectives got into the Jeep, Rimmer surprised a broad grin on his Inspector's face:

'You look happy, boss?' Russell looked across, the grin still in place:

'Yes! I don't like bullies, and that Gidding boy strikes me as a bully of the worst kind. I'm going to enjoy scaring the shit out of him!'

'What'll we do with him?'

'Arrest him – for indecent assault!'

'Can we make it stick? It'll be his word against Brad's, unless we find Hannah alive, won't it?'

'Oh, I doubt if it'll come to that. I think Spike'll fold up like a pack of cards as soon as he's under any kind of pressure.'

'Then what?'

'I don't know, yet. I'll think about it.' He checked his watch: 'I'd like to stop by Olsen's house on the way back to the station; then we'd better get his car over here for little Taylor to see it. Let's go, Doug.'

Rimmer started the car, and drove away. As they headed across the town, Russell asked:

'Who's in charge of the SOCO team?'

'The Mad Professor.'

'Oh, excellent! If there's anything to find, he'll find it!'

* * *

Terry Owen had joined the police force in his early twenties. During his time as a beat copper, he'd become more and more fascinated with the scientific approach to solving and preventing crime, something his superiors had soon realised; their offer of a transfer into Scenes of Crime, with its heavy reliance upon forensic science, had been eagerly accepted. Now, aged forty-nine, he was a highly respected scientific policeman – nominally a Detective-Sergeant, Terry showed no apparent respect for rank, his own or anyone else's. His round, ruddy face was surmounted by a shining bald pate, around which his remaining, bushy grey hair stuck out in all directions, giving him something of the demeanour of a crazed Benedictine Monk; clad in white protective clothing, he became everyone's image of the mad scientist, hence his accepted nickname.

In number 27, Newtown Road, he was just tidying up after his team's day-long examination of the premises when the Detective-Inspector's car pulled up outside. He opened the door to the two plain-clothes officers:

'David! Doug! Come on in. We're just finishing up in here.'

'Hi, Terry. What have you got for us?' Owen shook his head:

'Not a lot, I'm afraid. I've taken samples from all over the place, but at this point in time I can't say that there's anything much to place your little girl here. I'll tell you more when I've had a closer look, of course.'

'Doug said you'd found some hairs?'

'Mm, right. Black hairs – on that chair over there' he indicated a grubby armchair in one corner of the living room 'but I don't know if they're hers. Could be, maybe, but they're shorter than I'd have expected. Tell you tomorrow, all being well, when I've had 'em under the microscope.'

'Okay – soon as you can, Terry?'

'Of course, David.'

'You're about done here?'

'Yep – just about to leave. Kit's back in the van.'

'Olsen's car?'

'At the station. I've had two of my boys going over it – nothing to show, I'm afraid.'

'Can we borrow it?'

'Sure! I'm done with it, do what you like!'

Owen made a last check around the house, then the three left together, Rimmer locking up and taking the keys with him. Outside, the SOCO Sergeant got into the van with his two assistants; it started with a billow of diesel smoke, and took off down the road like a World Rally competitor on a special stage. Rimmer grinned at his superior:

'He really is crazy, isn't he?' Russell laughed:

'I reckon so, Doug!'

Andrew Dorman was still on duty at the garden gate; as Russell approached, he accosted him:

'Mr Russell, sir?'

'Everything all right, Andrew?'

'Fine, sir – but – I don't know if it's important: You see those three kids, over there?' He indicated the three youths, once more sitting on their garden wall, cans of drink in their hands, casually watching the proceedings.

'Yes?'

'Earlier in the day, they came over for a chat, asking what was going on. I told them I didn't know, played the ignorant foot-soldier, you know. From what they said, it seems they know all about Olsen's record, what he was in prison for; and they sort of intimated that they've been keeping a bit of an eye on him. One of them, I think it's the coloured lad, has a younger sister, and they obviously don't trust Olsen when there are girls around. I just thought, maybe they were watching him on Friday? Maybe they know if he was here, what time he came in?' Russell clapped the young Constable on the arm:

'Good thinking, Andrew! You could be right.'

'Perhaps they even saw him with Hannah?' Rimmer suggested.

'I don't think so, sir' the P.C. replied: 'I think they'd have said something, in that case. But it might still be worth talking to them?'

'You're right! Thank you, Andrew, we'll tackle them while we're here. Are you going off duty, now?'

'Yes, sir. A soon as I get back to the station.'

'You wouldn't like to do me a favour, would you? Earn yourself a bit of overtime?' An eager light appeared in the young man's bright blue eyes:

'Of course, sir! What do you want me to do?'

'Wait for us here while we talk to your friends; then I'd like you to come back to the station with us, and drive a suspect car to Alderley Park for our witness to see it. I'll square it with Mr Armstrong tomorrow, okay?'

'Yes, of course!' He stood to one side, as the two detectives crossed the road, headed towards the youths.

As they approached, Russell looked over their potential informants. All three looked to be around fourteen or fifteen; all were clad in casual jackets, jeans and trainers, the styles the same, only the colours differing. The uniformity of youth, Russell thought! Two were white; one tallish, slender, dark-haired, the other shorter, more stocky, and blond; the third lad was coloured, not the black black of the African or the Caribbean, but a warm chocolate brown, suggesting a mixed-race background. As the two officers came close, the taller boy stood up, looking at them almost defiantly.

'Good evening, lads.' He acknowledged Russell's greeting with a nod of the head.

'My Constable over there said you'd been chatting with him, earlier.'

'Yeah, we did. So?'

'He said you know all about our friend Mr Olsen?'

'Kinky Kev? He's no friend of ours.'

'Is that what you call him? I gather you, sort of keep watch on him, make sure he's not up to no good, is that right?' The boy shrugged:

'Kinda. When we can.'

'This is where you meet up, is it, this garden?'

'Yeah. I live 'ere.' The stocky lad stood up as he spoke.

'Mm. What's your name?'

'Barton. Al Barton.'

'You?' Russell looked at the tall boy.

'Darren Morgan. I live down there, number 46.' The coloured boy also rose to his feet:

'And I'm Will Christie, before you ask. That way – number 20.' Russell smiled:

'Right – thanks.' He paused; then asked: 'I don't suppose you were all here last Friday, were you?' Suspicion flickered in Darren Morgan's eyes:

'Why d'you want to know?' Before Russell could reply, Will Christie cut in:

'It's about that little girl, isn't it? The one that's missing?' Of the three, he was the only one who took any real interest in the world around him, watched TV news programmes. Neither Morgan nor Barton could be bothered with anything outside their own little sphere, anything which didn't affect them directly. Russell turned to the coloured boy:

'That's right, Will. Like you, we know all about Mr Olsen – and we're trying to find out if he had anything to do with her disappearance.'

'Bet 'e did, too!' Al Barton interjected: ''E fucked a little kid last time, didn't 'e? Bet 'e's done it again!'

'We don't know, yet.' Russell told him: 'But if you *were* here, and saw what time he came home, it might help us.'

'She disappeared after school, didn't she?' Will asked.

'Yes – between about five and six, that night.' The two white boys quickly exchanged glances:

'So if 'e was 'ere, 'e couldn't 'ave done it?' Russell nodded. Will opened his mouth to speak, but Darren grabbed him by the arm, and spoke first:

'We didn't see, did we, Al?'

'You mean you didn't see Olsen? Or you weren't here?' Russell asked.

'We – didn't notice, when 'e got in, like.'

'So you can't help me?' The lie was transparent, but Russell had no way of defeating it. Darren Morgan shook his head:

'No – sorry, but…' He shrugged his shoulders. Russell gazed into his eyes for a moment, a hard glint sharpening the hazel colour of his own:

'Okay – but think about this, lads: If Olsen *didn't* take that little girl, *someone else did!* If he goes inside for it, the real culprit might still be walking around loose – around *here,* in the Warren, maybe. How safe will your little sisters be then?' He turned his eyes on each boy in turn, then swung around and stalked back to the car, the Sergeant trailing behind. He took the keys from Rimmer, and got into the driving seat, beckoning Andrew Dorman to join them; the young Constable got into the back as the Inspector started the engine. His departure was only marginally less rapid than Owen's had been.

Will Christie rounded on his friends:

'Why didn't you tell him? You both *know* Kinky Kev was here, when that kid went missing!' Morgan shrugged his shoulders again:

'Why should we care if he goes in the knick again? It's only what 'e deserves!'

'Yeah – bloody prervert! 'E should be be'ind bars, shouldn't 'e?' Barton concurred.

'It's *pervert,* you ignorant sod! And if 'e does? What about what that copper said? The bastard who *really* had that kid gets off scot free, does 'e?'

'Oh, don't be so soft, Will! They'll get 'im, they don't need our 'elp. I just don't see why we should do anythin' for *that* bloody nonce.' Darren gestured across the road. Will gazed at the other two in disgust, then turned and walked away in the direction of his own home. Darren and Al looked at each other, their expressions seeming to ask what had got into their friend.

* * *

At the police station, Andrew Dorman picked up the Fiat and followed Russell to Alderley Park Avenue. They stopped, across the road from the Goldman house and several doors down. The Inspector got out; Andrew wound down the window as he approached:

'Right – wait here, Andrew. When I call on the radio, swing the car round, and pull up outside number 139, over there. Lean across, and open the passenger door, okay?'

'Very good, sir.' He closed the window again as the two detectives got out of the Jeep and walked across to the house. Rimmer rang the bell; Goldman opened the door to them, waved them inside, led them into the lounge where his wife and daughter were waiting. Tarah stood to greet them; Taylor looked up, and smiled when she saw Russell:

'Hello! Have you come to talk to me again?'

'That's right, Taylor.'

'Oh, goody! Come and sit next to me.' She beckoned him over. Russell gave his Sergeant a sheepish look as Rimmer's chuckle followed him across the room. The little girl took his arm in hers as he sat down; he smiled down at her:

'I want you to do something for me, Taylor.'

'What?'

'You remember the car you told me about? The one the little girl got into?' She nodded.

'Well, we've brought a car I want you to look at. I want you to tell me, if you can, whether it's the same one you saw before. Is that all right?' Taylor nodded again, thoughtfully:

'What if I'm not *sure?*'

'Just say so. If you think it is, that's fine. If you think it *isn't,* well, that's fine, too. Just tell me what you think, okay?'

'Okay.' He nodded to Rimmer, who took out his radio and called the waiting Constable. Taylor turned round in her seat, letting go of Russell's hand as she knelt up to look out of the window:

'Is that how you were looking out, when you were waiting for Daddy?'

'Mm-hm.' The Fiat drew up outside; the passenger door swung open, the interior light coming on as it did so. Russell asked:

'What do you think, Taylor? Is that the car you saw on Friday?' She didn't reply straight away, but went on looking, her head tilted in her usual thinking pose; then she looked around at him:

'I don't *think* so. It – might be, but – I think the other one was *bigger;* and more – more *swoopy.*'

'More streamlined, do you mean?'

'What's *streamlined?*' She frowned at him, her pert nose puckered up.

'Oh – sort of…' he gestured with his hands, indicating a sleek, smooth shape.

'That's right – *swoopy!*' The little girl's voice was triumphant. Russell laughed:

'Okay! We both know what we mean, don't we?' She giggled with him, turning round to sit down again, snuggling against his side. He grinned down at the child:

'So – we don't think it's the same car?'

'No.'

'But it *might* be, is that right?' Rimmer interjected his question.

'Mm-hm – that's right. It *was* a long time ago, you know.' Russell nodded solemnly, aware from conversations with his own children how their perspective of time differed from that of an adult – six days was an age, to a six-year-old! They were lucky the child remembered as much as she did.

'All right, Taylor – that's great. Thank you very much, you've been an enormous help.' He went to rise, but she kept hold of him; gently disentangling his arm, he smiled down apologetically:

'I'm sorry, Taylor – I've got to go, now.'

'Oh! Will you come and see me again?' He was aware of Rimmer's barely concealed amusement as he replied:

'I'd love to, Taylor. I'll pop by again soon, I promise.' She let him go, reluctantly. Harvey Goldman showed them to the door, apologising for his daughter's uncertainty; Russell assured him that they hadn't expected her to be certain, but that the indication she'd given them was still very helpful. As Goldman closed the door behind them, Rimmer burst out laughing:

'You're a real hit with the girls, aren't you, boss? First Emily, now little Taylor!'

Russell cuffed him playfully around the head, his mood more than restored after the recalcitrance of the youths earlier.

CHAPTER FIFTEEN

'Come on, Doug, let's go and stamp on young Spike!' Russell beckoned Police Constable Dorman from the little Fiat; the young uniformed officer got out and came over to the two detectives:

'Sir?'

'Would you come with us, Andrew? We're going to arrest a youth, and the sight of a uniform wouldn't go amiss. Leave the car there, we'll take it back to the station later.'

'Very good, sir.'

The three got into Russell's car, and drove the short distance along Alderley Park Avenue to number 188. Rimmer knocked at the door; Gidding opened it to them:

'Oh – Good evening Inspector, Sergeant. What can I do for you?' The diplomatic welcome in the man's voice was belied by the obvious annoyance on his face.

'Is your son in, Mr Gidding?' The Sergeant asked.

'He is – he's up in his room. What do you want with him?'

'Can you call him down here, please sir?' Gidding's anger at having his evening disrupted shone in his eyes, but he turned and shouted:

'Charlie! Get down here!' The fifteen-year-old emerged from his room, and stomped down the stairs, clad in a smart but rumpled casual shirt and new-looking denim jeans:

'What is it?' Before his father could speak, Rimmer addressed him:

'I'm Detective-Sergeant Rimmer, this is Detective-Inspector Russell, and Constable Dorman. We're from Grancester Police Station.' Caution lit the boy's eyes:

'What do you want with me?' Russell took up the proceedings:

'Charles Gidding Junior – I am arresting you for the indecent assault of Hannah Buckland, perpetrated at number 197 Alderley Park Avenue on Friday March the 15th at around five p.m. You do not have to say anything at this time; anything you do say will be taken down and may be given in evidence. However, I should inform you that your defence may be harmed if you later rely upon information which was not disclosed during the investigation.' Father and son appeared to be competing to see which could look the more stunned. Chuck Gidding recovered first:

'What is this bloody nonsense? Charlie's never done anything like that, for Christ's sake!'

'I'm afraid he has, Mr Gidding. We have a witness to the whole incident; and corroborating information.' Spike at last recovered his voice:

'Bradley fucking Farncome! I'll kill him, the bloody little sneak!'

'Shut up, you idiot!' His father rounded upon him. In a calmer tone, Russell told the boy:

'You'll do nothing of the kind, young man! Right now, you're coming with us. Constable, would you take Charles to my car, please?'

'Yes, sir!' There was a twinkle in the bright blue eyes as the young policeman turned to the deflated bully: 'Come along, son.'

Looking somehow bedraggled, Spike grabbed a coat from one of the pegs in the hall as he was led outside. Gidding, still looking dumbfounded, turned to Russell:

'Can I go with him, Inspector?'

'You could follow us, in your own car, if you wish, sir. I'd like to have you present when we question Charles, in a little while, but you'll understand that we can't allow you to be with him in the meantime.' The man looked ready to argue the toss; but, thinking better of it, he just nodded his head:

'I'll be along right away – I'd better tell his mother what's going on.' He turned and went into the kitchen. Russell waved his Sergeant to precede him through the front door; outside, he told him:

'You take Olsen's car back, Doug – I'll drop you off along the road. Dorman can ride with Spike, then get away home when we've deposited him in a cell. We'll talk to the brat later.'

'Okay, sir.' They climbed into the Jeep, and Russell drove off, pausing to let Rimmer get out near the little Fiat.

At the Police Station, they went through the formalities of placing Spike in custody. Andrew Dorman, still elated at his opportunity to work with Russell, an officer for whom he had the utmost respect, left to go home; the two detectives retired to Russell's office to confer.

'I think we'll let him cool his heels for a while, Doug. Won't do him any harm – nor his old man, for that matter!'

'Right, sir. What do you intend to do with Spike?'

'I'm not really sure. On the one hand, I suspect that a really severe shock at this stage will probably cure his antisocial tendencies, at least for the time being, so letting him off with a caution would do as much good as anything – and I don't like the idea of saddling a lad his age with a criminal conviction. But if what he did had anything to do with what happened to Hannah afterwards...? I don't know. Suppose she was so upset that she forgot her common sense, got into a car with a stranger because she grabbed the first opportunity for some sympathy? Doesn't sound like her, I know – but who can tell? The poor kid must have been absolutely distraught, after the way he treated her.'

'Yes – it could complicate things. This doesn't get us any closer to finding her, does it?' Russell shook his head.

'No, Doug. I'm glad we know at last what happened at that

house, but we're no nearer to knowing what followed. We need to trace that car!'

'If it wasn't Olsen's, sir. Little Taylor seemed to leave that possibility open, didn't she?'

'Mmm – maybe. I'm inclined to trust her first instinct, that it wasn't the right car. Not that, as we said before, her identification is actually worth a lot as evidence in court. If those hairs the Professor found *are* Hannah's, we've got our answer. If they're not, then I think we're looking for a largish silver estate car, with a streamlined shape.'

'*Swoopy,* you mean, boss!' The two laughed.

'Right!'

'What about a biggish hatchback? Something like a Vectra?' Rimmer suggested.

'Mm – possible. But they have a bit of a boot, don't they?'

'Yeah, but – her standard of comparison is the big Jag, remember, and they have a large, very definite boot. I reckon a Vectra, maybe one of the mid-sized BMW's, might be possible.'

'Or any number of Japanese models, Doug.' He snorted: 'Speculating over the type of car's not really going to help – there're too many possibilities! The only mention of something suitable is Andrews' Mercedes estate, and Brian Buckland reckons he's no longer got it, anyway.' He thought, then continued: 'Would Hannah have known the car?'

'I guess so – why?'

'Well – suppose a *car* she recognised pulled up beside her? Might she have got into it, even with a strange driver?'

'I doubt it, boss! She's not a silly kid, by any account.'

'But suppose – if the new owner knew its history, knew the girl, knew that she'd know the car – he could have said he was on an errand for Mr Andrews, or something, got her into the car on the promise of taking her home, maybe?'

'Oh come on, sir! That's a pretty wild idea, isn't it?'

'Yeah, I know – but still, it *could* be. We need to find out what happened to Andrews' car – did he trade it to the dealer, sell it privately, what?'

Rimmer looked almost pityingly at his superior, unconvinced by this, as he saw it, wildly speculative line of thought. But then, the Inspector was in charge:

'Yes, sir. Should I go and see him tomorrow, ask him about it?'

'We'll both go, Doug. No, Dammit! I'm in court at ten, over those corner shop robberies. You go, see if he can tell you where it is now.'

'Okay, sir. He'll be at the shop, I imagine?'

'I'd think so – call him, make sure. And talking of calling…' he reached for the telephone, dialled the Farncome's number.

In Alderley Park Avenue, John Farncome answered the phone's ring:

'Farncome?'

'Mr Farncome – D.I. Russell. I imagine Brad's told you about our visit, earlier?' The reply was grim-voiced:

'He has, Mr Russell. I can't tell you how ashamed I am of him, allowing something like that to happen in my house.'

'Don't be too hard on the boy, Mr Farncome. He *did* step in to stop it, after all – and I think he's suffered quite badly at that bully's hands, for a while now. I know he's desperately upset, thinks he's let you and his mother down very badly. It might pay you to be gentle with him, if you don't mind me making the suggestion.'

Silence fell at the other end of the line, followed by a sigh:

'You might be right, Mr Russell. I know I've been hard on him recently – but for so long he's been getting into trouble at school; and he wouldn't tell us why! Now we do know what's been going on…. I suppose it's unfair of me to blame the boy for giving in to that kind of pressure. If only he'd come out and told me in the first place!'

'Thank you, Mr Farncome. I like your boy – oh, he's been pretty stupid, especially in not telling *us* what happened there before now. But we can all get things wrong, can't we, from time to time?' He paused: 'Can I speak to him?'

'Of course – I'll get him for you.'

After a few seconds, the boy's voice came on the phone:

'Mr Russell? You want to talk to me?'

'Yes, Brad. Do you think you could come to the Police Station sometime, give me a proper statement about Spike?'

'Yes – I suppose so. When?'

'How about after school, tomorrow? I could pick you up, perhaps, then drop you at home when we're finished.'

'Er – yeah, I don't see why not. We get out at three o'clock.'

'Okay – You know my car? The dark green Jeep. If I can't make it myself, I'll have officers in a marked police car collect you, all right?'

'Oh, wow! That'd get people talking! I'll see you then.'

'Right – thanks, Brad. Goodnight.'

'Goodnight, Inspector.' Russell replaced the receiver:

'Come on, Doug – let's go and talk to Spike!'

* * *

As Russell and his assistant clattered down the stairs to the cells, Mary Parrott was walking slowly up the stairs in her house. She went into the back bedroom, turned down the sheets on the bed, and went to close the curtains over the window.

A small, sprightly woman of seventy-six, Mary had taken to sleeping in the smaller room since the Doctor had died the previous year. Oh, she'd been tempted to remove herself from his bed many times – but then, through it all, she'd regarded his string of affairs with a kind of amused disdain, and a supreme, and totally justified, confidence that he would sooner or later return to her arms, full of apologies and remorse. Until the next time his overgrown libido got the better of him, that is. Now that he'd gone, she was simply carrying on with her life as always;

the only difference was that he was probably chasing after the prettiest angel he could find. She hoped that Saint Peter would have more success than she had had, keeping him under control.

As she turned to the window, movement in the next-door garden caught her eye. Poor Mr Andrews! Whatever was he up to, out there at this time of night? Mary was not the kind of person to keep a watch on her neighbours, like some elderly people who live alone – the occasional media interest in her husband's affairs had taught her the value of privacy – but now her natural curiosity got the better of her. She watched him set up the incinerator, pile in a load of garden rubbish, pour some old engine oil over it, and drop in a lighted match. A satisfying 'whump' of flame went up, and the contents settled to burning steadily. It seemed a strange time to be having a bonfire – but then, with all his troubles, maybe it was the only time he had.

They had chatted over the garden wall earlier in the week: She had asked after Sheila, and learnt only that she was much the same, no better – not that she would ever get better, poor dear! – but not noticeably worse, either. And about the missing girl, of course; she knew that the child was the daughter of the man who ran Mr Andrews' shop in Barfield – she and the Doctor had bought several items there, before the Andrews' had come to live next door. Poor Mr Andrews was having to go there every day at the moment, to fill in for the girl's father, as well as having to visit his wife – so perhaps his nocturnal incineration was understandable. You'd have thought he might have left it until the weekend, perhaps – but then, that was his affair, after all! She pulled the curtains across, and turned her back on the rosy glow outside.

* * *

The interview with the youth went pretty much as Russell had foreseen. Once the boy understood that he wasn't going to be able to bluster his way out of trouble, he became the weak, frightened character that lies at the heart of all bullies. To his father's obvious disgust, he admitted tearfully to his assault on the little girl, confirming Brad's story in every detail, confirming that she had run from the house while he was incapacitated, on the floor of Brad's room. Despite Chuck Gidding's protests, they returned the youth to a cell for the night, saying that they needed to check one or two details of his story, that he could probably go home in the morning. Once the father had left, Rimmer asked his superior:

'We don't need to keep the boy, do we, sir?' Russell shook his head, grinning:

'No, Doug! But it'll do him the world of good, won't it? Spare me another half an hour, will you – I'd like to have another quick go at Olsen.'

'Right, sir!' That's more like it, the Sergeant's tone of voice seemed to say.

They collected the mechanic from his cell, took him to the interview room. There, the two went over his story yet again; then, Rimmer sprang the news on him that they'd found the hairs on his armchair:

'What d'you mean, 'airs? What sort of 'airs?'

'Black hairs, Kevin – like Hannah's.'

'Oh Christ! They ain't 'ers! They can't be – I keep tellin' yer, she ain't been near me 'ouse!'

'How do you account for us finding them, then?'

''Ow should I know? I tell yer… The bloody cat! It's 'is 'airs! Next door's bloody cat, Charlie! 'E's alwes comin' in, 'anging round!'

'A *cat,* Kevin?'

'Yeah – like I tell yer, 'e's alwes comin' in the back door, or in the winder. I s'pose I should'a sent 'im packin' – but 'e's so friendly, like, rubbin' round, purrin'. 'E sometimes curls up in the old chair in me livin' room for a sleep. They're 'is 'airs, they must be!' Rimmer was losing patience with what he saw as the man's continual evasions:

'Come on, Kevin! Stop trying to lead us up the garden path. We *know* you grabbed Hannah – you knew her, you could easily find out where she lived, she was seen getting into a car like yours! Why not get it off your chest? Tell us where she is, let the kid's parents off the hook, for pity's sake!' The man buried his face in his hands, then looked up again, tears of anger and frustration in his eyes:

'I *can't,* for 'eaven's sake! 'Ow offen d'you want me to tell yer, *I didn't do it!'*

Russell, tiring of the fruitless exercise, gestured his Sergeant to let it go:

'Okay, Kevin. The sergeant and I are going home, we've had a long day. We'll talk to you again in the morning, I expect. Interview concluded at 21.37.' he added for the sake of the tapes.

CHAPTER SIXTEEN

The following morning, after the Inspector had departed for Northampton Crown Court, Rimmer called the Mad Professor in his scientific lair:

'Terry – anything for us on the Olsen case?'

'Not yet, Doug. I'm only just starting to go over the samples we brought back. All I can tell you for sure is that your little girl's not buried in the garden – none of the soil there has been disturbed for years, by the look of it. Not your keen gardener, Mr Olsen. I rather doubt if she's been in that house – but I'll confirm that when I know for sure.'

'What about the hairs?'

'Hm! Possible, but I don't think they're hers. I'll call you, all right?'

'Okay – soon as you can, Terry?'

'Yeah, yeah! Soon as I can.' Rimmer smiled as he replaced the receiver; Owen's dislike of being interrupted in his domain was well-known.

The Detective-Sergeant called Barfield Antiques next, confirming that George Andrews was there, and arranging to see him. He drove out to the village in his Astra, and walked into the shop, savouring its heady atmosphere of dust and french polish. An elegant woman in her thirties stepped forward to greet him; he showed her his warrant card:

'D.S. Rimmer, to see Mr Andrews.'

'Oh yes, Sergeant, come on through, he's in the back room.'
She led the way. In the rear of the shop, Andrews rose to meet
the plain-clothes officer:

'Sergeant! Welcome to our little emporium. You've met
Stephanie?' They exchanged greetings; the proprietor went on
as she left them to talk:

'Steph's a God-send, believe me! Don't know where we'd be
without her – or Peter, of course. It's his day off, today. Brian
Buckland usually runs the place, as I'm sure you know, but as
things are…' He smiled apologetically.

'Of course, sir, I understand.'

'Tell me, is there any news of poor Hannah?'

'Not yet, I'm afraid. We've narrowed down the time when
she disappeared, thanks to a witness who saw her in Alderley
Park Avenue, but we still don't know what's happened to her.'

'Oh, that's too bad! I'm sure you're doing all you can, mind.
Now – how can I help you?'

'I wanted to ask you about your car, sir.'

'The Mercedes? What about it?'

'What type of car is it, sir?' Andrews grinned a little
sheepishly:

'A convertible, Sergeant – metallic Crimson, leather trim,
matching soft-top. A bit pretentious, I suppose – but my wife
wanted one like it.'

'It sounds quite something, sir. You don't have an estate car,
as well?'

'No – we did, but it's gone.'

'You traded it in for the convertible, did you, sir?' Andrews
laughed:

'No! It's quite a saga, I'm afraid – we were going to, but then
I decided we might as well hang onto it. For the business, you
understand. But after a while, I found I wasn't using it – Brian
has an estate car, and if we have any bigger things, furniture or
anything like that, to collect, we use Braggins, in the town. They

deliver for us, long-distance, as well – they're very good, we've never had anything damaged, and they're always on time, deliver when they say they will. Anyhow, I advertised the estate – sold it straight away! Must've made it too cheap, I suppose!'

'Who bought it, Mr Andrews?'

'Oh, dear! I don't think I kept a note of his name and address. He came from Bedford, I think – I'll have a look at home for you, Sergeant, see if I can find it. Is it important?'

'Probably not, sir – how long ago was this?'

'Oh – six or eight weeks. Just after Sheila went into St Mungo's. I'm afraid, I perhaps wasn't thinking terribly straight, around that time. My wife's… very poorly, you see.'

'I know, sir – I'm very sorry. About the car – it's just that someone saw little Hannah get into a big silver estate car, or possibly a hatchback, the night she disappeared; and we wondered if it could possibly have been your old one.'

'Oh, I doubt that! She wasn't the sort of girl who would get into a car with a stranger, I'm quite sure.'

'She would have known your car, though?'

'Of course! But it wasn't the only silver Mercedes estate around here, I'm certain. And from what you said, it could have been a different model altogether, couldn't it?'

'That's right, sir. Could your wife confirm what you've told me?' Andrews hesitated:

'I expect so, Sergeant. She knows I sold the car – but – they are controlling her pain with pretty strong medication, and it sometimes leaves her, a bit confused, if you know what I mean.'

'Could I speak to her, sir?'

'Oh, I don't see why not – just don't expect too much of her, please? And you can check in our garage, if you want to! You'll only find the convertible there, though!'

'All right – thank you very much, Mr Andrews. I'm sorry to have troubled you. If my superior wants to talk to your wife, I'll tell him to contact you, shall I?'

'Please do, Sergeant! I go to see her every afternoon – I try to get there in time to have tea with her, so if you would like to join us? I expect Sheila would enjoy seeing a new face or two.'

'Very good – thank you again.'

'Any time, Sergeant!'

The antique shop owner showed his visitor to the door, shaking his hand as he left.

* * *

The Sergeant was not long back in the office when a call came through from the forensic team:

'Doug? Terry Owen. Bad news, I'm afraid.'

'Oh?'

'Yeah – those hairs, from Olsen's place? Cat hairs. Must have a long-haired black cat.'

'Oh, damn! I thought we'd got him nailed, when you found them. Was there anything else to put the girl there? Anything at all?'

'Nah! Not a thing. If you're right, and he was the one who grabbed her, he disposed of her before he went home.'

'Bugger it! I was certain he'd taken her. Still could have, mind....'

'Sure you're not letting your dislike for the man cloud your judgement, Doug?' The Sergeant sighed:

'Maybe I am, Terry. He's a disreputable little runt – and I suppose knowing what he did before doesn't help you like him. Maybe Dave's right; maybe it was nothing to do with him. But dammit, he's our only real suspect!'

'Well, there you go, mate! Keep digging, you'll get there in the end!'

'Yeah, right!' He heard the other phone go down, replaced his own on the rest. He sat and stared at it for a moment, and then got to his feet and headed for the canteen for some lunch.

He was just finishing a cup of mediocre coffee when Russell entered, and sat down next to him:

'All right, Doug?'

'Yeah. How'd the case go?'

'Pretty good – jury's out now. I reckon we'll have a conviction before the day's over.'

'Oh, good! That's one off our plate, then!'

'Did you see Andrews?'

'Yeah. He confirmed more or less what the Bucklands told you. They did have a silver Mercedes estate, but he sold it a while ago, after his wife went into the hospital. He's quite agreeable to us talking to her – but he said to remember that she's under pretty heavy medication, and sometimes gets confused. And we're welcome to inspect his garage, if we want to.'

'Hm – sounds kosher, doesn't it? Where'd the car go, did he say?'

'No – says he didn't keep a note of the buyer's name or address, that he was not thinking too well at the time. You can understand, I suppose – his wife just into hospital with a terminal cancer, he'd not be at his best, would he?'

'No, I guess not. He didn't trade it, then?'

'No – sold it privately. Buyer was from Bedford, he thinks.'

'Okay. Might be possible to trace it – but I doubt if it'd be worth the effort. We might just contact the local dealer, though, see if they've any knowledge of it, just in case it did stay somewhere nearby.'

'Yes – I'll call them this afternoon.'

'Right, Doug. I'm going to grab a quick sandwich – I'll join you in the office shortly.'

A little later, in his office, Rimmer brought the Inspector up to date, including the news that the hairs in Olsen's house had indeed turned out to be from a black cat:

'Hm. We'll have to let him go, Doug.'

'Can't we apply to hold him another 36 hours, sir?'

'On what grounds? We've no real case against him, have we?' The Sergeant shook his head:

'No, I suppose not. I was sure those hairs would turn out to be Hannah's, but…' He shrugged.

'Pop down and turn him loose, Doug. He can take his car, as well. Oh, and tell him, will you, that I spoke to Mr Frost? He's put it about at the garage that he's not well, for the moment.'

'Okay, sir.' Rimmer rose to go, but Russell stopped him:

'You let the Gidding boy out, did you?'

'Yes – I called his father first thing, he came and collected him. I wouldn't want to be in that kid's shoes right now, if the old man's expression was anything to go by!'

'You made it clear he's on police bail for the time being?'

'Yes, sir! That didn't go down too well, either. You thinking of prosecuting him later?'

'Maybe – We'll take a proper statement from young Brad, keep it on file until we know what happened to Hannah. We can pick the boy up and charge him any time, if we want to go down that route.'

'Okay, boss. I'll go and see to Olsen.'

As Rimmer left, Russell picked up the telephone, dialled the number of Barfield Antiques:

'Hello – can I speak to Mr Andrews, please? It's D.I. Russell.' The shop's owner came on the line promptly:

'Inspector – what can I do for you?'

'Sorry to trouble you, Mr Andrews. You spoke to my Sergeant earlier, about your old car?'

'That's right.'

'Would it be possible for us to speak to your wife? I hate to impose, but I'm sure you'll understand, we have to double-check everything in a case as important as this.'

'Of course, Inspector! I told the Sergeant, I'd be only too pleased to take you to meet her. But you have to accept that she might not be much help – she's in a lot a pain at times, and they're using very strong medication to control it. It can leave her rather – out of touch, if you know what I mean?'

'Of course, Mr Andrews – we'll try not to tire her. When would it be convenient?'

'Today? You could meet me at my house, check the garage while you're there!' Russell laughed:

'That would be fine, sir! What time? I'll be busy until about four thirty, maybe a little later.'

'Come around at five, then, Inspector. Number 85, The Embankment. I'll show you the garage, and then we can go to St Mungo's – I'll call them, see if they can give us some tea, shall I?'

'That'll suit us, if it's not putting you out?'

'Not at all! I'll see you then, Inspector.'

CHAPTER SEVENTEEN

At three o'clock that afternoon, Bradley Farncome's street cred took a great leap forward with his school-fellows. Having heard the eagerness in the boy's voice at the idea, Russell had arranged with the traffic division for one of their highly-visible cruisers to collect him after school, from the main gates. Brad was delighted – it didn't matter to him if his peers thought he was in trouble with the law, or their honoured guest, either way, they'd treat him with respect!

At the police station, Russell took the boy up to his office, where Doug Rimmer went over everything he'd told them the previous day. When both were happy with the details, Brad signed the document; the two detectives ran him home in Russell's Jeep on their way to meet Andrews.

The antique dealer showed them over the house quickly, and then took them down to the garage, in the rear ground floor. The space, large enough for two cars, stood empty; outside on the drive, the crimson convertible gleamed in the late afternoon sunshine. Russell questioned Andrews again about the estate car, where he thought the buyer had come from, and got only the same vague, apologetic answers his Sergeant had received earlier in the day. Then, at the dapper entrepreneur's suggestion, they went out to their car and followed him to the hospice.

As they left the cars and entered the low building, a white-coated figure intercepted them:

'Mr Andrews?'

'Yes, Doctor – what is it?' The grey-haired specialist glanced over lowered spectacles at the two plain-clothes policemen before returning his attention to his patient's husband and continuing:

'Your wife, Mr Andrews – I'm afraid she's taken a bit of a turn for the worse, a little while ago.' A look of deep concern clouded Andrews' face:

'She's not…?'

'No, no! She has been in a lot of pain; we've given her as much as we dare to ease it, but she's still rather uncomfortable. I just didn't want you to walk in unawares, you understand?'

'Of course – thank you, Doctor. I've brought…a couple of friends, to meet her – is she up to it?' Again, the sharp, appraising eyes passed over the two detectives:

'All right – but not too long, you hear? And you must be careful not to excite her, is that clear?'

'Very good, Doctor – we'll only stop a minute or two, I promise.' Russell assured him. The grey head nodded; the incisive grey-green eyes followed them across the lobby.

In the room, the policemen couldn't but feel a surge of sympathy for the frail, wasted figure in the bed. Sheila Andrews seemed little more than skin and bone, her skin a translucent white, pale, wispy strands all that remained of her once-luxuriant golden hair. Nevertheless, the faded green eyes lit up with pleasure at the sight of her husband:

'Hello, Mac!' Her voice was little more than a whisper. He took her hand gently in his own, smiling down at her:

'Hello, Darling. I've brought Mr Russell and Mr Rimmer to see you – are you up to talking to them?' She nodded, smiling at each in turn:

'It's nice to see new faces – thank you for coming.' Russell glanced at his subordinate, uncomfortable with what he needed to do:

'Mrs Andrews – I'm sorry to trouble you. Doug and I are

policemen – we're looking for little Hannah Buckland.' A troubled look came into the pale eyes:

'Poor child! Where is she, do you suppose?'

'We've not much idea, I'm afraid. We're following every possible line of enquiry, however unlikely.'

'I'm sure you are. How can I help?'

'We're trying to trace your old car, Mrs Andrews, the estate car. Do you have any idea where it might be now?' A puzzled frown crossed her face as she looked at her husband:

'Isn't it in the garage, Mac?' The pain in his eyes was clear as he gently chided her:

'No, my love – I sold it, you remember? When you moved in here; I told you all about it.'

'Oh – yes, perhaps you did.' The puzzled look remained as her eyes turned to Russell's:

'I'm sorry – I'm afraid I don't remember things too well, sometimes. They keep me rather drugged up, these days – I'm a kind of legitimate junky!'

'That's all right, Mrs Andrews, we understand – I'm sure it isn't important. Tell me; your husband comes to see you every tea-time, does he?'

She smiled at the man by her side:

'He does, almost always. He misses every now and then – but I forgive him!'

'He was here last Friday, do you recall?' A frown of concentration crossed her thin face as she hesitated; Andrews intervened:

'You remember, Darling – cheese sandwiches and Swiss Roll?'

'Oh, yes, I remember! It was Wednesday you were late, wasn't it? And Saturday, after you went to see poor Brian and his wife.' She sounded childishly pleased with herself, turning her smile upon Russell; he smiled back:

'Thank you, Mrs Andrews. I'm sorry to have intruded – we'll

leave you in peace now.' He reached down to take her free hand briefly, then turned and beckoned Rimmer to follow.

Andrews also followed them out of the room; in the lobby once more, he apologised for his wife's inconclusive answers, but Russell waved his words aside:

'I'm only sorry to have disturbed her, Mr Andrews; I hope she feels a bit easier, soon.' The man smiled sadly:

'It won't be much longer, she'll be out of it at last.' He paused, his eyes averted; when he raised them again, the sheen of anticipated grief shone in them:

'I've made my life, my living, dealing in beautiful things, Mr Russell. But that poor, faded shadow in there is still the most beautiful thing in my life. I owe her everything, perhaps even my own life – when I was much younger, not long after we were married, I did a lot of... very stupid things. It was Sheila's strength, her love and support, that got me through then; and it's been her devotion that has kept me on the right track ever since. When she's gone...' He shook his head; the smile that appeared reflected only his sorrow:

'I must go back in to her. I'm sorry to burden you with my troubles, gentlemen.'

'Not at all, sir. Thank you again for your help; and please thank your wife for us.'

Andrews nodded:

'I will, Inspector. We wish you well in your search for poor Hannah. Goodbye, now.' He hurried away with a last smile at them both.

As they returned to the Jeep, Rimmer asked:

'What did you make of that, sir?' Russell snorted:

'Not a lot! The poor woman's obviously so befuddled with drugs she isn't sure what day it is. It's a good thing Andrews doesn't need an alibi. Or does he?'

'He couldn't have snatched Hannah, could he? And why?'

'He *could* – if her memory's at fault, perhaps. If Andrews

wasn't there on Friday. We should try to trace his car, just in case – try DVLA at Swansea in the morning, Doug, see if it's been re-registered in a new name.'

'Okay – have we got the number?'

'Switchboard'll have it.'

'What? No, the *registration* number!' Russell grinned at the result of his jest:

'If we haven't, call Andrews for it, first. He'll be at the shop again, I assume.'

'Right.' He paused, the asked: 'She kept calling him 'Mac', did you notice?'

'I did. Some kind of pet name, I expect.'

'Yeah – I suppose so. What do you think he meant, that last speech as we were leaving?'

'About doing stupid things in the past? I've no idea, Doug. You didn't find anything on record against him, did you?'

'No – he was on the list I checked, along with anyone who knows Hannah and her family, but there was nothing against his name.'

'Hmm – probably some shady dealings. You know what the antiques trade is like! Perhaps he was a bit of a Lovejoy in his youth.'

'Yeah, that's probably right.'

They climbed into the Jeep, Russell driving:

'I'll drop you at the station for your car, Doug, then I'm off home for an early night! There's not much more we can do today.'

'Right, sir. Let's hope the TV appeal will get us a few sightings of the car we want.'

'They're repeating it tonight?'

'On the news bulletins, yes. There was nothing useful came in from it after last night.'

'Oh, well – let's see what tomorrow brings.'

Sunday 4.00pm

Hannah stood, gazing out of the window. It had never occurred to her before just how miserable, how scared, how completely alone, she could feel. She shivered, hugging her arms around herself; and not with the cold – the room was quite warm enough to be comfortable, despite her nakedness.

How were Mummy and Daddy? And Josh? What were they thinking, what were they doing? Worrying about her, hunting for her, she knew – but how were they feeling? There was a television in the room, she'd seen the news reports, the stories of the search for her, the appeals for witnesses; she didn't know, of course, that as she stood there, her parents and brother were facing the cameras in the police station's press room.

How long had she been here? It would be getting dark again, soon, and she'd passed another night since the man had brought her here – so that meant it must be Sunday, now. How much longer would he keep her? How many more times would he…. The horror of what he'd done to her made her shiver again.

She didn't even know for sure where she was. On Friday, when he'd brought her here, they'd driven straight into the garage, and he'd closed the door. They'd gone upstairs; he'd made her a cup of cocoa while she'd had a shower. It was only when she realised he'd taken her clothes, that she began to worry, even through his reassurances that he'd only put them in the airing-cupboard to dry out. They'd drunk their cocoas, Hannah wrapped only in a towel, in the soft leather armchair; then he'd suggested she lie down for a while, rest before he took her home, and led her up to this room at the top of the house.

When he came back, she'd thought he had come to take her back to her parents. But instead, he'd taken his clothes off and got into bed with her. She shuddered again at the memory of what he'd done then. And when he'd finished, finally left her, crying and ashamed, he'd locked the door behind him. It had stayed locked ever since – he would open it to bring her food;

burgers, sausages, pizza – or to come in and do those horrible things to her all over again. The window was locked, too; and double-glazed, so she had no hope of even making someone hear if she shouted, or beat her fists on the glass. With a toilet and shower en-suite in the corner, she couldn't even hope to make a bid for freedom by asking to go to the loo.

He'd gone out, earlier – she'd seen the red car drive away, before dinner time. Soon, she thought, he'd be back. He'd get her a meal, leave her to eat; then he'd come up to the room, and her terror would begin all over again.

CHAPTER EIGHTEEN

Nine o'clock Friday morning saw Russell and Rimmer in the D.I.'s office once more. The previous afternoon's sunshine had given way to a grey, chill morning, and both had their hands cupped around mugs of steaming canteen coffee. They had hardly closed the door behind them when the telephone on the desk rang.

'Russell?'

'Sir – there's a young man down here asking to talk to the men in charge of the Hannah Buckland enquiry.'

'Oh? Who – did he give you a name?'

'Yes, sir. Says his name is Christie – he's got a young lady with him, too.'

'Okay – I'll be right down.' He replaced the receiver:

'Hang on here, Doug, I'll be right back. It's one of those kids we spoke to outside Olsen's house the other day.'

He hurried down the stairs to the station's main reception area, where the desk sergeant indicated the coloured youth, sitting to one side hand in hand with a girl of around his own age. The boy rose as he saw the Inspector approach; Russell greeted him:

'Mr Christie – Will, isn't it? I'm Detective-Inspector Russell. We met the other day.'

'Er – yes, Inspector. This is Ronnie – Veronica Marchent. She's my girlfriend.' He glanced nervously at the girl, who now stood close at his side, their hands still entwined.

'You wanted to see me?' The boy nodded, hesitantly:

'Yes – that is, Ronnie's persuaded me I ought to talk to you. About Mr Olsen.' Russell caught the movement as the girl squeezed his hand encouragingly, her deep brown eyes smiling into the boy's face.

'Okay – why don't you both come up to my office? It's more comfortable there, and we can talk without getting disturbed.'

He ushered them through the security door which the officer behind the barrier released for him, and then led the way upstairs. In his office, he introduced his Sergeant, and waved the two youngsters into the vacant chairs facing the desk. Rimmer, as always, perched on its edge; as Russell took his seat, he asked:

'Okay, Will – what is it you wanted to tell me?' The youth still hesitated, glancing at the girl for moral support; then he began:

'You were asking us about Kinky Kev, whether we knew when he got home last Friday?' Russell just nodded.

'Well – we *were* there, outside Al's house, like always. Darren had 'is bike out – he's got an old trials bike, he's been fixing it up, like, and he brought it out to try it. Anyway – we saw K.K. come home, and get out of 'is car – Al was on the bike, goin' a bit fast, like – he had to swerve to avoid 'itting the car door.' It was noticeable that, as the youth settled into his story, his manner of speech relaxed, became more slipshod.

'What time was this, Will?'

'Oh – 'bout 'is usual time, around twenty past five, I reckon.'

'Did Mr Olsen go out again, that you saw?'

'Nah! 'E was in, s'long as we were there. 'E never draws the curtains in 'is kitchen – p'rhaps 'asn't got any – and we could see 'im movin' round in there, getting' 'is dinner, I s'pose. We wasn't *watchin'* 'im, you understand – but you couldn't 'elp seein', from where we was.'

Russell sat back, with an appraising glance at his subordinate. Rimmer turned to the boy:

'You're sure of the day? It was pretty unpleasant out, on Friday, hardly a day to be chatting out of doors?' The youth shrugged:

'Yeah – we're used to it, I s'pose. We meet there 'cos Al's is in the middle, like. 'Is Mum don't like us indoors – tell the truth, she don't like Darren, thinks 'e's a bad influence…'

'*I* keep telling you that, too, Will!' the girl whispered into his ear, making Russell smile. The boy went on:

'My house is no good – Katie – that's my little sister – she'd be under our feet all the time. Any'ow, like I say, we don't mind the weather much.'

'And you're sure of the time?'

'Yeah – give or take a few minutes, like.'

'The others – Al and Darren – they'd know about this, too?'

''Course! I boll… I mean, I told 'em off for not tellin' you the other day. But none of us like K.K., 'e's a f… a nasty little pervert. So they don't want to get 'im off the hook, like. But – like I said, I got a little sister; and Ronnie said the same as you, what if 'e goes to jail, and the guy who *really* 'ad that little girl's still around? Might be our Katie, next time, mightn't it? I mean, she can be a f… a bloomin' nuisance, but she's still my kid sister, ain't she?'

'Do you think Al and Darren would confirm what you've told us, Will?' Russell asked.

'Yeah – maybe. If they know I've told you already, they might. At least, Al probably would – I dunno 'bout Darren, 'e's a bit anti-police, if you know what I mean?'

'Yes, I do! We find a bit of that, especially round the Warren.' Russell got to his feet:

'Thank you very much for coming forward, Will. I'm grateful for your help, you've saved us wasting a lot of time over Mr Olsen.' The youngsters rose as well; the girl gave Christie's arm a determined shake as she told him:

'You should have told them before, Will!' The boy grinned down at her:

'Yeah, I know! But I've done it now, okay?' Russell smiled at the pair:

'Now – I guess you two ought to be in school, didn't you?'

'Yeah, I s'pose we should. But it's only Geography and French 'fore break – as long as I'm there for chemistry, later. That's what I want to do, when I'm older' he confided.

'He's going to be a famous scientist, one day' the girl told the Inspector.

'Good for you, Will! It's good to have an aim in life – and you listen to this girl of yours, she's got the right ideas!' The boy grinned:

'Don't worry, I do! She won't even let me swear, hits me if I do when she's around!' Russell laughed with them:

'Right, go on now. The Sergeant here'll run you into school – don't worry, it's an unmarked car!' He'd caught the look of trepidation in the boy's eyes: 'And thank you again for your information.' He turned to Rimmer:

'Take the Jeep, Doug – and see if you can get a word with either or both of the other two, find out if they'll confirm what Will's told us. I'll see you back here in a while.'

'Right, boss.' Rimmer took the keys, and led the two young people down to the car park.

It was nearing lunchtime when the Sergeant returned from the Addison Community College, the one-time comprehensive school on Glebe Farm where Will Christie and his girl went to school. He joined Russell in the D.I.'s office, carrying two fresh mugs of canteen coffee to help their deliberations; the Inspector looked up as he entered:

'Any joy, Doug?'

'Yeah.' Rimmer adopted his perch on the desk's edge, sipping his coffee:

'The Head Teacher called each of the other boys to his office for me. The Barton kid backed up what Will had said straight away, when he knew that we knew. Darren Morgan didn't want to, at first – he obviously had a problem in talking to the police, as Christie suggested – but he gave in in the end.'

'Good. That girl of Will's is something else, isn't she?'

157

'Yeah! How old is she – fourteen, you reckon?'

'No more, surely. Strong-willed kid – she'll keep that boy out of our hair, as long as they stay together, if I'm any judge.' He leant back in his chair, running a hand through his own hair:

'So Olsen's out of the picture, Doug.'

'Sounds like it. How wrong can you be? I was sure he was our man!'

'He was always in the frame, Doug – but it never did feel right to me. Somehow.'

'You were right, boss – we can forget him, now.'

'Write him off.'

'Chuck him down the well.' Russell looked up at the laughter in the Sergeant's voice; a twinkle came into his eyes – the two shared an appreciation of the old Goon Shows. His voice took on a high, nasal tone, in fair imitation of Peter Sellers:

'Let us play a game, Bluebottle!'

'Okay, Eccles – what shall we do?' Rimmer, as Spike Milligan.

'Let us throw him in the well!' Both stood up, harmonising the fading scream as they walked to the door, and echoing the sound of a heavy splash at the end. The two stood, laughing at their own idiotic humour, as the door beside them swung open. Russell stepped hurriedly aside, as Detective-Superintendent Wilson entered:

'Something amusing you, Russell?' The D.I. stifled his grin:

'Just sharing a private joke, sir.'

'Hm. Well, I suppose you need a sense of humour sometimes, in this job.'

'Doug and I were about to go over the Hannah Buckland enquiry, sir – do you want to join us? I was intending to come and brief you later, anyway.'

'Okay – if you don't mind, David.'

They returned to the desk; Russell to his chair, Wilson to one of those facing him, Rimmer to his habitual perch.

'We've had to eliminate Kevin Olsen, sir. Three youngsters

saw him come home on Friday, before the last sighting of Hannah, and can place him there beyond the time she was taken.' Russell brought his superior up to date.

'So what are we left with, David?'

'That's what we were about to assess, sir. We have the girl's trail up to around twenty to six, when little Taylor Goldman saw her picked up by a car outside their house. Even if her testimony is a bit shaky – she's only six, sir – the other facts we have bear it out.'

'No trace of that car?'

'No. We don't have any clear indication of make or model, as you might imagine. No-one else appears to have seen it – all we know is that it was silver in colour, probably a large car, and either a hatchback or estate, with smooth lines. Could be almost anything.'

'Not a bad description, from a kiddie so young, though. Can we trust it, do you think?'

'I believe so, sir. I'm sure the child is truthful, and not elaborating for the sake of the attention, the way some kids might.'

'The abductor has to be someone local, don't you think, sir?' Rimmer addressed the Inspector.

'I think that's the most likely, yes, Doug. That part of the Avenue, beyond Turner's Lane, doesn't see any through traffic – there's only the residential roads, those closes on the South side, and the Crescent at the end – so the only people who go there are the locals themselves, the Post Office, services, deliveries and the like.'

'You've checked them all out?' Wilson asked.

'Yes – Gas, Telephone and Electricity providers all say they had no vehicles in the area Friday afternoon or evening. There were a few taxis, called to pick up, or bringing people home from town, but all the drivers can account for their time, with the support of their despatch records. There might have been the odd delivery van, but not that we've been able to trace; and none of the residents recalls having any deliveries, or seeing anything unusual.' Rimmer responded.

'Does anyone around there have a car that fits the description?'

'We have a list of possibles, sir' Russell answered: 'I was going to get Doug to check each one, make sure of their whereabouts during the time in question. But the Bucklands say that they don't know anyone else in the Avenue, or that area; and it's not likely that Hannah would have got into a car with someone she didn't know.'

'She might have got to know a few people there, herself, sir?' Rimmer suggested: 'I mean, she spent a lot of time around there, with Emily Farncome, didn't she? She might have got to recognise some of the locals, perhaps enough to have trusted them, especially when you remember how distressed she was, after what happened to her?'

'You're quite right, Doug. When she was so upset, even a vaguely familiar face might have seemed like a refuge. You'd better follow up those cars as soon as possible.'

'I'll get onto it right away, sir. Where does Andrews fit in, do you think?'

'I doubt if he does, Doug. All right, Hannah knows him, presumably she would trust him enough to get into his car. And we have to take his alibi with a pinch of salt.' He turned to Wilson: 'Andrews' wife supports his story that he was with her for tea on Friday, sir – but she's suffering from terminal cancer, and with the level of her medication, I doubt if her memory is really that reliable. They did own a silver Mercedes estate, which would fit the description, as well, but he claims to have sold it about eight weeks ago – privately, so it's proving difficult to trace or confirm. We're intending to contact DVLA, and the local dealers, to see if we can find it. But, in all honesty, I can't see him as our abductor. It's quite obvious when you talk to him that under his act as the charming entrepreneur he's desperately upset about his wife, to the point that even if he was inclined to go after little girls, I can't imagine there being room in his life for such antics right now. And we've no reason at all to think he's that way inclined, any way.'

'What he's told you hangs together, given the uncertainty about his wife's memory?'

'Yes, sir. There's no trace of the other car at the house – he has a red convertible now, no chance of confusing that with the one we want to find. And I've no reason to doubt what he's told us, otherwise.'

'Hm, I see. Whoever did grab the child, must have done it on impulse?'

'That's right. Hannah didn't even decide to go and visit Emily until after school, so no-one could have planned to be there to take her. It has to have been a chance encounter.'

'Right. I should get after all those possible local cars, if I were you, David – that sounds like your best approach, now.'

'I agree, sir. Doug and I will get right on it.'

'Good. Keep me posted, right?' Wilson got to his feet.

'Of course, sir.'

CHAPTER NINETEEN

Friday afternoon, and the first week of torment for Hannah Buckland's family was drawing to a close. After a hurried lunch in the staff canteen, the senior investigating officer and his assistant returned to their respective desks.

In the incident room, given over to the search for the child for the seventh day, Doug Rimmer set to, trying to trace the whereabouts the previous week of every silver car registered in the vicinity of Alderley Park, according to the records of the Driver and Vehicle Licensing Authority. About half of the total could be eliminated straight away, as not coming close to the description required; but that still left a surprising number. And if none of them proved suspect, the Sergeant had a pretty good idea that the next suggestion would be to widen the enquiry to all silver cars in Grancester as a whole. Then the surrounding area. Then the County? He could envisage his work programme for the foreseeable future, unless they had some kind of break!

A whole raft of other work was still going on in the background, of course. The Uniform branch were still pressing forward their own part of the investigation, dealing with continuing searches of the area, correlating incoming information from all over the country. Inevitably with such a high-profile case, involving a missing child, reported sightings were appearing from all directions, to be checked out by the police forces of every city and county, and a record of each forwarded to Grancester's incident room. So far, every one had proved false – a few, perhaps, deliberate hoaxes, the majority the result of genuine mistakes – but nevertheless, each day, David Russell received a summary noting each report in brief detail, and its conclusion.

That afternoon, he sat in his office, apparently at ease, his feet swung up onto the edge of the desk, hands clasped behind his head. Behind half-closed eyes, his brain was again going over what he knew of Hannah, her family, her friends, all the people who knew her, trying to find a spark of light in the gloom. But all he could see were questions.

Had the girl been taken? Could there be any other explanation of her disappearance? It didn't seem so – there was nothing in the background to give the slightest hint that she might have been unhappy at home; far from it, in fact. And if she'd been hiding out for some inexplicable reason, surely she would have heard of the search for her, and at least got in touch with her parents? No, she *had* been kidnapped, for a certainty.

Why? He could see only one reason, the darkest he could imagine. Not for ransom – the Buckland's were not particularly well off. Andrews was obviously moderately wealthy – but it seemed a remote way of putting a squeeze on him, to abduct his employee's daughter. And anyway, there would have been a demand by this time, surely? Not as any kind of revenge attack – no-one had spoken any ill of her family, they seemed to have no enemies. Could someone be trying to get at Andrews by this distant route? He'd mentioned doing stupid things in the past – had someone taken a long-delayed blow at him, for some ancient evil, real or imagined? But again, why target Hannah? And however you looked at it, given the circumstances of her disappearance as they were now coming to light, any kind of premeditated kidnap had to be ruled out, didn't it? So – the only sensible conclusion: A little girl, not especially pretty perhaps, but quite cute, at least in her photographs with those bright blue eyes, her freckled face, and that mane of jet-black hair. Ten years old, and attractive, in all probability, to a passing paedophile. Enticed into a car, taken away – he didn't want to dwell on what might have, must have, followed. Then what? Where was she now? Was she, could she be, still alive? He wasn't sure whether yes or no was the preferred answer – if she was dead, at least *her* troubles were over, even if they were only just beginning for all those she had left behind in this world. But – what if she was alive, captive, abused, terrified out of her wits? *Please God, let her be all right! Let there be some stupid reason we've missed, why she's hiding out, laughing at us all!*

Russell dropped his feet to the floor, sat forward, his head in his hands, turning his back on those thoughts, knowing his prayer would go unanswered. The big question, then – who? Who was it, in that silver car? Who had Hannah trusted enough to go with them, only to have that trust betrayed? Damn and blast Spike Gidding! His attack on the child had thrown a considerable spanner into the investigation. Had the girl been so upset as to grab at any port in a storm, the first friendly face that had come by? Had the face in the car been that of a dimly-recognised acquaintance, someone she had seen around the Avenue, as Doug had suggested? His assessment of the child told him that, if things had been normal, she would have politely declined any such offer of help – but, thanks to Spike, things *hadn't* been normal. He felt his resolve harden, at least in one respect: What that bully had done constituted a serious sexual assault, and he deserved to face the full penalty for it. They had Brad's statement, and the boy's own confession, so a prosecution was almost a formality; he'd discuss the matter with the Super, see how he felt about things.

But that got him no nearer to knowing who had taken little Hannah. Now that their chief suspect (their only suspect!) had been eliminated, however reluctantly, by his self-appointed watchdogs, they were questing in the air like hounds in search of a scent. Not that Russell had ever felt that Olsen was the culprit – the case against him had never amounted to much, and the little man's almost pathological fear had all but convinced the Inspector, at least, of his innocence. And who else was there, in the frame?

Most sexual abuse cases involve someone in, or very close to, the child's family. But in this case, he was more than happy to rule out all of the people who fell into that category – the Bucklands, the Farncomes, the families of other children she was friendly with like Briony James, her teachers, everyone. Except – maybe – George Andrews? His thoughts returned to the suave, elegant antiques dealer; there was something about the man he distrusted, something in his manner that made him less than comfortable. But, in fairness, what? The man had made a career, a very successful one, selling people things that, in most cases, they probably didn't need. His personable charm, his vaguely ingratiating habit of speech, had no doubt been a part of his success, had probably developed over the years until it had become a part of his outward persona, a habit put on like his smart jackets and his cravats as a part of his public image. To take exception to it was as silly as, for example, judging the Mad Professor's abilities by his wild appearance.

And anyway, could he be regarded as a suspect? There was no hint, certainly no record, of him being in any way attracted to children; on the contrary, he was so obviously devoted to his dying wife. He *could* have taken Hannah, she would have trusted him, surely – but there was nothing to suggest he'd been around Alderley Park that evening. With Sheila's doubtful memory, his alibi might be suspect; but that in itself almost told in his favour – if he'd needed an alibi, wouldn't he have contrived to make sure she *was* certain to tell them the right thing? And the car – he'd claimed to have sold the silver estate long before Hannah's abduction, but they hadn't been able to substantiate that: Earlier, he'd contacted DVLA, only to be told that the car had not so far been registered to a new owner.

Grancester did not justify a Mercedes Benz dealer of its own – the nearest was Bellevue Motors, in Northampton. Russell had contacted them, to learn that they had been dealing with Mr Andrews for some years. Their sales manager had handled the sale of the new convertible, and remembered the indecision regarding whether to trade in the estate, but he knew no more – he had not seen the car in new hands, nor still in Andrews' for that matter, since. And the service department were no more help – they had had the convertible in for servicing and a little warranty work, but likewise hadn't seen the estate for six months or more.

So – all they could do, for the moment, was to press on with the routine of the enquiry, and hope for a glimmer of light to appear somewhere along the way. The best chance, as Wilson had agreed, was that they would come across a car that matched little Taylor's observations, which either lived around, or had been in the vicinity of, the Avenue last Friday, and belonged to someone whom Hannah would have possibly recognised.

And in the meantime, Brian and Harriet Buckland lived in torment for their missing daughter; young Josh lived in anguish for his missing sister; little Emily, and her other friends, wondered and feared for their missing playmate; and most of the population of Grancester, along with a large part of the country, held its collective breath.

But not for much longer. Russell couldn't know, as he sat ruminating over his investigation, that very soon a number of his questions would be answered, even if those answers still left him groping for a total truth.

Sunday 11.30pm
Hannah slept. Her pain and horror submerged by exhaustion, she slept soundly, her mind taking refuge in dreams of home, parents, brother, friends, even school. She slept, her exhaustion, the result of hours of unwanted, enforced, sex, reinforced by the

sleeping tablet the man had slipped into the mug of cocoa he'd made her when it was all over. She slept, never to wake.

She slept, as he gently pushed back the covers, rolled out of the bed to stand there, looking down at her. She lay, so slender and fragile, curled into a foetal ball, her pale skin sheened with sweat – he had kept the heating up quite high, so that the naked child would be comfortable in the room. He walked around to her side of the bed on silent, bare feet, bent over to gently - oh so gently! – roll her onto her back. His eyes ran over her sleeping form, so young, so slim, so arousing, and a swell of sadness rose in him at what he had to do. But he had no choice, not now. It had to be done. The knowledge didn't ease his feelings of regret; it took him some effort to harden his resolve. But, she would leave him some incredible memories, wouldn't she?

He reached across her, carefully lifted his own pillow, held it in both hands while he took one last, lingering look at her cute, fascinating face, the amazing blue eyes hidden now as she slept, the scattering of freckles across her nose, the spreading fan of glossy, jet-black hair on the pillow…. He lowered the pillow, slowly, gently, as if merely covering her lovingly against the chill of the night; but he lowered it across her face, held it there, one hand pressed over her nose and mouth.

Hannah didn't stir. Her drugged, exhausted mind too slow to react to the knowledge that she was dying – or did she welcome death, an escape from the horror her life had become since Friday night?

When the child was dead, he sat on the edge of the bed, and wept.

CHAPTER TWENTY

Joanne Halifax woke to the cool, grey light of dawn. She swung long, shapely legs from under the quilt and sat up on the edge of her bed, reaching arms equally long and limber above her head to stretch her slender back, then dropping her hands to her head, running her fingers through her thick, auburn hair.

It was good to be home, if only for a couple of days! Cambridge was fine, she was enjoying the work and her friends there – but even so, to come home to the farm and the countryside gave her the welcome opportunity for a total mental change of gear. The oldest of the three Halifax children at twenty-one, Joanne was in her third year at Girton College. Tall and elegant, she was attractive in an athletic, outdoor kind of way – hardly surprising, perhaps, for a farmer's daughter. Young Len, her junior by just over a year, was attending the agricultural college in Moulton, near Northampton – he was staying there for the weekend, working on his project. He'd be taking over the farm, some day, when their father decided to retire; if he ever did! Joanne could hardly conceive of the bluff, robust man ever giving up his land – what on earth would he do?

Smiling at the thought of her father, big and strong as an animated granite statue, she stood up. Slipping off her nightdress, she peeked out onto the landing, and, finding it unpopulated as she'd expected, padded silently along to the bathroom. After a quick wash, she was making her noiseless way back to her room when a door cracked open as she passed, and a slightly bleary face peered out:

'Jo? What're you doing?' The twelve-year-old giggled at the sight of her older sister with only a towel around her middle. The older girl put a finger to her lips:

'Ssh! I'm going out for a ride. What are *you* doing awake at this hour, Bellie?' The youngster giggled again at the unofficial nickname:

'I just woke up – I guess I heard you, or something. Can I come?' Joanne smiled at her sister, youngest of the Halifax clan, but she shook her head:

'Not now, Sprat. I want to be on my own, just for a bit. Tell you what, we'll go out together later on, shall we?'

'Oh! Okay, I guess.' Annabel's disappointment was clear in her voice

'You don't mind? I don't get much peace, at college – we'll take Saracen and Marmaduke out in the fields, after lunch, maybe?'

'All right – promise?'

'I promise! Now go back to bed, it's only six o'clock.' Satisfied with her sister's promise, the younger girl pulled back into her room and closed the door quietly. Shaking her head with a smile, Joanne went back to her own room and sat to quickly brush through her hair before dressing and making her way down to the stables, across the yard from the kitchen.

Saracen, the tall, limber bay, nuzzled her affectionately when she went into his stall to greet him. The three labradors had followed her, and fussed around as she saddled him, looking at her all the while as if to tell her to hurry up, they were quite ready for a good long run. She led the horse out into the yard, vaulted easily into the saddle, clicked her tongue at him to give him the go as she gathered the reins in her hand; the dogs led them off through the gate, eager to be running free in the open country.

* * *

In the little terraced house in Bedford Road, Kim stumbled sleepily downstairs to the kitchen. Her mother was still snoring disjointedly in the front bedroom – if she got down first, she could make some breakfast, brew a pot of tea. That way, her mother might at least start the day with some food in her stomach, and a little caffeine to counteract the alcohol which would inevitably soon follow it.

As she filled the kettle, she thought sadly how different this was to the previous Saturday. Then, she'd been woken in bed by the diminutive, ever-laughing Liu, bearing a tray with toast and coffee; and, before she could even start on her breakfast, had found herself with a small boy snuggling under each arm. The contrast couldn't have been more dramatic, more poignant – now, she was back to the eternal, dismal routine of trying to care for her sick mother. To Kim, the woman's unacknowledged alcoholism *was* an illness – one she had to try to help to cure, somehow, even if the patient didn't know she needed curing. Her life had become a constant round of trying to make her mother eat, trying to keep her drinking to a minimum, trying to keep the house presentable, and at the same time cope with her schoolwork. Perhaps it was no great surprise that, although an intelligent girl, her grades were less than brilliant.

There were times, it was true, when she resented the lot that life had cast for her. If only she could go and live with her father! He wanted her to, desperately; he would let his feelings show, every now and then, even if he tried not to let on too often, acknowledging her acceptance of the duty of caring for Martha. She had caught herself, more than once, on the brink of wishing her mother dead; even then, pulling herself up guiltily, she'd wondered if it wouldn't be a blessed relief for the woman herself, if the truth were told. But, while she lived, she had no-one else to look after her; and, despite it all, Kim did love her.

The kettle boiled – she filled the teapot, let it brew for a minute or two, then poured a mug. Plenty of milk, two sugars – she took it upstairs, and gently roused the sleeping woman. Martha peered at her daughter out of sleep-encrusted eyes, struggled to sit up in the bed, and took the mug:

'Thanks, Kim – you're a good girl. What would I do without you, eh?' The girl smiled at her:

'Take your time, Mum – I'm getting some breakfast. Would you like some toast and marmalade? I'll bring it up for you, if you like.'

'Oh, Kimmie! Why are you so good to me, the rotten life I lead you sometimes?'

'Ssh! You're my Mum, and I love you. Besides, you're not rotten to me – it's only…'

'The drink' her mother finished the sentence for her: 'I know, darling – but – I can't help it! I need a drink or two, each day, to get me through…'

'Hush, and drink your tea. I'll be up with the toast in a minute.'

If it *was* only a drink or two, we could cope with it, Kim thought as she went back down to the kitchen.

* * *

In Ivy Cottage, Josh Buckland sat at the kitchen table in his pyjamas, rubbing his eyes. His parents were still asleep – or at least, they were still in bed; he doubted if they were sleeping any better than he was. Like the grown-ups, after a week with no word of Hannah, he was trying hard to cling to a desperate hope that she would still be found alive – but suddenly, as he sat there, in his heart he knew she was dead, knew that he would never see his bright, chirpy, irritating little sister ever again.

He leant forward, resting his forehead on his folded arms. His sadness was too much for him to bear – he gave in to it, sobbing quietly, his shoulders shaking. He hadn't been to school all week, staying home because he could never have focussed on lessons with Hannah missing, and trying to be strong like the Inspector had said, to help and support his Mum and Dad. But it was all too much for him! Harry had come round a few times, tried to help cheer him up – but even his best friend's company had given him no respite, the underlying sympathy of his manner, the careful avoidance of certain subjects only serving to remind him of the awful situation he was in.

So he sat at the table, the tears soaking through the fabric to his skin, grieving for the pretty black-haired girl and his own loneliness in about equal measure.

After maybe half an hour, his tears began to subside. He raised his head, sniffling, wiping his eyes with already-soaked pyjama sleeves. He got up unsteadily, and went to the fridge to pick up a pack of tissues off the top, returning to his seat with them. As he dried his eyes, he found a strange calmness settling over him – it was as if, in finally letting his feelings go, he'd achieved a kind of acceptance, a kind of peace with the idea that Hannah was gone. *She might still come back!* He told himself fervently – but though the hope still existed, he could at last face the fact that it was a very slim hope, a very slim hope indeed. He drew in a deep breath, held it, let it out again as a long, shuddering sigh.

In command of his own feelings, his thoughts turned to his parents. Yes, maybe now he could do what the Inspector had told him, and be strong for Mum and Dad, help them to cope with things. And he could start by getting them breakfast in bed, they'd like that!

With a new confidence that would have surprised his parents, he stood up, filled the kettle and put it on the stove, took out the toaster and inserted four slices of bread. Putting a tray on the worktop, he got the butter from the fridge, jam and marmalade from the cupboard, two plates, two knives, two cups, two saucers, milk and sugar, and arranged them ready to take upstairs, smiling to himself at how surprised Mum and Dad were going to be!

The toast made, the tea brewed, he carried the laden tray

carefully up, knocked on their door, and pushed his way in when he heard his mother's voice.

* * *

In Bevington village, David Russell sat at the kitchen table, surrounded by his own family. It was unusually quiet – Sarah had just turned huffy and indignant because, in a pause in her incessant chattering, Daniel had asked if his sister could be fitted with an on-off switch. Looking from Tracy's amused but disapproving expression to the cheeky glint in his son's eyes, Russell was reminded again of just how lucky he was. He wondered what the scene in the Buckland household was like at that moment; the thought sobered him, and he looked across the table at his own daughter, feeling a surge of love for the little dark-haired replica of her mother:

'Let's all go shopping together today, shall we?' The little girl instantly brightened up, knowing full well that if Daddy came with them, that meant treats for her and Daniel.

'Don't you need to go into the office, David?' He shook his head at his wife:

'There isn't a lot I can do, right now; the search for Hannah's pretty much stalled. The team in the incident room can cope with the routine stuff; until something breaks, all I can do is wait.'

'You sure?'

'Yeah – they'll call me, if anything happens. Let's all go into town, I could do with the change!'

'Right – I'll go and get dressed!' Russell grinned at the eagerness in Daniel's voice:

'No hurry – there's plenty of time!' He called as the boy disappeared through the door. Tracy stood up with a smile:

'Come on, Sarah, finish your tea darling. Then we'll get you ready, too.'

'Okay, Mummy.'

CHAPTER TWENTY-ONE

It was a beautiful morning – so very *English,* somehow. Still and silent, bright despite the mist drifting across the fields, swirling around the trees as Joanne rode by, the bay trotting easily, ears pricked, happy to be out in the fields with his mistress. You felt that Spring, if not quite arrived, was at least peeking around the next corner, ready to jump out at you, giggling and sparkling with new life, all green shoots and dewdrops.

They rode South from the farmhouse, following an ancient way which led right across the lands of Pury Home Farm, crossing the modern paved road and on to the distant village of Lillingstone Lovell. The Halifax family had owned and managed the Home Farm for several generations, and looked fit to continue the tradition and the business well into the future. They farmed much of the land between Paulerspury and Whittlebury, most of it their own, a few fields leased from other landowners. The bridleway crossed a belt of trees, and then skirted an area of woodland, before approaching the back-road which ran between Whittlebury and Deanshanger.

The dogs had been thoroughly enjoying themselves, ranging free across the fields, chasing each other, laughing and leaping like excited children, sometimes disappearing into the woods for a while before reappearing with a lolling grin at their mistress, looking to make sure she was still with them. Joanne rode on, relaxed, happy, at peace with herself and the world; the labs dashed across in front of Saracen, headed into the trees once more, and she watched them go with an indulgent smile.

It was a little while before she noticed that they had not returned. She looked around, only slightly concerned when she didn't see them anywhere:

'Tess! Fern! Where are you? Blue!' No labradors appeared at her call. She reined in, waiting for them:

'Come on, girls – where are you?' Still no sign. Muttering about damned dogs under her breath, Joanne turned Saracen back along the trail, imagining that they had found some interesting smell, and hoping that they wouldn't decide to bring it home with them. Peering in under the trees as she passed, she called them as she rode; but then she spotted them, all three nose down, pawing at the ground in front of them, their backs to her:

'Fern! Tess! Blue! What have you got there?' The golden bitch raised her head, as if to say come and see; then turned back to scrabble again at their discovery.

'What is it, then, Fern? Something good?' Accepting that they were not going to come away easily, Joanne slid from the saddle, leaving the reins over the horse's neck.

'Wait there, Sarrie' she told the bay; he ducked his head with a soft whinny as if acquiescing to her command, and she patted the strong neck as she turned to follow the dogs. As she approached, Fern looked up at her again, the expression on her face eager and excited:

'What is it, girl – show me!' The dog took a pace towards her, revealing a part of what it was they were digging at. Joanne frowned, peering for a closer look at what at first appeared to be a mound of earth, twigs and dead leaves. Something pale showed under the covering, fabric of some kind – and....

Joanne stepped back in horror, one hand pressed to her mouth, her knuckles between her teeth to stifle the scream:

'Fern! Blue! Tess! Leave! *Leave, I say!* Come here!' At the sudden tone of command in the girl's voice, the three dogs obeyed, if reluctantly. They came to her, to sit in a row at her side as they had been trained.

'Stay! Stay there!' She stepped forward again, to be sure of what she had seen. Where the dogs had been worrying at the fabric, it had torn through, and something was poking out of the hole: A small, white hand. Joanne felt terror rise in her heart – a child's hand!

For a moment, she just stared, unbelieving. Then she turned and ran back to the horse, leaped into the saddle, urged him to flight. They wheeled around; ignoring the bridleway they rose to a full gallop, headed straight as an arrow for the farmhouse as she called the labs to follow. Saracen raced for home, his ears alert, breath surging into his lungs as he eagerly took to his mistress's sudden, if unexpected wish to have a race. On his back, Joanne was offering her thanks that she hadn't given in to Annabel and let the youngster come along for the ride.

They were still going full-tilt through the gate into the yard. Joanne wheeled him to a skating halt near the kitchen door and vaulted from his back without pause. Her father, about to enter one of the barns opposite, gaped for a moment and then ran to see what she was about. In the house, she dashed through into the hallway, grabbed up the phone, tried to dial 999 with fingers that shook so much that she couldn't find the buttons.

Leonard Halifax ran up behind his daughter. Realising that she was in a near panic, he gently took the receiver from her trembling hand, put his other great paw over the hand on the dial:

'What is it, Jo?' The girl was almost sobbing for breath:

'Dad! There's – a body – by the twelve-acre – in the trees!'

'What! What sort of body?'

'Oh, Dad! It's – it's a kiddie! It's….' She collapsed against his shoulder:

'We've got to call the police!'

'All right, Jo – take it easy for a moment. Let me.'

He punched the three nines, heard the operator answer:

'Police' he replied to her question. When the police control-room came on the line, he told them:

'This is Halifax – Home Farm, Paulerspury. My daughter's just come home – she says there's a body on our land, beside a field near the Deanshanger road. A child's body, she thinks.'

'Yes – you'd best come here, to the house, I can show you where to look. She's very upset, but by the time you get here she'll be ready to talk to you.'

'Okay. Thank you.'

He replaced the receiver, slipped an arm around the girl's still-trembling shoulders and led her gently back to the kitchen where her mother stood by the cooker, open-mouthed:

'Oh, Len!' Rachel Halifax was a robust mentally as her husband was physically, but her daughter's sudden, distraught appearance, and what she had heard of the telephone call had shaken her badly.

'It's all right, mother. Just get her a cup o' tea, right? Where's Annabel?'

'In the bathroom, having a shower, Dad.' He nodded:

'Right. You look after Jo – I'll tell Annie to stay in her room for a bit, we don't want her getting upset too. I'll fetch her down when Jo's herself again.' He headed for the stairs, then looked back over his shoulder:

'Police'll be here pretty quick, I expect. Let 'em in, 'n I'll take 'em over the twelve-acre.'

* * *

David Russell was just ushering his children out of the front door to the Jeep when the mobile phone in his pocket rang:

'Russell?' Daniel turned to look at his father, saw his eyes close as if in pain, his free hand raised to his brow as he listened;

'I'll be right there.' He closed the connection without another word, his eyes still closed.

'Dad? What is it?' The hazel eyes opened, to look down at the boy with an expression full of sorrow:

'I've got to go, Daniel. I'm sorry about our shopping trip.'

'What's wrong, Dad?' Russell hesitated – his son deserved some explanation:

'They've found – a body, Dan.' It was the boy's turn to look upset:

'Is it – the little girl?' Russell nodded:

'Probably.' Daniel gazed at him for a moment, his pain at the idea of a child's death clear in his eyes. And then, without thought for his action, he stepped forward and put his arms around his father as if to comfort him:

'Oh, Dad! That's awful – I'm so sorry.' Russell hugged the boy, surprised and touched by the words mumbled into the cloth of his jacket:

'So am I, Dan, so am I.'

After a moment, the boy released him, stepped back, looking up with a brightness in his eyes:

'You'd better go, hadn't you? Mum can take us to the shops.'

'You're right, Dan. Tell her I'm sorry when she comes downstairs, will you?'

'Sure, Dad. See you later.'

Russell hurried out to the car, told Sarah, who was waiting there patiently, to go back in doors and wait for Mummy. Daniel beckoning her from the doorway, the little girl obeyed, despite her puzzlement at the sudden change of plan; Russell got into the Jeep, started the engine and drove off towards Northampton and the South of the county.

CHAPTER TWENTY-TWO

The Spring sunshine lit the backs of the group who gazed forlornly into the shade of the woodland on Halifax's land. Its warmth failed to dispel their chill, did nothing to raise their spirits, as they watched the raincoated figure of the County Pathologist, bent over the now-uncovered body.

First to arrive had been a young uniformed constable. Halifax had driven him straight out to the spot in his Land Rover; the lad had needed no more than to touch the small, limp hand to know that they did indeed have the body of a child; he had immediately radio'd in to inform the incident room, and pass a message to the Inspector and the Sergeant. From the farmyard, Russell had driven Rimmer out across the fields in the Jeep, closely followed by the Mad Professor and his SOCO team in his van. Whether the latter would get back to the road without a tow seemed debatable; Halifax had grinned and offered the use of a tractor if it was needed.

Russell had begged a penknife from the still-trembling hands of the constable, giving him a reassuring smile and a terse word of thanks, and gone to the pathetic bundle. Steeling himself, he had slit it carefully, peeling back what appeared to be the linen fabric of a bedsheet, exposing what he already knew he would find.

'That's her, boss?'

'Yes.' They spoke almost in whispers, perhaps not trusting their voices at any higher level. They gazed down at the dead child for a brief while before returning to join the gathering beyond the trees. Russell spoke to Owen without raising his eyes::

'Is the pathologist coming?'

'Yes, sir.' Russell looked around in surprise – it wasn't like the Mad Professor to acknowledge anyone's rank.

'Okay – you'd best hang on until he's taken a look.'

A few minutes later, a second Land Rover had bumped across the young crop, and Doctor Iain Somerfield, forensic pathologist to the county of Northampton, had climbed out. Now, the good doctor was examining their find. After no more than a few minutes, he arose and returned to the group:

'That's Hannah Buckland?'

'Yes – we'll need a formal ID, of course, but yes, it's her.' Russell replied.

'Mmmm. Been dead quite a while, four or five days, at least.'

'How – can you tell yet?'

'No. No apparent injuries, that I can see. No marks on the neck, as if she'd been strangled. Might have been some form of asphyxiation, if you're expecting that kind of thing, but I can't tell until I take a look inside. One thing, though – come and see.' He beckoned the Inspector forward, pointed down:

'See those marks, like bruises? I assume she was lying like this when you found her? No-one's turned her over, have they?'

'No.'

'Then she's been moved. She lay on her face, after death, probably for a day or two. Blood's accumulated at the lowest points, congealed there, giving you those marks. Then, I'd guess that she was brought here, dumped on her back as you see her now.'

'Right, I see. When can you let us know more?'

'When your SOCO boys'll let me take her away, I'll get her into the mortuary. I suppose you're going to expect me to work on Sunday, are you?'

'We need to know what you can tell us as quickly as possible, so if you can...?'

'All right, all right! I'll call you, okay? Maybe Sunday, maybe Monday – depends what I find.'

'Thanks, Iain.'

'Humph!' The pathologist strolled back to his vehicle; he called across as he got in: 'Tell me when I can pick her up, right? I'll have the mortuary boys standing by.'

'Will do!'

As Somerfield drove away, Russell gave Owen the nod for his team to get started. He turned to the farmer:

'Mr Halifax? How would someone bring a body to this spot, would you think?'

The man pursed his lips, thinking:

'Well, there's no sign of a vehicle about here, other than ours, today. The only way would be from the road, down that way.' He pointed in the direction away from the farmhouse.

'Can we take a look?'

'Surely!' He led off, along the bridleway; Russell and Rimmer fell in behind him. After a few paces, he glanced over his shoulder at the two detectives:

'Bad business. Death of a kiddie's never right, even if it's natural. Something like this….' He let his words tail off, before going on:

'On a farm, we live with life and death, Mr Russell, even when your business is only arable, like us. But there's still things can shock you. Our Annabel's not much older than that child lying there – how can anyone do something like that, to an innocent kid? You wonder what the world's coming to, don't you?'

Neither felt qualified to reply. They walked on in silence, until they reached the edge of the field, and the gate which opened onto the country road. Halifax quickly checked the padlock, confirmed that it hadn't been disturbed; the loose growth along the bottom of the gate itself also told its tale – no-one had brought a vehicle through here in a long time.

'You don't use this gate?' Russell asked.

'No. Haven't opened it for years – with the house and the yard at the other end of our land, we bring the machinery here along the tracks, no need to use the road.'

Rimmer had climbed over the gate, stooped to examine the ground outside:

'Sir? There's tyre tracks here.' Russell and the farmer leant over the gate. In the soft mud at the edge of the tarmac, a clear impression of tyres could be seen:

'Looks like a heavyish car, sir. Wide tyres, tread pattern looks expensive, too.'

'We'd better get Terry down here, get casts and pictures of those, let him check the area.' Rimmer straightened up, nodded:

'I'll go and tell him.' He climbed back over the gate, set off back the way they'd come, walking on the edge of the field itself to avoid over-stepping any possible footprints on the path. The Inspector and the farmer followed at a more leisurely pace.

When they got back to the site, they found that the Mad Professor's team had erected their tenting to protect the area around the body, and were setting to inside, apparently turning over every blade of grass individually to see if it might conceal a vital clue. Russell poked his head in:

'All right, Terry?' The bald head with its wild grey fringe looked up:

'Fine, Dave, just fine!' The man's casual attitude to rank had returned.

'Let me know when we can move her body, won't you?'

'Of course! We'll take the cloth to the forensic lab, the doc shouldn't need it, should he?'

'Doubt it. Let him take it if he asks, we can always get it back later.'

'Right-o.' He returned to his examination of the sheet wrapping the child's body. Russell turned to the farmer:

'Can we go and talk to your daughter now, Mr Halifax?'

'Of course – follow me.'

Jeep followed Land Rover along the wide bridleway to the farmhouse. In the kitchen, they found Joanne sitting at the table, a fresh mug of tea in her hands; opposite, twelve-year-old Annabel sat with her own cup, her light grey eyes wide as she gazed at her still-tense big sister. Their mother turned from the sink, where she stood washing the breakfast dishes:

'Tea, Inspector, Sergeant? It's just brewed.'

'Thank you, Mrs Halifax. I could use it.'

'Sit you down then, Mr Russell. You too, Mr Rimmer. Len, you as well – get out from under my feet, man!' The big farmer sat down as he was told, grinning ruefully at the two detectives. The immense oak table, in proportion to the cavernous room, still had room for several more. Russell looked across at the girl:

'How are you, Miss Halifax?' the dark green eyes looked up into his; she smiled, a little tentatively:

'I'm okay now, thank you. And it's Jo, please?' Russell smiled back:

'Jo – do you feel up to telling me about it?' She nodded:

'Of course. I know how important it is. It was just – such a horrible shock, to come across something like that. On such a glorious morning; it just makes it seem – so much worse, if you know what I mean?'

'I understand, Jo.' She held his eyes for a moment:

'Is it – that little girl? The one who's missing?' Russell nodded slowly:

'I'm afraid it is.' She hesitated before speaking again:

'I'm – so sorry. Will you tell her family, for me? I'm just so sad for them.' Len Halifax leant across the table, took her hand in one of his own; he spoke to the Inspector:

'That goes for us all, Mr Russell. I wish we could have found their kiddie alive, instead of this.' Russell nodded:

'I will tell them, of course. They may well ask if they can come here, see where she was found – would you have any objection?'

'No, of course not!' the farmer replied: 'They would be

welcome, any time, if it would help them. Anything we can do, anything at all, Mr Russell, just ask.'

'Thank you, Mr Halifax.' He turned to the girl again: 'Now, Jo…?'

The girl took a deep breath, and began to talk. Her sister sat gazing at her, her eyes getting wider by the minute as she listened to the awful tale. When Joanne had finished, she reached across with both hands, took her older sister's free hand in them:

'Oh, Jo!' she breathed. The older girl smiled at her:

'I'm just glad you didn't come with me, Annie.' Annabel nodded:

'So'm I!'

Russell rose to his feet:

'You got all that, Doug?' The Sergeant looked up, nodded.

'Thank you very much, Jo. You too, Mr Halifax; we'd better be getting back to the incident room. We can contact you if we need to talk to you again?'

'Of course. We'll be here, but Jo ought to go back to University on Monday?'

'I don't think that'll be a problem – we can get hold of you there, can we?'

'Oh, yes' the girl replied: 'I'll give you my number at the flat. I share with a couple of the other girls, they'll get hold of me if I'm not there.' She scribbled on a piece of paper her mother passed to her: 'There's my mobile number, too.'

Rimmer took it from her hand:

'Thank you, Miss.' He slipped it into his notebook.

'Come on, Doug. Let's get back to the office.'

The farmer rose to show them out; at the door, Russell looked back:

'Thank you for the tea, Mrs Halifax.' She looked around from the sink, where she had returned to her chores:

'Rachel! And you're welcome, Inspector.'

CHAPTER TWENTY-THREE

From the farm, Rimmer headed back to the police station to hold the fort in the incident room, while Russell took the turning at the edge of Grancester which would lead him to Elwood village. On the way, he radio'd through to let the local C.I.D. chief know that Hannah had been found.

At Ivy Cottage, he found the Superintendent's black Omega waiting outside for him. Wilson's short rotund figure clambered out as he drew up behind:

'Morning, David. Rotten show.'

'Yes, sir. Thanks for coming – I'm sure the Bucklands will appreciate it.'

Wilson nodded, removing his spectacles, to polish the lenses on his handkerchief:

'Let's get it over with – I hate being the bearer of bad news.'

'Me, too, sir. It's the one part of this job I'd happily live without.'

'Mmm.' They walked up to the front door.

Brian Buckland answered the Inspector's knock:

'Mr Russell! Good morning – come in.' Neither officer moved:

'Is Sergeant Wells here, sir?' Russell asked; Brian looked puzzled:

'Not right now – she said she'd look in later.'

'Ah. Let's go inside, please.' By now, Brian had realised that something was wrong. His face a picture of anticipated pain, he led the way into the lounge, where Harriet got up from the settee to greet the policemen. The moment she spotted the Superintendent behind Russell, she guessed at their news, and turned to her husband with a look of despair in her eyes; he turned to the Inspector:

'You've found Hannah.' It wasn't a question; Russell just nodded, his sympathy for their plight etching lines around his mouth. He needed say no more – Brian took his wife by the hand, sat her gently down on the settee again. Beside her, he drew her silently into his arms; her eyes hadn't left Russell's – now, she buried her face in her husband's shoulder as she found her greatest fear realised. Wilson spoke quietly over the Inspector's shoulder:

'I'm so sorry, so very sorry. We would all have given anything not bring you this news.' Brian looked up at him, tears glistening in his own eyes; he nodded, not trusting himself to speak. Silence held sway for a minute or more, only broken by the sound of Harriet's muffled sobs.

The kitchen door burst open, and Josh rushed in. He'd been filling the kettle for a pot of tea – hearing an unfamiliar voice, once it was on the stove, he came to see what was happening. He almost skidded to a halt, seeing his parents in each others arms, the solemn expressions of the two policemen. The hope vanished from his face as he looked at Russell:

'Hannah's dead, isn't she?' He asked quietly.

'I'm sorry, Josh. I've let you down – I promised to bring her home.' The boy averted his face, looking down at the carpet; then he looked up again:

'You would've – if you could, I know.' He swallowed hard, grey eyes blinking as he fought back his tears. His gaze switched to his parents, huddled in their grief; he turned and walked over to the sideboard. Forgetting the tea, he opened the left-hand cupboard and groped inside, took out two glasses, and his father's best single malt. Uncapping it, he poured two large measures, and took them to the settee. Brian looked up, startled; he took one glass from the boy with a smile of thanks:

'Here, drink this, mother, it'll do you good.' Harriet took it from him, obeying without thought; Josh handed him the second glass, and turned to the policemen:

'Would you like a drink, Mr Russell? Sir?' the last directed to Wilson:

'No – thank you!' The Superintendent sounded quite taken aback: 'Is there anything we can do for you? Shall I call Amanda, get her to come straight here?'

Brian looked up, shook his head:

'No – thanks. I think we're best on our own, for a while.' He smiled round at the boy: 'Josh'll look after us!' Pride shone through his sorrow.

'Will you be all right? Are you sure?' Russell's heart went out to them. The man nodded:

'We're okay – just get whoever did this for us. Please?' Russell nodded:

'We'll see ourselves out.' Despite his words, the boy followed them to the door, saw them out; before he could close it behind them, Russell turned:

'Are *you* okay, Josh?' The youngster nodded:

'I'll be all right' he hesitated, then explained: 'I *knew*. Don't ask me how – I was in the kitchen this morning, before Mum and Dad were up, and I knew she was dead. I...cried for her, then.' He looked apologetically up at the policeman, gave him a faint smile: 'I'll be all right' he repeated.

At the garden gate, Wilson looked back at the closed door:

'That's an impressive child, isn't he?' Russell smiled:

'He's changed, in the last week, grown up.'

'Mmm. Reminds me of your lad, after that Evans business, last year.'

'Me, too, sir!'

* * *

After the morning's shocking revelation, little of any import happened for the rest of the day. Owen's Scenes of Crime officers spread their pinpoint searching out from the tented enclosure where Hannah's body had lain into the surrounding field and woodland, taking a very special note of the area around the roadside gate with its impressed tyre-tracks. Somerfield returned, when Rimmer passed on the word that the body could be removed; with two men from the mortuary team, he had lifted the child into a zip-up body bag, placed her gently into the back of his Land Rover and taken her back to Northampton ready for his post-mortem examination.

Wilson had called Amanda Wells, the family liaison officer, and had her go out to Elwood, alert the immediate neighbours to the latest development before going in to the Bucklands. Later that afternoon, she had contacted Russell to ask if it would be possible for the family to go to the spot where their daughter had been found – he called Halifax, and made an arrangement with him for the following morning.

In the incident room, he had conferred with the Sergeant, the two putting in place the expansion of the enquiry to cover the villages and habitations around the farm, accepting the possibility that the killer lived in that vicinity even though their suspicion still remained that he was more local to the child's home.

Returning home, he found his family long returned from their shopping expedition. Tracy had taken the children to Northampton as a special treat, going to the Old Orleans restaurant at Sixfields for a late lunch on the way home. Sarah showed him two new dresses, and the horse to go with her Barbie doll; Tracy had added to Daniel's saved pocket-money so that he could afford some new trainers (the *right* brand, of course!) and a pair of superbly soft jeans in a grey-green colour. Russell's eyebrows went up when he saw the Armani label on the back:

'We can afford *these?*' Daniel laughed, his eyes sparkling:

'*I* can, Dad!' Russell turned to his wife:

'We're giving this boy too much pocket-money!'

CHAPTER TWENTY-FOUR

Nine thirty Sunday morning saw the Jeep Cherokee once more bumping over the fields from Pury Home Farm. Silence reigned inside; conversation between Russell and his passengers had been desultory at best, all the way from Elwood, Brian, Harriet and Josh all wrapped in their own thoughts, and the Inspector reluctant to intrude upon them. In front, Len Halifax and his two daughters were jammed into the cab of the elderly Land Rover pick-up, bouncing their shoulders together with every lurch over the uneven ground.

Conscientious about causing as little damage to the farmer's crop as possible, Russell stayed carefully in the already-created wheel tracks until they jounced to a halt at the side of the twelve-acre field. Halifax swung his robust frame out of the Land Rover, and approached the Jeep; Russell killed the engine, and got out to meet him, the Bucklands following suit:

'We're here?' Brian Buckland asked.

'That's right, Mr Buckland. She was over there, just in under the trees.' The farmer replied; he led the way to the edge of the tree-line, where the sombre group stopped to gaze at the disturbed undergrowth where the girl's body had lain. Harriet clenched her husband's hand in her own, making him wince; no-one spoke for a while.

Joanne and Annabel had got out of the truck, and now came to stand, silently respectful, behind the others. Without looking

189

around, Brian asked:

'She didn't…die here, Mr Russell?'

'No, sir. The doctor is certain she was brought here, later.'

'And he still doesn't know…how?'

'We might know later today; he's examining her now.' Brian nodded his thanks. In the ensuing silence, Josh suddenly let go of his father's hand, and took a few steps forward, to stand close to where his sister had been found. He clasped his hands as if in prayer, bowed his head. A faint choking noise came from behind the grown-ups, and Annabel squeezed past; she went up to the boy, halting just by his shoulder. As he unclasped his hands, she took the one closest to her in her own; he looked around, startled, but then smiled at the girl, returning his gaze to his sister's temporary resting-place.

Taking her cue from the children, Joanne stepped closer to Harriet. She rested one hand sympathetically on the woman's shoulder; Harriet turned, and the next moment the two were in each other's arms, both crying quietly. Halifax turned to Brian, who still stood gazing at the spot, and took one of the man's hands in both of his own great paws, his sympathy and understanding alight in his eyes. Words were unnecessary, as Brian looked around and their eyes met.

At last the tableau broke up; the groups returned to their vehicles, and drove slowly back to the farmhouse. Rachel welcomed them all, fussing around with an enormous pot of tea; gradually, the atmosphere relaxed, although the underlying pain and sorrow remained. The adults spoke together in quiet tones, Joanne and the Bucklands talking of her morning ride, Len and the Inspector listening to the soft conversation.

At the far end of the huge table, Annabel and Josh sat together, each cradling glasses of Pepsi-cola. After a few minutes of silence, the girl, unsure if she ought to broach the subject, asked about Hannah, what she was like; the boy looked up, dark grey eyes gazing into her own light grey ones, his pain evident in their expression. But he began to talk, trying to tell her how bright, how lively, how funny, how wonderful, his little sister had been. And once more, Annabel found herself blinking back tears, listening to his soft voice, feeling his sorrow as her own, sensing the oddly youthful maturity, the strength and resilience of her companion.

After around half an hour, Brian got to his feet, taking his leave of their hosts:

'We should be getting home – we've taken up too much of your morning already. Yours too, Mr Russell.' Rachel protested that they were not to rush away on that account, but Harriet rose too, beckoning Josh to join them:

'You've been very kind, Mrs Halifax…'

'Rachel, I told you!'

'…but we really ought to go. You've your own lives to get on with; and the Inspector will be wanting to get back to work.'

'I should indeed, Mrs Buckland.' Russell concurred. Halifax walked with them out to the Jeep, stood watching in sympathetic silence as they drove away. He returned to the kitchen, where Rachel was turning to the preparations for their Sunday dinner:

'Terrible! To lose a child, like that.' He spoke to no-one in particular; Annabel, still seated at the table, her eyes on the worn, scrubbed wood, looked up:

'Dad?'

'Yes, love?'

'Could we…ask them here again, one day? I could show Josh around, maybe teach him to ride?'

'You like him, don't you?'

'Yes – he's…nice! And it just seems so unfair, for them to be hurt like this, doesn't it?' The big farmer smiled at his youngest:

'It does. All right – not yet, but when they're maybe getting over this terrible business a bit, we'll invite them, okay, Annie?'

'Okay, Dad!'

* * *

191

Russell dropped the Bucklands back in Elwood, where Amanda Mills was waiting for them in the cottage, and returned to the office. Rimmer had little to report; no news from the mortuary, and not much from the Mad Professor. The SOCO team had found little of any significance in the area around the body, and no footprints on the bridleway, where the grass would take no impression of a shoe. They had photographed and made casts from the tyre tracks, and of one partial, and very smeared, footprint, in the soft mud by the field gate – the tyres, in Owen's opinion, were a low-profile design of Continental origin, such as would be found on many high-priced foreign cars. He would confirm this, with more detail if possible, on the Monday.

Around four o'clock, long after he had sent the Sergeant home to join his wife for the remainder of the day, Russell's telephone rang. He grabbed it up:

'D.I. Russell.'

'Inspector? It's Iain Somerfield here.'

'What have you got for me, Iain?'

'Not everything yet, David. But I can tell you how Hannah died, and pretty much what happened to her.'

'That's great – fire away.'

'Well, my guess in the field was spot on, for a start' the doctor sounded quite pleased with himself: 'She died from asphyxiation. There're fibres in her nose and mouth, and in the pulmonary tract, which look like cotton, possibly from something like a pillow or a sheet. Perhaps the one she was wrapped in, or one like it.'

'Did she struggle?'

'Not then, I think. There're marks, bruises, scratches, from what I think are previous attempts to defend herself, but they look to have been caused a little while before death. I suspect she might have been drugged, possibly with nothing more elaborate than a proprietary sleeping pill, and then killed while she slept – the lab analysis will tell us, when I get it back.'

'How long had she been dead when we found her?'

'First estimate would say about five or six days. I'll tighten that up for you when I can.'

'Previous attempts – what else had happened to the poor kid?' He heard the pathologist draw a deep breath:

'She'd been raped. Not once, not twice. A number of times, within a short space of time, presumably between when she was taken and when she died.'

'Oh, God! Poor little beggar!'

'Yes. Well, the good thing is we've got plenty of D.N.A. evidence. All you need is a suspect to match it to, David.'

'Huh! That's easier said than done, right now!'

'Yes, well, not wishing to be unsympathetic, but that's your problem, mate! I'll get the samples analysed, make sure if we're dealing with one or more attackers. We should know more in a day or two, but the D.N.A. test will take a bit longer, say the end of the week. I'll keep you posted, as the results come back to me, okay?'

'Yes, thanks, Iain. God, I hope we nail the bastard who did this!'

'Yeah – me too. Oh for the death penalty, eh?'

'Right! I'll talk to you soon.'

'Yeah – 'bye, David.'

* * *

At home that night, Russell remained quiet, withdrawn. His family, sensing his sombre mood, left him in peace, even little Sarah playing quietly in her room, accepting that her Daddy needed to be left alone for a while. He'd apologised to his son – the two had missed out on their sailing club for two weeks running, now – but the boy had shrugged it off, understanding that his father's job had to interfere with their shared pleasure sometimes. At ten o'clock, he'd looked into the study, where Russell had been half-heartedly tinkering with one of his radio controllers:

'I'm off to bed, Dad.' Russell glanced up:

''Night, son.' The boy hesitated:

'Are you all right, Dad?' He was treated to a rueful smile:

'Yes, I'm fine! Sorry I haven't been much company, tonight. This case is getting me down, a bit.'

'Yeah – I understand. It's…pretty awful, isn't it?'

'It is. I'll be happy when we catch whoever killed that poor girl. I hope they lock him up for all time.'

'You'll get him, Dad, I know you will!' Russell laughed at the boy's self-assurance, wishing he felt half as confident:

'Go on, brat! Off to bed with you!'

''Kay, Dad. See you in the morning.'

'Sleep well, Dan.'

* * *

In Bedford Road, Kim Lee Hsung was struggling up the stairs, half helping, half carrying her mother. Martha was no great weight, she didn't eat enough to keep most people alive, but the girl was no athlete, and getting the semi-conscious woman up there and easing her into bed left her gasping for breath.

That morning, Martha had beaten her daughter to the kitchen, which meant that she'd been already started on the vodka before breakfast. Not that she'd eaten much breakfast – Kim had had to be very firm with her to get her to eat even one slice of toast. And the day had gone downhill from there.

Kim went back downstairs, leaving her mother snoring loudly, still fully clothed, on her bed. She put the kettle on, made herself a mug of coffee, and sat in front of the television, not even pretending to watch the news. She felt so miserable; another weekend over, a time when most kids her age would have been out playing with their friends, enjoying the first real Spring sunshine of the year. She'd gone out for a bit yesterday, gone to see Amy, her only real friend, out in Glebe Farm. But then, when she'd got home in mid-afternoon, her mother had laid into her for leaving her on her own, shouting at her until the eleven-year-old had run crying to her room. She'd stayed in for the rest of the weekend, wondering if her life would ever improve, if her mother would ever accept that she had a real problem, and seek the help that her daughter and her ex-husband both agreed she so desperately needed.

Once or twice in the past, she'd got so fed up with it all that she'd walked out, spent a night or two at Amy's. Her friend's parents knew how difficult her life was at times; they'd told her to come and stay whenever she needed a break. But her loyalty to her sick mother kept her at home, along with the knowledge that if she wasn't there, Martha would just drink until she collapsed. Even leaving her alone for the monthly visit to her father's house made Kim uneasy; although, perhaps surprisingly, Martha seemed able to take some kind of control of herself for those pre-arranged days.

She finished her coffee, turned off the TV, left the mug to be washed up in the morning and took herself off to bed, ready for school the next day.

* * *

George Andrews awoke with a start, looked around. He was slumped in the chair in his wife's room; she was sound asleep in the bed next to him. He must have dozed off!

He'd been there most of the day – the shop was closed on Sundays – had lunch with Sheila, sat with her all afternoon in the garden, enjoying the growing warmth of the gathering Spring. One of the orderlies had helped her back into bed in time for tea; after buttered crumpets and jam, Sheila had settled back for a rest. Andrews himself had begun to nod, tired from a heavy week, and the constant worry over her health. Since Friday, her deterioration had been noticeable, her face thinner, her skin paler day by day; the house doctor, the same who had met him with the detectives, had waylaid him again that morning, gently warning him that his wife was probably on her final decline, telling him to be prepared for her not to see the week out. He'd managed to keep up a brave face for her sake, even if he'd felt like crying inside whenever he looked at her lying so helpless and vulnerable in the crisp white sheets.

Now, she was sleeping peacefully. He got to his feet, padded silently to the door, turned for one last look before he left for his own bed.

CHAPTER TWENTY-FIVE

The recovery of Hannah Buckland's body should have taken the enquiry forwards dramatically. But the truth of the matter was that it made very little difference, a fact that David Russell found increasingly frustrating as the next few days went by.

Despite the impetus given by the knowledge that they were now engaged upon a murder investigation, any police enquiry can only progress on the basis of knowledge and information. Nothing has changed substantively since the days of Sherlock Holmes – the discovery and interpretation of clues is necessary to give focus and direction for the enquiry to move on. Modern technology can make the finding of clues easier, their interpretation more accurate and definitive – but insufficient clues still means a stalled investigation.

The new evidence that resulted from the discovery of the dead child was vital, of that there was no doubt. But it all required a standard for comparison: As the pathologist had mentioned, D.N.A. evidence needs a suspect to be matched against, although Russell had suggested in a meeting with Wilson on the Tuesday that a genetic check of all adult males living in the relevant area might have to be considered. The C.I.D. chief was reluctant to sanction such a prolonged and costly effort if it could be avoided, but conceded that it might prove to be the only way forward in the end. Similarly, the tyre tracks needed a vehicle for comparison – Owen had come back to confirm that the type and size were commonly used as original equipment on some European models, notably from Mercedes Benz, BMW, Volvo, Peugeot and others. The same tyre was available from British sources, and could equally well be found as a replacement on many other cars, effectively leaving the field pretty well wide open as to what make and model had been involved.

Once a reasonably believable suspect had been identified, both D.N.A. and tyre casts would soon prove guilt or innocence – but the suspect, man or vehicle, had to be found, first.

The location of the girl's body, more or less at the far end of the county from her home, had resulted in a part of the effort being expended in the triangle of countryside defined by the villages of Whittlebury, Paulerspury and Deanshanger, in an attempt to see if her killer could be from that neighbourhood. However, Russell remained unconvinced – the circumstances of her abduction still made him cling to the idea that the murderer was more local to her home, someone who had come across the distressed child purely by chance, picked her up and then taken advantage of the situation, and possibly her state of mind.

Even the timescale of Hannah's ordeal remained rather vague. On Wednesday, Russell bearded the pathologist in his den to hear the latest lab results; Somerfield had by then been able to confirm that the girl had been drugged with a commonly-available proprietory sleeping tablet:

'Someone had given her what looks like being an adult dose, David. Wouldn't have done her any long-term harm, but it does suggest that she would have been very deeply asleep when she was smothered.'

'How as it administered? Did she just swallow it in tablet form?'

'Doubt it. I'm pretty sure she was given it in a cup of hot chocolate, probably ground up into a powder, to judge from the stomach contents.'

'So the killing was obviously planned?'

'Yes. I'd assume he'd been having his fun for a few days, and decided that the time had come when he had to get rid of her.'

'Sounds horribly clinical, put like that, Iain.' The pathologist peered at the policeman over the rims of his spectacles:

'Does, doesn't it? But it's the logical conclusion, Mr Spock.'

'Huh! I guess so. Can you tighten up the time at all?'

'When she died? Not a lot, to be truthful. If we knew she'd been where you found her since she died, I could be more certain – but that's the problem, you see. If she'd been there all the time, I'd put it around Monday afternoon or early evening, but we know she wasn't. Trouble is, temperature and humidity have a big influence on what happens to a body – if she'd been out of doors all that time, then that would be a good estimate. But was she?'

'I take it there's nothing on her body to tell us where she was?'

'Nothing – but I have my suspicions. If she'd been indoors, somewhere warm, I'd have to shorten that time a bit, put her death maybe into Tuesday morning; but I don't think that's the case. I'm wondering if she might have been somewhere cold – a deep-freeze, perhaps? – while that post-mortem lividity was developing. If that was the case, then I'd say she could have died Sunday evening – or Sunday night, which would fit with the sleeping-tablet, perhaps?'

'I see what you mean, Iain. Do you have any idea just when she might have been taken to the farm?'

'Not clearly. Depends on when she died! Sorry if that's not very helpful. Let's try to put what we do know together: She was abducted when, Friday evening?'

'That's right, about half past five.'

'So, given the number of sexual attacks she suffered, and the state of her injuries, she must have been held for a couple of days at least, I'd say. Ties in with Sunday night for her murder, as well. If I'm right about the freezer, let's say a couple of days there, while he decided what to do with her – Tuesday night? But its really little better than guesswork, David.'

'Okay – thanks, Iain. Even guesswork gives me something to work from!'

So the middle of the next week arrived, and despite all the intense effort put in in the background by the team of detectives and uniformed officers at their disposal, Inspector and Sergeant found themselves little if any closer to identifying the perpetrator of such a horrifying crime. They desperately needed a breakthrough, a hint, a glint of light through the darkness which would give them the direction, the focus they required to draw closer to their quarry.

And at last, it came. It came from an unexpected direction, as such things often do. A sceptic would call it blind chance; a believer might see the hand of God; for most of us, the all-encompassing word coincidence can cover a multitude of fortuitous events.

* * *

That Thursday night, a couple of teenage car thieves scrambled over the barbed-wire-topped back fence of Bellevue Motors. They spent the best part of an hour, forcing doors on a row of cars parked in the corner of the yard farthest from the workshops, grabbing anything they could find which might be of value, forcing the boots also to rip out the occasional CD multichanger. They escaped the way they had entered, taking their prizes away in the over-tuned, wide-tyred Escort XR3i they had left outside.

Next morning, the Service Manager discovered their depredations, and called the police. During the morning, the cars were examined, fingerprints taken, the damage to each assessed, the owners traced and informed of what had happened. Except for one.

When he checked the registration numbers against the service records, Peter Willetts, the workshop foreman, discovered that one of the cars shouldn't have been there. There was no job card for it, no record of the owner having brought it in. Puzzled, he checked with the Service Manager:

'Norm?' Norman Mitchell looked up as the foreman's head appeared round his office door:

'Yes, Pete?' The foreman dropped the list of numbers on the desk, pointed to one of them:

'Do you know why that car's here?'

'Isn't it booked in?'

'Doesn't look like it, there's no card for it anywhere.'

'Unh. How long's it been there?'

'No idea.'

'You've asked Jayne?' Jayne was the service receptionist.

'Yeah – she's got no record of it coming in.'

'Okay – leave it with me for the minute, I'll see what I can find out.'

The foreman withdrew, to return to more pressing jobs. Mitchell pushed his glasses up into his thick, blond hair as he got up from his seat and turned to the filing-cabinet. He riffled through the files, came upon the one he wanted, withdrew it and took it to the desk.

The cars which had been attacked were all ones being held at the dealership for one reason or another, awaiting the delivery of parts from the factory or diagnostic information or the resolution of other problems. Several of them had been there for a number of weeks; the presence of an interloper might easily have gone unnoticed for a considerable time, anyone who spotted it naturally assuming that someone else would know all about it. Mitchell opened the file – when he read the name of the car's owner, he sat back in surprise; then, after a minute or so spent deep in thought, he picked up the telephone and spoke to his Sales Manager, confirming what he thought he remembered. Then, even more thoughtfully, he dialled an outside number.

CHAPTER TWENTY-SIX

'D.I. Russell's office – Sergeant Rimmer.' He'd leant forward from his usual perch on the desk-edge to scoop up the handset. It was mid-afternoon; Russell looked up from the report in front of him, saw a puzzled frown cross his assistant's face as he listened:

'Who left it there – and when?'

'Ah – right – thank you. You'd best not touch it, if you don't mind, I'll call you. Thanks again.' He looked up, his puzzlement still evident.

'What is it, Doug?' The Sergeant didn't reply immediately, his expression saying that he was trying to get his thoughts in order:

'They've found Andrews' car, the estate.'

'Really?' Russell's interest was fired.

'Yeah – but...' Rimmer paused, thinking, then explained:

'That was D.C. Ames, in Northampton. Someone got into the service yard at Bellevue Motors last night, broke into a number of cars – cars which were there for long-term work, right, parked at the back of the yard? Well, one of them turns out to be his old car. Thing is, no-one knew it was there.'

'What do you mean?'

'There's no record of the owner bringing it in, no details of whatever work it's there for.'

'How long's it been there?'

'They're not sure – a few days, they think.'

'So – what the devil…' The light of inspiration suddenly flared in the hazel eyes:

'Doug! Suppose you wanted to lose a car, what would you do?'

'Take it out in the country somewhere, jemmy the door, set fire to it and report it stolen.'

'Yes, but – if you needed to lose it *after the event,* so to speak? It would be no good reporting it stolen on Tuesday, if you needed people to think it was gone on Saturday, see what I mean?'

'Okay – dump it in the river?'

'No good – how would you be sure the water was deep enough to cover it? Anyway, you'd probably leave tracks.' By now, Rimmer had cottoned on to his superior's train of thought:

'You couldn't just leave it somewhere, even right out in the sticks, someone would soon spot it, and then you'd be faced with a lot of embarrassing questions.'

'Right! So – where would be the best place to hide it? What could be better than a yard full of similar cars? There must be upwards of a hundred Mercedes in Bellevue's yard most days – who'd notice one more?'

'Chancy, surely?'

'But if you were a regular customer, knew where to put it among the long-term jobs, it might easily stay there for weeks, months even, before someone realised it shouldn't be there at all!'

'You could be right, sir.'

'Okay, Doug – let's get out there. Call Ames back, tell him we want the car, they're not to touch it. And call Terry, tell him we want him to go over it ASAP, and fine-tooth-comb! We'll need an interview team, to talk to all the staff at Bellevue, find out as much as we can about how long it's been there, see if any of them know anything about it, if there is a valid reason for it's being there.' He'd got up as he spoke, slipped his jacket on; the two departed from the office with a new sense of urgency.

In the Jeep, on the way to Northampton, The Sergeant glanced at his superior from behind the wheel:

'How significant do you think this car is, sir?' Russell thought before replying, in his typically cautious manner:

'I don't know, Doug. If Andrews is on the level, if he really *did* sell the car two months ago, then it's probably irrelevant. I know, I had wondered if a new owner could have taken advantage of the girl's familiarity with it to entice her inside, but that rather presupposes that Andrews must have sold it to someone he knew – the chances of him selling the car to a complete stranger who just happened to know the Bucklands, knew that Andrews was Brian's boss, and had a yen for little girls: The odds would be too long to make any sense.'

'But you think he's lying.' It wasn't a question; Russell laughed:

'I don't know, Doug! I suspect he is, yes. Either he sold it to someone he knew, someone he's now protecting for some reason; or he didn't sell it at all. Let's assume he's lying through his teeth for a moment – look where that puts us: The car matches little Taylor's description. Hannah knew him well, would have got into his car without a qualm. His alibi is far from solid. He's been a customer at Bellevue for some years, probably knew their routine to some degree at least. And he's alone in the house, with his wife in the hospice, probably feeling lonely and depressed. The only part missing is whether he fancies little girls; and it could be just the depression showing itself in that way, perhaps? Maybe he didn't mean to hurt her, just let his state of mind take over?'

'I suppose it's possible, sir. If he had any kind of record of perversion, even a warning or two, it would support the idea, wouldn't it?'

'It would – but you tell me he hasn't.'

'Mmm.' They drove on in silence for a few minutes; then Russell spoke again:

'We need a thorough examination of the car, Doug. Is there any trace of Hannah having been in it recently? Do the tyres match our casts from the farm? Who's fingerprints are inside it?

I'd expect we might still find Andrews', even if he's telling the truth – but if they are fresh? And are there any from another driver, his supposed buyer?'

'Yeah. The Mad Professor's waiting for it, I've asked for the piggyback to collect it as soon as possible. Maybe the people at Bellevue will be able to pin down how long it's been there?'

'That would be useful. Maybe someone saw it left there, saw the driver. Mind you, if it's been there a couple of weeks or more, we're barking up the wrong tree, aren't we?' Rimmer laughed:

'Yeah! That would be just our luck, wouldn't it?'

'Have we got a picture of Andrews, Doug?'

'No, sir.'

'Hmm. We could do with one, see if anyone recognises him – but then, I guess a lot of the people there would know him anyway, if he was a regular customer.'

'I expect so.'

'If he did dump the car there, my guess is that he'd have had a ready excuse, a reason for going there. We need to ask if he's been to the garage in the last week or so, for any reason at all; and did whoever spoke to him notice what he was driving?'

'I'll make sure the team are primed on that, sir.' He glanced in the mirror, to be sure that the C.I.D. car was still following.

A little later, they swung onto the forecourt of Bellevue Motors, in the Kingsthorpe district of Northampton. The dealer principal, big heavily-built man by the name of Anderson, hurried across to meet them:

'Inspector Russell? Sergeant?' He shook hands with the two officers:

'Norman Mitchell, the Service Manager, and Pete Willetts, the foremen, are waiting for you. I'll take you through to the after-sales area, if you'll follow me.' As they followed the broad back through the showroom and along corridors, Russell told the man:

'We'll need to talk to everyone on the site, sir, if that's all right with you?'

'Yes, I suppose you will. I'll make sure everyone knows to co-operate in any way they can; but I'd appreciate it if we can carry on our business today, Inspector?'

'We'll try to interfere as little as we can, sir. The police piggyback truck will be along shortly, to take the car for forensic examination; we have to try to establish, if we can, how long it's been here, and who left it here. I take it you haven't come across a good reason for its presence?'

'Not that I know of – Norman will know better than I.'

'Thank you, sir. We'll probably only be able to complete a few of the interviews today – I'll have our team out here first thing tomorrow, get finished and leave you in peace as early as we can. You know Mr Andrews, the car's owner, sir?'

'I do, of course. He's bought several cars from us over, oh, seven or eight years, I think. We haven't contacted him about this, since Norman recalled your enquiry about this car last week, thought we should leave it to you, perhaps?'

'That's absolutely right, sir. It may well be that there is no connection with our enquiry, in which case we'll return the car here and leave you to call him. You weren't aware of him selling it, were you?' Anderson looked around, surprised:

'No! He had thought of trading it, as I recall, when they bought the convertible, but then he decided to keep it, for his business. Paid cash, for the other car.'

They arrived in the aftersales office, where Anderson introduced the Service Manager and foreman. He left them to it; the interview team set to, beginning with the mechanics, any of whom might have information about the car, when it had arrived, who had brought it. The Inspector and the Sergeant spoke to Mitchell and Willetts, and then the receptionist, quickly establishing that none knew of the car's presence, or of any reason for it's being left with the dealership. By now, the afternoon was running on, the garage's workforce looking forward to knocking off and going home.

The two interview groups, at their temporary homes in the back of the showroom, had spoken to each mechanic, and were about to turn to the parts department staff; some of the company's employees had opted to stay on, get the interviews out of the way that evening, others would be spoken to the following morning. The piggyback had arrived, loaded up the estate car, and left for the police forensic department, when Russell decided to call it a day, feeling that there was nothing to be done that couldn't wait until morning. He and Rimmer walked back through the almost-deserted garage to the car, got in and drove off to return to Grancester.

'You want to come back here tomorrow, sir, or leave things to the team?' Rimmer asked as he drove off.

'I think we'll come back, Doug. Looks better, for our P.R., for one thing – and I want to talk to the parts people myself. You noticed that the parts department is round the back, in the service yard? If neither Andrews nor anyone else spoke to the workshop staff, maybe they went to the parts counter? He could have driven into the yard, parked the car, gone in, maybe asked about something for the convertible, and then just walked out, leaving the car there.'

'Could be. You're certain it was Andrews, aren't you, boss?'

Russell laughed:

'I will be, if we find proof that kid was in the car, and no trace of another driver! But yes, I'm beginning to think he's our man.'

'Should we pull him in, give him a grilling?'

'Not yet. He's a very different proposition from Olsen, much more sophisticated, much more self-confident. At this stage, all he'll do is be very apologetic, tell us that maybe the buyer *was* from Northampton, not Bedford, and deny all knowledge of the car's whereabouts. We'll need proof, solid, incontrovertible proof, before we'll shake his story, Doug. Best leave him for the moment, bring him in when – or do I mean if? – we're in a position to nail him to the wall.'

CHAPTER TWENTY-SEVEN

Sheila Andrews died at fourteen minutes after midnight on Saturday morning. Her husband had been at her side for the best part of twelve hours; he had driven there straight from the shop in Barfield after a couple of hours at work, to find her very weak. The staff at the hospice had brought him meals, which he had mostly ignored; he had sat by her bed, her hand in his own, talking quietly to her, not knowing whether she could hear him or not.

When she died, her last breath escaping in gentle silence, he didn't move. He sat, her hand still clasped in both of his, gazing at her peaceful face, remembering: Remembering the beautiful girl he had met in Hastings, on the seafront, all those years ago. Remembering the way she had stood by him, through all of his shame. Remembering how she had started their new life all alone, while he was detained by Her Majesty. Remembering how, together, they had gone on through the years, never falling out of love, always side by side, enjoying all that life could throw at them. As he remembered, the tears ran unnoticed down his cheeks until the collar of his shirt grew damp.

At last, after he knew not how long, he laid her still, cold hand on her breast and stood up. He went to the night nurse's station, told her quietly what had happened; as the girl hurried off to find the doctor, he slipped out of the door to his car and drove away. He couldn't face their sympathy, their well-meaning fussing over him; and he knew that Sheila was in safe hands – at least, that part of what had been Sheila which remained in the room he had left.

He drove back to the house on the Embankment, went upstairs to the lounge and poured himself a large brandy. Sitting in the armchair, he sipped it slowly while the remembering went on. He thought he dozed, from time to time – but waking and sleeping blended seamlessly together, memory and dream becoming a continuous process of grieving. The dawn came up outside, without him being more than distantly aware of the brightening sky; it was some hours later when, feeling stiff from sitting so long, he got up, put the now-empty glass on the sideboard and went downstairs. His subconscious need for fresh air drove him out of the front door; he walked slowly, blindly, across to the riverside, wandered along its bank as the two of them had done so many times.

* * *

Josh Buckland rose early that Saturday. He had been sleeping better of late, less disturbed, at least subconsciously, by the fact of his sister's death than he had been by the uncertainty of her fate; but he still found himself waking in the early hours, unable to doze off again.

And when he woke, the same thought returned to puzzle him. It was scary, really – but a scariness which excited rather than frightened: When they'd visited Pury Home Farm last week, to see where Hannah had been found, he'd listened to Joanne talking about her morning ride in the fields. And, as he listened, it had come to him that at just about the exact time she must have found Hannah, he had been sitting at the kitchen table, when that sudden certainty of her death had hit him and left him sobbing. He didn't understand – he wasn't sure he wanted to – and he hadn't told anyone, feeling that whatever ethereal message he'd received, it was something very personal, very private.

He sat at the table again, for a while, thinking about Hannah. He missed her terribly, still – but now it was different kind of missing, somehow, a quieter, less anguished feeling, a kind of constant ache deep inside him that he knew would never go away, but that he would be able to live with, in time. And, in quiet moments like this, he almost felt that a part of that ache was because she was with him, *in* him, seeing what he saw, feeling what he felt. He realised that he was crying, brushed the tears away with a smile – even crying didn't feel so bad, now – and got up to put the kettle on. A little later, he carried the tray upstairs, knocked at his parents' door, pushed his way in at his mother's sleepy greeting.

* * *

In another cottage, in another village, Daniel Russell sat across the breakfast table from his father. Dad had come home the night before, not *too* late for dinner, a new excitement evident in his face and his manner; he'd told his son that they might be getting closer to catching the little girl's murderer, a prospect which pleased the boy almost as much as it did his father. At twelve, Daniel still had a sharply-defined image of right and wrong, and a great belief in his father's part in the struggle between the two. But now, his excitement at the gathering pace of the pursuit was tempered by a more personal consideration:

'Dad?' Russell looked up from his own eggs and bacon:

'Yes, Daniel?'

'Where's the club meeting tomorrow?'

'Linford Lakes, Milton Keynes.' The boy hesitated to ask the next question:

'Will we be going?' His father smiled apologetically:

'I wouldn't bank on it, Dan! I'm up to my neck in a murder enquiry, remember – it'll depend on what happens today.'

'Yeah – I suppose.' Russell saw the disappointment in his

son's eyes, felt the boy deserved more of an explanation:

'We've got a lot to do today, interviews and the like – if that leads on to more things, I'll probably have to work tomorrow. But it might leave us stuck again, even if we are a bit further forward – in which case, maybe I'll be able to get away, and we can go sailing. No promises, mind!'

'Okay, Dad! If not, there's next week, isn't there?' Daniel sounded brighter.

'That's right – I don't like having to keep tell you next week, next week; when we've got Hannah's murderer, I'll take a few days off, and we can always go somewhere, just the two of us, okay?'

'Yeah – it'll be the Easter holiday soon, we can go then!'

'We will – I promise!'

'Can I come?' Sarah joined in; Russell turned to his daughter:

'We'll all go, shall we? Have a day or two out, you and Mummy as well?'

'Mm-hm!'

* * *

Kim overslept that morning. She'd been up late, sitting with her mother, watching television, trying to slow the woman's alcohol intake as best she could, knowing that if she didn't there would be trouble in store the next day.

And she was right – she stumbled downstairs, half-awake, in a light shirt and jeans, to find her mother already up, sitting in the kitchen, a glass at her elbow, the opened vodka bottle in front of her. She gave an inward groan, but put a smile on her face as she said, as breezily as she could:

'Hello, Mum!' Martha looked up, smiled at the girl:

'Hello, Kimmie!'

At least we're starting the day okay! the girl thought, as she replied:

'I'm having some coffee – shall I make you one? And how about some breakfast, egg on toast? It'll set you up for the day.' Not waiting for the reply, she filled the kettle, lit the gas under it, went to the fridge for the eggs.

Martha didn't want any breakfast, didn't want coffee – all she wanted was another drink. But she let the girl fuss about, preparing a breakfast, recognising that this ritual dance had to be adhered to – for her daughter's sake, she would make a token attempt to eat, sip a little of the coffee. But there were times when she tired of the whole charade, only her love and respect for the capable eleven-year-old making her acquiesce in the whole silly business. The drink didn't *really* do her any harm – and it did help her to cope with each day, insulate her from a life which had no purpose that she could any longer determine. She poured another glass of vodka, swallowed it in one when the girl's back was turned. Just one more, and she'd be able to face the day – this shot emptied the bottle, and a frown of annoyance crossed her face: Did she have any more? Where had she put it?

Kim chose that exact moment to put a plate of egg on toast in front of her mother. Her mind on the whereabouts of her spare bottle, Martha looked down at the food:

'Don' want 'ny breakfast! Kimmie, I need a drink – where's 'nother bottle?'

'Come on, Mum, don't be silly – eat up, it'll do you good. And have some coffee – you can have a drink in a little while, okay?' The sudden aggression of the drunk flared in Martha; she swept the plate from the table, to shatter in a mess of egg on the floor:

'I tol' you I need 'drink, you stupid child! Don' like bloody eggs!' The girl had jumped back to avoid the projectile, her face crumpling:

'Oh, Mum!' It was a cry of pain; she ducked aside as the mug of coffee flew against the wall, cracking a tile as it too shattered.

'Bloody kid – can' you do 'nything righ'?' Kim just stood

staring, her face a mask of anguish, the pain as much for her mother as for herself, as the woman continued to let rip, unthinking:

''N don' look at me li' that! You look just like 'im! Why did 'e 'ave to gi' me a bloody kid? All you do is remind me of 'im, ev'ry time I see you! Bloody li'l wog, I should never 'a married 'im – then I wouln't 'ave *you,* remindin' me of 'im all the fuckin' time!'

Faced with this tirade, Kim had backed slowly away, her hands to her mouth, eyes wide with pain and fear. At her mother's sudden, awful rejection of her, she turned and ran. With no thought for where she was going, she ran out of the front door, tore the gate open and ran, tears streaming down her face, along the street. The enormity of her own words blew Martha's anger out like a candle caught in a gale; she leapt to her feet, almost falling in her hazy unsteadiness, and ran after her daughter, to stop in the doorway, calling after her:

'Kimmie! Kimmie! I'm sorry, darling – I din't mean it! Come back! Please, baby, come back!'

But the girl didn't hear, her senses swamped by the depth of her anguish. She ran on, headed unconsciously in the general direction of the town centre. Martha turned back inside the house – God, she needed another drink now, for sure! There was a bottle upstairs, in the bedroom, somewhere, she was sure; she made her way, carefully unbalanced, up the stairs; just near the top, she missed her footing, grabbed for the banister and missed that too, felt herself falling, toppling backwards, unable to save herself….

* * *

At Bellevue Motors, the interviewing of the staff was proceeding steadily. Russell, following his hunch, had been talking to the parts department employees; two of those who were not in fact on shift that day had come in specially, and he had dealt with them first to allow them to get away. He had then spoken to the manager; now, he was in the sales counter area, talking to Helen Bradshaw, one of the on-shift staff while the other dealt with customers. He asked if the girl knew Mr Andrews; her brow furrowed:

'I don't think so…'

'Yes you do!' her colleague , overhearing, put in: 'He's the smart guy, with that crimson C-Class soft-top. Came in last week.'

'Oh, yeah, right! I know.' Russell turned to the young man at the counter, his excitement growing:

'You say he came in last week?' The lad looked around; he had no customer at that moment:

'Yeah – asked about a boot liner, you remember, Helen! We had to e-mail Milton Keynes 'cos there wasn't one in the catalogue for the convertible.'

'Oh, yes, that's right, I remember!' the girl confirmed.

'What day was that, can you tell me?'

'Oh. Now, let me see – Tuesday? No, Wednesday, wasn't it, Perry?'

'Yeah, that's right. Nutty Norm – sorry, Inspector, I mean Mr Mitchell – was off from then 'til the weekend, which was why we had to contact the factory; normally, he'd deal with that kind of thing.'

Russell found himself almost disbelieving how things were beginning to drop in his lap; his elation rising, he confirmed:

'So Mr Andrews came in here on Wednesday of last week? You're certain?'

The two young people looked at each other, turned back to him:

'Yeah, sure.' The young man spoke; the girl nodded:

'Definitely!' She concurred; both were surprised at the grin on the policeman's face:

'I don't suppose you saw what car he was driving?' The young man shook his head:

'No; I assumed he was in the convertible, but I didn't see it, did you, Helen?'

'I didn't, either.'

'Thank you, both of you! I'll have my Sergeant take a full statement from you both during the course of the morning, if that's all right?' They nodded their agreement; he hurried out, to find Rimmer.

Leaving the Sergeant to take formal statements from the two of them, he went out to the car and set off to return to his office. Owen had promised to get him at least a preliminary result from the estate car by lunchtime; and he'd not heard from Somerfield about the D.N.A. results. In the car as he drove, his thoughts were revolving around their latest discoveries, circling like mental planets around a central sun which was the great word 'if': If Andrews had been the one who left the estate car in Bellevue's yard, then it gave the lie to his claim to have sold it. If he'd left it there on the Wednesday, that fitted with the pathologist's theory that Hannah's body had been dumped on Tuesday night – assuming he'd used that car for the job. And if those two ideas were correct, the only sensible conclusion was that Andrews was the girl's abductor, wasn't it?

He drove, in a state of considerable excitement, impatient to talk to both the pathologist and the forensic officer, but restraining himself from the temptation to use the car's radio for the purpose, realising that he would need his full concentration for those conversations.

CHAPTER TWENTY-EIGHT

It was a pleasant enough Spring morning. The overnight cloud cover was beginning to break as George Andrews wandered along the Embankment; near the Town Bridge, on the South side of the town centre, he stopped to rest, easing himself into one of the benches provided for sightseers. He huddled against its cast-iron arm, hunched forward in his grief, looking like a rather expensively dressed down-and-out; uninterested in the view across the river to the Cross Keys Hotel, or the meandering ducks, or the two students exercising their skills in a racing canoe, his gaze remained fixed on the ground a little way in front of his feet. He was only vaguely aware of the young girl who joined him a little while later, flopping into a similarly inattentive pose at the far end of the bench.

* * *

Kath Braham had been washing up when she heard the kerfuffle next door. She turned to Tom, seated at the kitchen table; her husband met her gaze, raised his own eyes to the ceiling as if to say *not again!*

They were used to such happenings. They knew about Martha Simpson's drink problem, knew and admired the little girl for the way she looked after her mother, even tried to help in small ways when they could.

Sounds carried quite clearly through the thin walls of the old terraced houses. This morning, they heard the shouting, Martha yelling at the child as usual, then the sound of feet running down the hall, the front door flying open. That was unusual – Tom got to his feet, went to their own front door, looked out. He saw the girl run off, her distress clear; he heard Martha yell her drunken, ineffective apology, felt no surprise when the girl ignored it – *she'll come home in her own good time,* he thought. He turned and went inside, knowing there was nothing he could do. He returned to the kitchen, sat down to finish his cup of tea, shrugging at Kath as she raised a questioning eyebrow.

A minute or so later, they heard a clatter and bang, from the next-door stairwell. Tom looked up in alarm, saw the same thought echoed in his wife's expression:

'That sounded nasty – you'd better go and see, Tom.'

'Yes, love. Reckon she's gone down the stairs?' He got to his feet again.

'Sounded like it.'

'Mm.' He went to the door, stepped across the low wall between the small front gardens and knocked at the door. It swung open at his touch, unlatched from when the girl had flown out; he leant through, called out:

'Martha? Are you all right?'

The door swung further back; he drew in his breath sharply as he caught sight of the huddled bundle at the bottom of the stairs. Hurrying forward, he bent over the prone figure, shook her shoulder; she didn't respond, but her head moved in a way he didn't like the look of. Rushing back next door, he grabbed up the telephone and dialled 999.

'What is it, love?' Kath asked.

'Martha. I think she's hurt. Ambulance, please, to number 44 Bedford Road – there's a woman, I think she's fallen downstairs.' He spoke into the phone.

'Okay, thank you.' He replaced the receiver, turned to Kath:

'They'll be right here.'

'What about little Kim?' He shrugged his shoulders:

'Not much we can do until she comes home, is there?'

* * *

Once out of the house, Kim just ran. Uncaring of where she went, it was only an instinctive tendency to follow familiar roads which took her to the town centre. A few turnings along Midland Road from her home, she slowed to a walk, breathing heavily, half sobbing in her distress. One or two passers-by looked at her, concern on their faces; but none took the next step of approaching her.

Her mother's words had left her desperately upset. She was scared, her usual quiet self-confidence shattered, utterly destroyed – the rejection of what she tried to do for her mother she could handle, she was used to that, but the sudden, awful rejection of what and who she *was*….

Kim was her father's daughter – she knew she looked like him, the Oriental cast was there in her face for all to see, despite her blond hair and blue eyes. If her mother hated her for *that*, what could she do?

Over the years, she had taken her mother's drunken verbal abuse, brushing it aside as just a symptom of her illness. But the terrible revelation that Martha hated her as a living reminder of her father had snapped something inside her – she found herself returning the hatred; her anger at all the years of trying to support the woman, of finding herself loaded with ever greater and greater responsibility as she had got older and more capable of bearing it, of giving up her own life and liberty to look after her, came to the surface at last. *I'm eleven years old! I want a life of my own, I want to have friends to play with, I want to enjoy myself!*

She found herself by the Bridge, at the end of the Embankment, unaware of how she had got there. Her anger and despair welling up inside her, she turned and almost fell onto the nearest of the benches, hardly noticing the man sitting at the other end, leaning on the arm almost as if in pain.

* * *

Back in his office, Russell was on the point of reaching for the telephone when it forestalled him by ringing. He snatched up the receiver:

'Russell!'

'David? It's Iain Somerfield.'

'Doc! What have you got for me?'

'You sound very eager this morning?'

'Yeah!' Russell had the grace to laugh at himself: 'I think we might have a lead on who grabbed Hannah.'

'Really? That's good. Maybe I can help – I've had all of the lab results, now. I reckon the timescale we talked about the other day is about right – there are indications in the structure of some of her cells we looked at which support my idea that she was kept in a freezer for a while, at least. So I think you're looking at Sunday night for her murder, probably Tuesday night for her body to be dumped at the farm.'

'That's fine, Iain – that fits with my theory, with the other information that's coming to light. Can you tell me any more about her killer?'

'Not a lot, as such:' As the pathologist went on, the office door burst open and the Mad Professor flew in, his grey tonsure even more wild than usual. Russell waved him to a seat, as he listened to Somerfield: 'The D.N.A. shows that there was only one attacker, as we'd maybe assumed. There's no match on any database, that I can see, though.'

'So we're not looking for a known offender?'

'Well, not a recent one, or not one who's had a D.N.A. sample taken, anyhow.'

'Okay – thanks. If I get a sample to you, how quickly can you check for a match?'

'Urgent?'

'Very.'

'Hmm. I suppose I can get the lab to work Sunday if necessary – twenty-four hours do?'

'Yes, that'd be fine. I'll call you, okay?'

'Sure. I'll be waiting.'

'Thanks again, Iain – bye!'

Russell replaced the receiver, turned to Owen, who was sitting there in a state of some agitation:

'What've you got to tell me, Terry?' The chubby face was even redder than usual, split by a huge grin:

'You're going to like this, Dave! Do you want the good news, or the good news?'

'Just get on with it, for Heaven's sake!' Although the forensic sergeant's enthusiasm was infectious, his manner could be aggravating at the same time.

'Right – well – I can place your victim in that car, for a start! There're traces of mud on the front passenger carpet, which match that on the footpath between Elwood and the Avenue - must have rubbed off from her shoes. And a hair, caught in the stitching of the passenger headrest.'

'Hannah's?'

'Yeah – no question!'

'Bingo! That's the car Taylor Goldman saw, then?'

'Has to be. And that's not all, Dave!'

'Yes?'

'There's mud on the tyres, as well.'

'And?'

'It matches the mud by the gate, where you found the tyre tracks. And, in case you haven't guessed, the near-side tyres on the car match the tracks – right make and type, right size – and there's even a small fault in one tread, which I can see in the matching track.'

'So that car was used to dump her body, as well?'

'That's the obvious assumption, yeah!'

'That's excellent, Terry. If I can knock over Andrews' story about selling it, we've got him, haven't we?'

The forensic expert didn't reply. He leant back in his seat, his grin if anything even wider than before, obviously keeping the Inspector on the hook; Russell sat forward, a grin on his own face:

'Out with it, man, before I arrest you for obstructing an enquiry!' Both laughed; then Owen sat upright, his face suddenly serious:

'You were interested in fingerprints?'

'Of course!'

'Well – we've got Hannah's, as you'd expect. Around the passenger seat area, on the inside door handle, places like that. Some quite clear, others partial, or smudged, or both.'

'And?'

'One – fore and index fingers, also pretty smudged, on the outside of the same door, presumably the yob who broke in. They forced the passenger door to gain entry. No match, not clear enough, really.'

'And what else? The driver's?'

'Yeah. Only one person, that I can see. Prints all over the place, some quite old, others very recent. On the controls, around the driver's door, on the tailgate, everywhere you'd expect.'

'So – Andrews'?' The forensics man hesitated:

'His prints aren't on record.'

'Are you saying they might be someone else's? That maybe he did sell the car, and we're looking for another man altogether?'

'Look – all I can do is give you the facts…'

'So what's your problem, Terry?' The other ran a hand through the fringe around each side of his bald pate, frowning:

'I don't know what you're going to make of this, Dave.'

'Oh?'

'Well, like I said, Andrews' prints aren't on file. But I thought I'd run them against the national database anyway, just to check. And I got a match.'

'What? Who?'

'Malcolm Mathers.'

'Who the hell's he?' The twinkle was back in Owen's eyes:

'Malcolm Andrew Mathers. Convicted in October 1974, sentenced to five years at Lewes Crown Court. No record since.'

'What for? Don't keep me in suspense, man!'

'You'll never guess: For a series of sex attacks on little girls.'

Russell sat back in his chair, stunned, trying to fit the pieces of the puzzle together:

'So what you're telling me is that this Mathers guy is the man who abducted Hannah, and presumably killed her?' Owen shrugged his shoulders:

'Like I said, Dave, all I can do is give you the facts. You're the detective – it's up to you to put the pieces together!'

'Yeah, fine! You come in here and blow my theory out of the window…' He shook his head: 'Oh well – back to the drawing-board. All I've got to do is find this Mathers fellow, I suppose.' He sat deep in thought for a moment, then looked up and asked: 'Is that all, Terry?' The other laughed:

'How much do you want?' Russell joined in his amusement:

'Okay! Thanks, Terry.'

CHAPTER TWENTY-NINE

The subconscious gnawings of hunger brought George Andrews back to reality. He straightened up, stretching his back painfully on the park bench, looked around – for the first time, he saw the child sitting at the other end, thought that she looked as dejected as he felt.

But he needed to eat. He didn't feel like it, particularly, but he knew he had to get some food inside himself, or he would be no use to anyone – and there were going to be so many things to be done, now that Sheila was gone. Death Certificate, funeral arrangements, family and friends to be informed; the thought of it all only depressed him further. One job at a time – food, for a start. He looked around once more, realised with a kind of mild surprise where he was; it was handy, really; just around the corner in Bridge Street there were a number of fast-food restaurants, a Deep-Pan Pizza on the corner itself – that would do!

As he stretched again, went to stand up, a snuffling from the far end of the bench caught his attention. He looked around; the girl seemed to be crying – he reached out, touched her arm; she looked around, startled, gazed at him out of huge, deep-blue eyes.

'Are you all right?' he asked quietly; she nodded, sniffing;

'Yes – I'm fine, thanks.' He looked at her for a moment; she returned his gaze, frankly, her eyes red-rimmed, her cheeks tear-stained.

'Forgive me, but – you don't *look* all right?' Kim tried to smile, almost succeeded:

'I am, really. It's just…' she shrugged inconsequentially. Andrews hesitated, asked:

'I was about to get some lunch – can I tempt you to join me in a pizza?'

Kim just looked at him, slowly shaking her head, remembering all the times her father, her teachers had told her never to talk to strangers.

'Are you sure? You look as if you could use a meal.'

'No, really…' But she *was* hungry – and what was she going to do? She'd run out with only a little small change in her pocket; and after all, this man seemed quiet, pleasant – and what was he likely to do, anyway? Strangle her in the middle of the nearest Pizza Hut?

'Well – if you're sure? I don't want to be a nuisance, but…yeah, I *am* hungry!' The man smiled at her, got to his feet, beckoned:

'Come on, then! I'm starving.'

* * *

When the Mad Professor had gone, Russell sat thinking hard for a few minutes. He reached for the phone, spoke to the control room, established that Rimmer and the interview teams had finished at Bellevue Motors and were on their way back to the station; he left a message for the Sergeant to join him in his office as soon as he returned.

Ten minutes later, he was occupying his habitual perch:

'We've got all we can from the people at the garage, boss. I took statements from your two in the spares department, like you asked – it sounds like we're building up a case against Andrews, doesn't it?'

'Hm – maybe.'

'I thought you fancied him as the killer?' Russell didn't reply immediately; he ran his fingers through his hair:

'I've heard from Somerfield – he's convinced the girl was killed Sunday, stored in a deep freeze for two days, and dumped at the farm Tuesday night. And he tells me we're looking for one attacker – there's only one D.N.A. trace from all the samples.'

'That fits Andrews, as far as it goes, doesn't it? He kills her, dumps her on Tuesday, loses the car Wednesday!' Russell nodded:

'So far, yes. Owen's been in, as well. He's got clear evidence of Hannah being in the car, *after* walking across the footpath from Elwood to the Avenue. And, the tyres match the tracks from the farm.'

'That clinches it, surely?'

'There's one small problem, Doug.'

'Oh?'

'Terry checked the fingerprints from the car. He's got a lot of clear prints, all around the driving seat, door, tailgate and so on. And he got a match, from the national database.'

'I thought Andrews' prints weren't on file?'

'They're not. The prints belong to a Malcolm Mathers – he's a convicted child molester, from the South coast somewhere. I've just been looking him up: He served four and a half years of a five year sentence, at Wellingborough. Convicted October 1974, released April 1979.'

'So Andrews was on the level? He *did* sell the car, to this guy Mathers?'

Russell didn't reply. He sat with his brow furrowed in thought for several minutes; then, releasing a long slow breath, he looked up:

'It just doesn't fit with what we know, Doug. Think about it – *if* Andrews is being entirely truthful, he sold the car to a complete stranger, he thought from Bedford. But this total stranger must have known the Bucklands, known them well enough for Hannah to have got into a car with him, without a qualm. Remember,

Taylor Goldman jumped to the conclusion that it was her father in the car – that suggests that she showed no hesitation at all in getting in; she must have recognised the man, trusted him. Given the relationship between the two families, how likely is it that someone that well known to the Bucklands, was totally *unknown* to Andrews? And remember, Brian Buckland didn't even know he'd sold the car – if it had been bought by a family friend, how likely is *that?*'

'So Andrews is covering for this Mathers?'

'That's the obvious thought – but why? And, if this fellow is so well known to the Bucklands, *why don't we know about him?* We should have found him in the course of tracing all their other friends – how could we miss him?' Rimmer raised his eyebrows, realising that it was his backside which would get the kicking if an obvious suspect had been missed during the initial enquiries:

'Perhaps we didn't, sir. With that sort of record, maybe he's changed his name since he came out.' Russell sighed:

'Yeah, maybe he…' Suddenly, he sat bolt upright, slammed his fists onto the desk: 'Christ Almighty! We're missing the obvious, Doug!'

'What? What do you mean, boss?' But Russell was deep in thought again. At length, he raised his eyes again:

'How long has Barfield Antiques been going?'

'Oh, hell! I've seen a date somewhere; where was it?' It was Rimmer's turn to run his hands through his hair in frustration – but then it came to him:

'Yes! On the shopfront! You know how they've got it all signwritten, made it look really old-fashioned? There's a scroll, painted over the doorway – established 1975.'

'You're sure?'

'Quite sure.'

'Damn! Damn and blast!'

'What are you thinking, sir?'

'You said it, Doug – what if he changed his name? What if he changed it to George Andrews?'

'Holy shit! Of course – that's it, it must be!'

'There's still a problem – how could Andrews be establishing a business here in 1975, if he was in Wellingborough prison until 1979?'

'Oh – yeah.' Rimmer sounded deflated.

'Job for you, Doug – check it all out. Can we trace Andrews back – where was he, what was he doing, before he set up the antiques shop? And Mathers – what trace is there of him, after he was released? Where did he go? Family, background, all the usual. And is there any way that the business could have been started while he was in jail. Can we account for that clash of dates?'

'Right! I'll get right on it. Should we pull Andrews in, do you think?'

'Not yet. He's a clever, sophisticated fellow, and pretty quick-witted, in my estimation; I'd rather not give him any more warning of what's coming than we have to. And we could be wrong, remember – if we arrest him, and it turns out he was happily selling his antiques while Mathers was still banged up, we're going to look pretty stupid! Besides…' he paused: 'The thought that any man could actually do the kind of things that were done to little Hannah utterly revolts me. Can you imagine what it would be like to be accused of something like that, if you were innocent? I wouldn't want to do that to anyone. No – we'll pick him up when we sure of the terrain, whip him in, get the fingerprint and D.N.A to back us up as quickly as possible after that. Get me those checks, show me we're standing on solid ground, and we'll take it from there, Doug.'

'Soon as I can, Boss! I'll make a start – will you be in tomorrow?'

'Looks like it. Daniel's going to miss his sailing again. See what you can get by then, will you?'

'Sure thing!' He departed for the incident room, only to put his head back around the door a few minutes later:

'Sir? I called the hospice. Sheila Andrews died this morning, some time in the early hours. He was there, but left straight away; they haven't seen him since.'

Russell looked up: 'I don't suppose he's going to go far. We'll find him when we want him.'

'Right. Sir – I was thinking – you remember, when we went with him to talk to his wife – she kept calling him 'Mac'?'

'Yes, so she did – short for Malcolm?'

'That's what I was wondering.'

'Hm – makes sense, Doug.'

'Yeah. I'll get back to work.'

CHAPTER THIRTY

Neither Andrews nor the girl spoke as they walked together around the corner into Bridge Street. Each was aware of the other's distress; both waited for the other to break the silence. Andrews led the way into the Deep Pan Pizza restaurant, asked the pretty dark-haired waitress who approached him for a table for two; they followed her as she smiled them into chairs at a small table in a far corner. She hovered as they perused the menus, jotted down their selections and retired to the kitchen with their order. A few moments later, she brought a glass of wine for Andrews, and one of orange juice for the girl.

Andrews looked up at his companion, really taking her in for the first time. She was a lovely girl, maybe twelve years old – not pretty in any classical sense, but striking, attractive, for all that; tall, slender, coltish in her juvenile grace, her face that blend of Europe and Asia which is so truly beautiful, surmounted by a flowing mane of golden hair. And her eyes! Blue, as Hannah's had been – but there the resemblance ended. The ten-year-old's had been a sharp, startling, almost turquoise shade; this girl's were a deep, soft colour, almost identical to the blue denim of her jeans.

Aware of his scrutiny, she gave him a wan smile, introduced herself:

'My name's Kim – Kim Lee Hsung.' She giggled at his expression, went on to explain:

'My father's from Vietnam; Mum's English. I live with her in Bedford Road, off Midland Road, you know?' He nodded:

'I know the area, yes.' He hesitated, then asked: 'What has got you so upset, Kim?'

The girl didn't answer straight away, not sure of how much to tell this stranger of her affairs, her problems; but then, almost involuntarily, she began to talk to him, telling him of her mother and her drink problem, how she had to spend most of her time looking after the woman, how her efforts had finally been rewarded with an awful rejection, that very morning. The man opposite sat and listened in silence, nodding occasionally, his face creased with his sympathy for her plight; when she finished, he didn't speak for a minute or so.

'How old are you, Kim?' He asked, at length.

'Eleven – I'll be twelve in May.' He nodded again:

'It's a terrible load for such a young girl, Kim. What do you want to do, now?'

The girl hung her head, then looked up, a hopeless expression in her eyes:

'I don't really know! I can't leave my Mum to cope on her own – but how can I go back there if she hates me for the way I look, for who I am? I was trying to think, before you spoke to me back there; I think the best thing I can do is to talk to my Dad, see what he says. But I can't get there, I haven't got much money.'

'Why don't you telephone him?' She sighed:

'I could, I suppose – but I'd much rather tell him about all this face to face. I haven't got the right change for a phone box, anyway.'

'I see.' Andrews thought for a moment, then suggested: 'You *could* use my phone – I live just along the Embankment. But – if you'd rather go and see your father, why don't you let me take you?'

'Oh no, I couldn't do that! It's very kind of you – but I couldn't let you go to that sort of trouble.' He smiled at her:

'Why not? It would be no trouble, really – Cambridge isn't so far away; and it would help me to get my mind off of my own problems for a while. I…could do with the diversion, believe me.'

'Well…I don't know. I shouldn't…my Dad'll shoot me if I turn up in a car with a complete stranger, he's always telling me to be careful – you know, don't talk to strangers, all that kind of thing. And it really is too much to ask…?'

'No it isn't! I mean it – I wouldn't offer, if I didn't.' He suddenly looked down at his glass, frowned: 'Mind you, it might have to be in the morning. I've drunk most of my wine – and I had a big glass of brandy, earlier, so I shouldn't drive today.'

The girl's face fell at this – not another night at that poky, depressing house! He saw, and responded:

'You don't need to go home, if you'd rather not – we've got a spare bedroom, you could use that tonight, if you like?'

She looked up, hope alive again in her face; but there was doubt there, too:

'That's very kind, but…I mean…I don't really know you, do I? I mean….'

'You're not afraid of me, are you? Oh, Kim! I don't know you, either, do I? You might run of with the family silver, or my wallet, or something! Tell you what – I'll trust you, if you trust me, how's that?' The girl smiled, wanting to take the man at face value, reassured by his disarming manner, by the knowledge that whatever happened, she would know where he lived, could point the finger at him.

'Well – okay, if you're sure' she agreed at last: 'But you haven't told me your name?' He looked surprised:

'Oh no, so I haven't! Sorry – I'm George Andrews, but…call me Mac, please? That was my wife's name for me.'

Kim felt slightly taken aback – she felt it would be too familiar to use such an intimate name for a man she'd only just met, and who was so much older than her:

'Would you mind – could I call you *Uncle* Mac? I mean, you're a grown-up, and I'm just a kid…and I haven't got any *real* uncles!'

'Okay – I expect that will be all right!' The two, man and girl, smiled at each other freely for the first time.

Their pizzas arrived, and they began to tuck in, relieving their hunger. As they ate, Kim plucked up the courage to ask her companion what it was he needed his mind taken away from. Andrews explained slowly about Sheila's long illness, the pressure of looking after her as well as running his business; he told the child how she had died in the early hours of that morning. The girl had stopped eating, gazing at him with a look of horrified sympathy on her face:

'Oh, I'm so sorry! That's terrible! But – don't you have things you need to do, rather than worry about me?' He shook his head:

'The people at the hospice will take care of most of it. Oh, I will have things I'll have to do, of course – but I can't face them just yet. Looking after you for a day or two will get my mind off things; I'll be ready to cope better later on, if I can get away for a while.' Kim, still stunned by his revelation, put down her knife and fork, got to her feet and went around the table to his side. She bent down, put her arms around his shoulders; he looked up, smiled at her, put his own arm around her waist, held her close. She quickly kissed him on the cheek, and returned to her seat, to finish her meal.

Neither spoke again until the waitress had cleared the table and brought the bill. Andrews rose to go and pay; Kim got up, followed him to the cashdesk and then out into the street. They wandered together around the shops for a while; Andrews bought the child a couple of small presents in his new capacity as 'Uncle Mac', and then they made their way gradually to the big town house on the Embankment.

Inside, the two sat talking for a while, becoming slowly more familiar with each other. As the evening began to draw in, Kim offered to cook them a meal; her host readily accepted, having had to fend for himself for so long. She rose with a smile, went through to the kitchen and began to rummage through the cupboards and the refrigerator.

Kim had never seen a house like this one before, where all the living accommodation was on the first floor, over the big garage. And her new friend was obviously pretty well off – she had glimpsed the red Mercedes Benz on the drive below, was quite keen to have a ride in it the next day. If it was nice, would he put the roof down? If the truth were told, she was still a little nervous of him, years of being told to avoid strangers at all costs had had their effect – but he seemed so *nice,* so honest and straightforward, that she felt no real fear that anything horrible could happen to her. And tomorrow, she'd see her Dad – she couldn't wait!

* * *

It was just after six o'clock when Rimmer returned to his superior's office. He slumped into one the spare chairs, ignoring his usual perch on the desk edge. He felt weary; his right ear was numb from having a telephone receiver pressed against it for most of the last three hours, the only respite from that pressure coming with the occasional trip to the fax machine, or foray onto the internet. But he had some, at least, of the answers that Russell had wanted:

'Right, boss – I can tell you a bit about Mathers, but not a lot about Andrews, so far.'

'Okay – let's have it, Doug.' Russell relaxed back in his chair.

'Well, first off: As you found out yourself, he served four and a half years in Wellingborough. He'd had counselling and psychiatric help during that time; he applied for parole at the end of his four years, but it was turned down, seems the psychiatrist wanted to keep him under observation for a bit longer, and the authorities went along with that. Six months later, he tried again; this time, the shrink decided that he no longer represented any danger to little girls, and they let him out. Shows how much they know, doesn't it?' He looked up at Russell, his expression mirroring his anger. The Inspector smiled at his assistant:

'Be fair, Doug – he's kept out of trouble for over twenty years. Unless there're other things we don't know about, of course.'

'Yeah – I suppose so. Anyhow, the prison authorities were under the impression that he was going back to Hastings, where he'd lived before; certainly, he was there during his parole period, signing on with the local probation service as he should. But, after that, he seems to just drop out of sight altogether – no-one down there has any idea where he is now, or has been since the end of '79.'

'Hmm – that fits, if he *is* Andrews. Is there a photograph on the file?' The Sergeant grinned ruefully:

'Sort of! It's pretty awful, and the fax transmission didn't help. But yes, I guess it *could* be Andrews, twenty-five years ago - if he's since grown his beard, and got rid of his spectacles!'

'Yeah, right! Both conceivable - contact lenses? Have you got it there?'

'Here.' They pored over the scrappy, black-and-white image for a moment:

'You're right, Doug, it could be him. It could also be a lot of other people! Can we get a better copy?'

'They're supposed to be sending one by e-mail, but I haven't got it yet. Knowing them, it's probably gone to Istanbul or somewhere.'

'Oh well, we'll take a look when it gets here. To move on: How did Andrews start a business *here* in 1975?'

'That I can't answer, boss. I think the best way to track that down is to get hold of the solicitor, the one who handled the purchase of the shop. It's the same office which are the company's lawyers today; but they won't tell me anything there, say that only the partner who handles Andrews' affairs can talk to me, if he decides he wants to. And he's out playing golf, they don't know where. I *have* got his home number – I'll try him later tonight, or tomorrow if that fails.'

'Okay, Doug. What do you know about Mathers' crimes – do they fit with Hannah's death?' The Sergeant grimaced:

'Well – yes and no. The girls Mathers attacked were the same age group; he was a swimming instructor, used to get their confidence, get them used to being touched in the pool, then molest them in the changing rooms when he could get one alone with him. There was a suggestion that he'd raped at least one of them, but they didn't have enough evidence to pursue it, by the time it came to light. He admitted to a total of sixteen offences, mostly indecent assault. But he never killed – presumably thought he was getting away with it, didn't need to.'

'Okay – thanks, Doug. I think we might as well leave it at that for tonight – let me know if you get hold of that solicitor, what he tells you.'

'Sure, soon as I can.' Silence fell for a few seconds, then Russell spoke again:

'Have you heard – uniform are looking for a missing girl, Doug.'

'Oh, God – not again? No, I hadn't heard.'

'I doubt if it's anything to do with us, mind. She's eleven, ran away from home this morning after a row with her mother – seems the mother is an alcoholic, lets rip at the kid every now and then for no apparent reason. Anyway, she ran off into the town today – problem is, right after she left, the mother fell down the stairs, broke her neck. Seems the father's remarried, lives near Cambridge - Jock Buchanan's contacted him, but there's no trace of the girl. They've put out an appeal on the local radio and TV, without saying anything about the mother's death, of course. Waiting to see if they get a response; and there's a W.P.C. at the house, in case she turns up back there.'

'Oh – I see. As long as she doesn't fall into his clutches, eh?'

'It's not likely, is it? With Sheila dead, I'd think he's got other things on his mind right now than grabbing another victim.'

'Yeah, I suppose you're right, boss.'

'Go on home, Doug – I'm off now, myself.'

'Okay – 'Night, boss.'

'Good night, Doug.'

CHAPTER THIRTY-ONE

'Police in Grancester are anxious to trace a young girl who left her home this morning after a row with her mother. The girl, named as Kim Hsung, is eleven years old, described as tall and slim, with long blond hair and blue eyes, and distinctively oriental features; she was wearing a casual shirt and blue jeans. Anyone who may have seen her since around ten a.m today is asked to get in touch with the police....' The newscaster went on to give the relevant telephone numbers, and then turned to a review of the weather.

Uniform division's search for the girl had been very low-key. The Braham's, the next-door-neighbours who had called the ambulance when Tom found Martha lying at the foot of the stairs, had been able to tell them that such rows were not uncommon, so the assumption was that she would return home voluntarily, probably before the day was out. They had contacted her father, informed him of his ex-wife's death, but he knew nothing of the row or of his daughter's whereabouts. He had confirmed Martha's state of health, which they knew from the neighbours, and promised to let them know should Kim get in touch with him.

They had no reason at all to connect her disappearance with that of Hannah Buckland, two weeks previously. Nevertheless, Sergeant Buchanan, when his patrolling officers had been warned to keep a lookout for the girl, and the appeal arranged with the local radio and television stations, had picked up his internal telephone and called through to D.I. Russell's office. He'd informed the plain-clothes officer in charge of the Buckland case in his soft highland accent that 'another wee girrl's gone adrift, sorr.' He quickly explained the circumstances, and then added 'it'll be nothing to do wi' yourr case, but I thought ye should know, sorr.'

Russell was inclined to the same opinion. A domestic dispute, in another part of the town, and a girl who had run away as a result, seemed irrelevant to his investigation – and yet, the coincidence of a young girl walking the streets in a distressed state left him somehow troubled. Even so, the possibility of Andrews happening across this child seemed so remote a chance as to be instantly discounted; although it had to be acknowledged that he still did not know how the man had come to pick up Hannah in Alderley Park Avenue that fateful Friday night, what he had been doing there.

* * *

That Saturday evening, the object of the search, and of Russell's deliberations, was enjoying the meal she had prepared in the old town house. They had, of course, missed the lunchtime news broadcasts; and the evening ones, with the repeated appeal for knowledge of Kim's whereabouts, happened to coincide with the time when she and her host were tucking in to the sausage, egg and chips she had rustled up after her exploration of the kitchen.

Over the meal, Andrews found himself warming to the girl in a way he hadn't anticipated. She had a quick wit, and, now that she had relaxed in his company, overcoming her initial doubts, they enjoyed a prolonged discussion, ranging across all kinds of subjects. As they talked, he watched her, the animation of her face, the abandon of her careless gestures; she was, he decided, the most beautiful child he had ever met. Without question. Her beautiful Eurasian features, the heavy golden hair which bounced on her shoulders as she tossed her head, those gorgeous dark blue eyes; and, when she stood up to take their abandoned plates to the dishwasher, her long, trim figure, the narrow waist and pert bottom emphasised by the tightness of her jeans, served to arouse him to a degree that was almost painful.

They retired to the lounge with mugs of coffee, continuing their conversation, ignoring still the temptations of the TV set in the corner. Kim curled herself demurely into one of the deep brown leather armchairs, her legs tucked up beside her, unconsciously exciting her host still further. At last, their talk ran down into a brief silence. Kim looked at the man who had befriended her so unexpectedly; suddenly nervous of his reaction, she quietly asked him about his wife, what she had been like, half expecting that this would upset him, that he would rebuff her interest.

Andrews looked up, caught off-guard by her question. He didn't reply straight away, but sat in thought – he was surprised to realise that, while his sadness at Sheila's death was as deep as ever, he could actually accept that she was in the past, that his life as going to be very different from now on, that he now had no-one but himself to lean upon. Just how he would manage without her by his side was the question he didn't want to face, for the time being at least. He looked up at the girl, curled so provocatively into the chair opposite, and began to talk, to tell her all about Sheila, how lovely, how strong, how caring, she had been. For an hour or more, he talked, pausing now and again to collect his thoughts; the girl listened, not interrupting, her face showing her understanding and sympathy.

At last, he stopped, his love and grief for his wife talked out at least for the moment. Kim said nothing; she smiled, rose from her seat and went to him, kneeling in front of him, reaching for him. He allowed himself to be drawn into her arms, leaning forward into her embrace, slipping his arms around her shoulders as he felt hers enfolding him. She held him, without words, for some minutes, then released him, rocking back onto her heels as he sat back into the chair; she smiled, and he responded, with a whispered 'thank you'.

Kim returned to her armchair, and they sat in companionable silence for a while. Eventually, he looked up and smiled:

'This won't do! We've got to think about being ready to get you to your father in the morning, Kim.' The girl shrugged:

'What is there to do?'

'Well, why don't you go and have a shower, for a start? It'll refresh you, and you'll be all clean and shiny for him tomorrow – or soak in the bath, if you prefer. Take as long as you like.' She nodded, smiling:

'Okay – that would be nice. But I think I ought to call my Mum first, see if she's all right, if you don't mind?'

'I don't mind – but will she answer the phone, do you think? Or, from what you told me, will she be in a fit state to talk to you if she does?' The girl hesitated, thinking:

'Maybe you're right – perhaps it would be better to talk to her in the morning, she's more likely to be sober then. Can I call her before we go?'

'Of course you can! Now, go and get that bath; and let me have your clothes, I'll put them through the washing machine so they're nice and clean for tomorrow, too.'

'Okay, thanks! I'll drop them outside the bathroom door, shall I?'

'That'll do. Come on, I'll show you where to go.' He stood up, led the way from the lounge, up the stairs to the next landing and the bathroom. His guest, a picture of innocent, childish beauty, followed him willingly.

* * *

In the study of Old Laundry Cottage, Bevington, Daniel Russell sat opposite his father at the big old oak desk. A cloth covered the wood and leather surface, pots of paint and varnish strewed the area, tools were scattered around; father and son were also sharing a companionable silence as each worked upon his own current project, readying a scale-model yacht for the next morning's session. With his deputy still probing the possible link between Mathers and Andrews, Russell had decided he could afford to take the time to go to the club's prearranged venue and take his son along, although, knowing he could be called away, he had refused to include Daniel's friend Jack Carter from the next village – the boy had accepted the explanation in good part, proud as he was of his father's job. Now, the two worked together, happy in their shared interest, requiring no conversation to enjoy each other's company. Sarah was already in bed, asleep after her story; her mother relaxed in the lounge, watching a drama on the television.

At ten o'clock, the news came on at the end of the programme. Tracy Russell got to her feet, went through to the study, knocked on the door, put her head around:

'Come on, Dan – time you were in bed, child!' The boy looked round:

'I'm *not* a child, mother!' The grin on his face gave the lie to his pretended anger: 'I'll be a teenager next year – then you'll be sorry!' She laughed:

'*This* year, even. Unless you're cancelling your birthday in October?'

'Eh? No, of course not! I'm expecting *lots* of presents, as it's a special one this time!'

'Nothing special about becoming a teenager' his father interjected 'you wait until you're thirty – or forty!'

'Of *course* it's special! It is for me, anyway. I won't be thirteen, ever again, will I?' His parents laughed; Tracy raised her hands in a gesture of surrender:

'All right – you win! But it's still time you were in bed, young man!'

'Okay!' The boy gave in, put his tools aside and stood up. At the door, he turned back to his father:

'I'm really looking forward to tomorrow, Dad.' Russell glanced up:

'So am I, Daniel. It seems like ages since we've been sailing together, doesn't it?'

'Mm-hm. We'll make up for lost time, won't we?'

'We will. And I still mean for us all to have a break together somewhere, very soon.' Daniel grinned, nodding enthusiastically:

'Yeah – that'll be great, won't it?'

'It will – now go on, get to bed or your mother'll be after you. And me too, for that matter, for keeping you talking!'

'Okay, Dad – good night.'

'Good night, son.'

* * *

Once again, Kim sat snuggled into the big leather armchair in Andrews' lounge. Now, the two were sipping mugs of cocoa which he had produced when she came down after her bath, wrapped in Sheila's dark blue bathrobe. The girl grinned across at her companion:

'You peeked!' Andrews laughed:

'I couldn't do much else, could I? Not when you opened the door and stood there with nothing on!'

'Well, I didn't know you'd be there, did I?' Kim giggled.

'I suppose not! I thought I'd leave that robe there for you to use, but you opened the door with your clothes just as I got there. I'm sorry if I upset you?'

'That's all right, you just startled me for a second. Thank you for lending me this – ' she hesitated: 'Was it your wife's?' The man nodded:

'Yes.' He smiled at the girl: 'It looks good on you, though. It's the same colour as your eyes. Would you like to keep it?'

The blue eyes lit up:

'Are you sure? It's so lovely and soft….'

'Of course. Sheila won't need it any more. I'd like you to have it, please.'

'Okay – thank you, Uncle Mac!' She beamed; he smiled back, touched by her honest pleasure.

They sat in silence for a while. Andrews studied the beautiful child, reliving in his mind the brief glimpse she'd given him of her nudity – she'd quickly dodged behind the partly-open door when she'd seen him, handing out her clothes, taking the robe from him before closing it again with an embarrassed smile. She was so gorgeous! He desperately wanted to see her naked again, to feel the softness of her bare skin, hold the slender strength of her young body in his arms….

More than once, the girl glanced up, to catch her host gazing at her; each time, he just smiled reassuringly – but she had caught a strange light in his eyes, which momentarily unsettled her. But each time, she dismissed her misgivings, thinking that she could hardly know every little quirk of someone she'd only just met, that it was just his curiosity about her showing through. They finished their drinks – Andrews rose to his feet:

'Come on, time for bed! I'll show you to the spare room.'

CHAPTER THIRTY-TWO

Sunday dawned bright and clear once more. Ten o'clock saw David and Daniel Russell excitedly involved in the flurry of activity around Linford Lake, getting their boats and the radio control gear ready for the morning's sailing.

At half past, David was doing well, holding second place in the first race, when his mobile phone rang. He cursed, quickly handing the controller to his son, and pulled it from his pocket:

'Russell!' His annoyance sounded in his voice.

'Sorry, sir! It's Doug Rimmer – I've just been talking to Andrews' lawyer.'

'Okay, Doug – what have you got from him?'

'Her, actually. Lady named Elizabeth Greener. She's handled the business affairs for them since they bought the shop in Barfield. Barfield Antiques is a partnership – the two partners being Andrews and his wife. They bought the shop in May 1975; she handled the transaction for them, and set up the partnership papers at the same time.'

'Damnation! How could he still be in jail, and be there as well?'

'Ah! It seems Ms Greener never met *Mr* Andrews until years later. He was supposed to be working abroad – Sheila didn't give much away, but the impression she had was that he might have been something to do with the F.C.O., a diplomat, or similar. Mrs Andrews took the papers away to get them signed – they were reaffirmed and witnessed later, when he supposedly came back to the U.K. And guess when that was?'

'Tell me?'

'The summer of 1979! *After* Mathers was released. It seems that Sheila ran the business on her own up to then.'

'That's brilliant, Doug! You did well to get so much information from a solicitor, they're usually pretty tight-lipped?'

'Most of that is a matter of public record, really. She told me the personal details when I pointed out we could subpoena her if we needed to, as it was a murder case. We've got him, haven't we, boss?'

'I reckon so, Doug! We'll arrest him, get the fingerprints and D.N.A. done pronto. It'll be good to see Hannah's killer put away for life. Maybe her family will be able to move on, then.'

'Yes, indeed. Do you want me to go and bring him in? You could finish your outing with Daniel, join me later?'

'Yeah – okay, if you don't mind. There's someone you can take along?'

'Sure – I'll find a spare D.C., or borrow someone from Uniform if I have to. I'll see you later, sir?'

'Right – I'll be there by about three, all being well. Bye, Doug – and well done!'

'Thanks! See you then.'

Russell cut the connection, a grin of triumph on his face. In the meantime, the race had finished – Daniel, lacking his father's experience, had slipped to fourth place at the end, but that was still good enough to qualify for the semi-final, later in the morning. He apologised, but his father congratulated him, thanking him for standing in so well. Then, it was Daniel's turn with his own yacht, in another qualifying run. Russell was standing, watching and encouraging, when the phone rang again.

It was Rimmer again:

'Sir! I was about to leave, to go and arrest Andrews, when this girl called in about Kim Hsung – you know, the other missing kid?'

'Yes?'

'Seems this girl is a waitress, in the Deep Pan Pizza place in Bridge Street. She was doing a double shift yesterday, didn't get home until late last night – she saw the appeal on the news today, rang in to say she saw the kid in the restaurant, yesterday afternoon. With a man.' Russell's stomach sank into his boots:

'You're having me on, Doug?'

'No, sir. From her description, it could well have been Andrews.'

'I don't *believe* it! Of all the God-awful things to happen! This is stretching coincidence to breaking point.'

'It is. We've no idea how they might have met, whether they knew each other before, where they'd been – or indeed, where they went. They left about half past two, according to the witness.' Russell heaved a deep sigh:

'Right, Doug – you'd better get over to the house straight away, pick him up, search it for the girl. And let's hope to God she's all right. I'll come right over, join you there.'

'Right, sir.' He heard the click as Rimmer hung up.

Daniel's race had finished ignominiously, when he had allowed the stiffening breeze to get the better of him and capsize his boat. Usually, the boy did much better, but he had been half-aware of the intensity of his father's telephone conversation, and that had served to distract him. He looked up at Russell, his expression concerned:

'What is it, Dad?'

'I've got to go, Dan. It's – very important. Tell you what, why don't I leave you here? You can take my place in the semi-final. If I can't get back to pick you up at the end, I'll call Mum, have her drive over in her car and fetch you?'

'You sure, Dad?'

'Yeah – you'll be all right on your own, won't you? You know most of the people here. Just be careful with the *Dragon,* okay? You know she's a bit sensitive in strong winds, mind she doesn't go over on you.'

'Yeah – right!' The boy's delight at being trusted to sail the *Flying Dragon,* his father's pride and joy, was clear in his eyes and his voice: 'Don't worry – I'll look after her!'

Russell grinned down at his son, patted his shoulder and turned to run across to the Jeep.

He swept out from the lakes into the main road, up past the Black Horse by the canal bridge and across the Northern bounds of Milton Keynes until he picked up the A5. Following the bypass around Northampton, he had the grille-mounted blue lights flashing to clear his path through the ambling Sunday morning traffic, his mind in turmoil.

Mostly, he was furious with himself. His desire to have all the t's crossed and the i's dotted had left Andrews on the loose for the best part of a day, when he could have pulled him in sooner. He'd allowed his awareness of the man's devious intelligence to make him hold back, wanting a solid foundation for his arrest – and now that had back-fired on him, in the worst possible way. He tried to console himself with the thought that he'd had no way of knowing that the other child was at risk from the man, that they knew each other – if, indeed, they did, prior to the events of yesterday! But most of all, he wondered how he could face the kid's family, knowing that prompter action on his part would have saved her from the pain and terror she must have suffered since the previous day. He'd let everyone down – himself, the force, the Bucklands – but most of all little Kim Hsung. She'd had her innocence destroyed, her childhood snatched away, just to satisfy his desire for a well-founded case.

The Jeep carved its way across the town, at last screeching to a halt outside the Embankment house. Rimmer met him at the door:

'Sir! They're not here, I'm afraid.'

'Oh, Christ! Where the hell are they?' The two detectives entered the house.

'We've no idea, sir. But the kid's definitely with him. The

neighbour, a Mrs Parrott, saw them arrive last night, about six o'clock – from her description, it must have been Kim with him. She – the neighbour, that is – assumed the girl was a relative, a niece maybe, come to stay with him for the weekend.'

'Oh, hell! Is there anything to give us a clue about what might have happened, where they might be now?'

'Not really. Mrs Parrott's in here, sir.' The Sergeant led the way into the upstairs lounge, introduced his superior to the elderly lady inside.

'Mrs Parrott – thank you for waiting to talk to me. You saw Mr Andrews come home last night?'

'That's right, Inspector. And leave again, today.'

'You've no idea where he might have gone, I suppose?'

'I'm afraid not.'

'Did he have the little girl with him?'

'That's right. I was just tidying my bedroom – I sleep at the back of the house, since my husband passed away – when I heard his car start up. I had the window open, to air the room, you see. I looked out, watched him fold the roof down – it's so clever, isn't it, they way they do that? – and she was in the car with him. Then they drove off, out of the drive.'

'Did the child seem…all right? I mean, was she upset or anything, that you could see?'

'I don't think so – she just sat there quiet, as I remember. Mind you, the drive is at the far side of his garden, so they were a little way away.'

'What time was this?'

'Oh, about ten o'clock, maybe a little before.'

'All right, thank you, Mrs Parrott. You've been a great help – I'll have my Sergeant take a proper statement from you, later, if that's okay. There's no need for you to stay here, I'll have him come round to see you in a while.'

'Thank you, Inspector.' She got to her feet, then turned to him, a sudden memory coming to her: 'I don't know if it's important, but I noticed Mr Andrews doing something a bit odd, the other week?'

'Oh?'

'Yes – one night, well after dark, he was in the garden, with the incinerator alight. I expect he was just getting rid of some rubbish – but it seemed a strange time to do it, that was all. It probably doesn't matter.'

'It may not be important – but then, it might, Mrs Parrott. Do you remember just when this was?'

'Oh, not this last week; the week before? About Tuesday or Wednesday, I think. I'm sorry to be vague, but I didn't give it a lot of thought at the time, you see.'

'Don't worry – we'll check what it was all about, when we find Mr Andrews. Thank you again for your help.'

'That's all right, Inspector. I'll be next door, when you need me, Sergeant'

Russell turned to his deputy:

'Who've you got with you, Doug?'

'There wasn't anyone spare in C.I.D. – I grabbed P.C. Dorman out of the canteen. He's looking through the bedrooms.'

'Okay – get him to go through that incinerator, see if he can find any trace of what Andrews was burning. We've never found Hannah's clothes, remember. I'll call in, get control to alert everyone to look out for his car. I guess I'd better expand that to the surrounding counties, too – he could be well over the border by now.'

'Right, sir. I called SOCO earlier, they're on their way.'

'That's fine, Doug. Let's hope we pick him up before he can do that kid any more harm!'

CHAPTER THIRTY-THREE

By lunchtime that Sunday, the ponderous machinery of the Constabulary had surged with dramatic urgency into top gear. Off-duty officers had been drafted in, helicopters were aloft, every available car, motorcycle and foot patrol was on high alert, primed for a possible sighting of the red convertible or its occupants; and not only in Northamptonshire. A similar state of alert existed in the neighbouring counties, and information regarding the hunt for Andrews and his latest victim had been disseminated through police forces nationwide. A new appeal had been sent out to radio and TV stations.

But no sightings were reported. Looking for a particular vehicle on Britain's busy roads, especially one which has such a good head-start on the search, relies almost as much upon luck as upon effort. Even in the relatively light traffic of a Sunday morning, the car escaped notice – Russell had remained at the Embankment house with the Sergeant, fretting over the painstaking work of the Scenes of Crime team, hanging on every radio call in the hope that it would signal his quarry's discovery.

Quickly after being given his task, Andrew Dorman had called the plain-clothes officers into the garden. Among the ashes in the incinerator, he had uncovered a part of what appeared to be the waist-band of a pair of trousers, singed and blackened, but still showing the dark blue colour of the slacks that Hannah had been wearing when she disappeared. This minor triumph put the case against Andrews beyond doubt, even in advance of the fingerprint or D.N.A. evidence.

* * *

Silence reigned in number 14, Elmfield Close, Cherry Hinton, except for the television set murmuring to itself in the corner of the lounge. Detective Constable Fred Barrett, a Cambridgeshire family liaison officer, sat in one of the comfortable armchairs; opposite him, Tran Quoc Hsung sat on the sofa, his arm around the diminutive figure of his wife; even the two boys were playing together quietly in the dining room, awed by the atmosphere they could sense but not understand.

At noon, the news programme replaced a repeated episode of a soap-opera that no-one had been following:

'Northamptonshire police are becoming increasingly concerned for the safety of a girl who ran away from home yesterday morning after a row with her mother. The girl, Kim Lee Hsung, is described as being eleven years old, tall and slim, with long blond hair and blue eyes. She was last seen wearing a casual shirt and blue denim jeans. She is believed to be in the company of an older man, possibly travelling in a red Mercedes Benz convertible motor-car; police wish to interview the man about another matter also. Any member of the public seeing the couple are advised not to approach them, but to get in touch with their local police.'

Liu raised big dark eyes to her husband; he smiled reassuringly down at her:

'They'll find her soon, don't worry' he whispered. Barrett glanced across:

'I'm sure you're right, Mr Hsung. It's only a matter of time.' He looked around at the sound of a car drawing up outside: 'It's one of our patrols.'

Liu leapt to her feet, ran to the door to meet the officers from the car, desperate for any possible news of her step-daughter; Tran's eyes followed her. The conversation from the hallway carried into the lounge:

'Have you found Kim?' Liu's eager voice.

'I'm sorry, Mrs Hsung' a man's voice replied: 'We've been cruising around the neighbourhood, in case she's in the area, trying to make her way here – but we've seen no sign of her. And there's been no report of her from elsewhere.'

'Oh!' The pain and disappointment were clear in her voice; she went on: 'Come in, anyway – would you like some tea?'

'That would be very kind, Mrs Hsung. Thank you.'

P.C. Anne Summerbee followed John Statham and the tiny Vietnamese woman into the house. Anne was in her mid-twenties; a policewoman for two and a half years, stocky and dark-haired, she radiated a kind of solid dependability. John was considerably older – a 'career constable', he had held that rank for almost twenty years, happy to be a front-line copper, wanting nothing more out of life or the force. The two, partners for the best part of a year, made a good team, even if at times Anne found her companion's total lack of ambition almost frustrating.

Liu waved the policewoman to the other armchair in the lounge; Statham stood close by, positioned so that he could see out of the window – just in case! Minutes later she returned, carrying a tray loaded with a pot of freshly-brewed china tea, cups, saucers, sugar and a milk jug. Statham stepped forward to help as she set it down on the coffee-table, leaving his vigil for a moment.

Doing so, he failed to see the vehicle which drew up a short distance behind his patrol car. The first they knew of it was when the front door flew open, and a voice called out:

'Daddy? Liu? Where are you?' The occupants of the lounge stared at each other in disbelief; Tran jumped up and ran out into the hall, to be almost knocked from his feet by the girl who threw herself into his arms. He staggered as hers went around his neck, and she kissed him long and hard on the cheek:

'Kim? How on earth did you get here?' She eased back in his embrace, joy evident in her face, as Liu joined them, the hug expanding to include her as well. Barrett and Statham stood behind them, equally eager for the girl's answer; Anne Summerbee had pushed gently past into the street, looking up and down for any sign of a vehicle – but she was just too late, the car which had deposited the child had vanished around the end of the close into the main road.

'Oh, Daddy! It's so good to see you! And you, Liu – where are Kai and Little Tran?' At that, the two little boys rushed out from the dining room; she released the grown-ups to bend down and gather them into her arms, kissing each in turn.

Tran looked around at the two police officers; Barrett went to speak, but he gestured to stop him, put a hand on his daughter's shoulder:

'Kim – it's wonderful to see you safe, but we must talk to you, now. These policemen need to know where you've been, what's happened to you.' She smiled up at her father, let go of the two children and stood up:

'Of course, Daddy – I understand.' He looked into her eyes, concern registering in his own:

'Kim – did that man…hurt you? Did he touch you?' The girl laughed, shook her head:

'*No,* Daddy! I'm fine, really – he didn't do anything to me. He brought me here.'

Statham intervened:

'Kim – it was Mr Andrews who drove you here, is that right?' She turned to the constable:

'That's right. I met him in Grancester, yesterday – he let me stay at his house last night, and brought me here today, to see Daddy.'

'He's just dropped you outside, now?'

'That's right. Oh, he's not there now, he drove off right away, when I got out of the car. He…knows you're looking for him – he said…there's something he's got to do.'

'What was that, do you know, Kim?'

'No – I did ask, but he wouldn't tell me.'

'You don't know where he's going, now?'

'No – back home, maybe? To Grancester?'

'All right – thank you, Kim.' He turned and hurried out, joining his partner by the patrol car.

Anne had already radio'd the news of the girl's return to their control room; indeed, at that very moment the message was being relayed via Northampton to Russell and his team. Now, she called in again to confirm that Andrews had dropped Kim at the house, and was now driving away from Cherry Hinton in she knew not what direction; Cambridgeshire control promptly alerted all of their cars in the area, as she and Statham got into theirs and set off in the hope of picking up the trail.

Inside the house, Tran was questioning his daughter about her ordeal, Barrett listening in, ready with questions of his own should he need them. Not that Kim seemed to view the last twenty-four hours as an ordeal – she had to reassure her father several times that she was unharmed, before he began to believe her, and relaxed:

'Oh, Kim, we've been so worried! The man you've been with – he's….' Tran was unsure how to explain to the girl, but she held him at arms length, her face suddenly serious:

'I know, Daddy. He's…done bad things, broken the law.' the girl smiled at him:

'He *told* me, Daddy. This morning, on the way here. We didn't know you were looking for me, until we heard it on the car radio. When it came on, I think he realised that the police were onto him – it said something about them wanting to talk to him. I asked him what that was about – he went kind of quiet for a bit; and then he told me he'd done some very silly things, things he was very ashamed of. He seemed to be really upset, really sorry about it. Then he said he'd drop me off here, like he'd promised to anyway.' Her father asked her:

'He didn't tell you what *sort* of things?' She shook her head:

'No. I did ask, but he said – it didn't matter. He said he'd have to go and talk to the police about them, but he wanted to go somewhere to think for a bit first.'

'He didn't say *where* he was going, did he?' Barrett asked; again, the child shook her head.

Tran still held her by the shoulders, looking into her smiling blue eyes. Then he released his breath in a huge sigh, smiled, and led her at last from the hall into the lounge. The three sat together on the sofa, the girl snuggled happily between her father and stepmother; the two little boys squeezed together into one of the armchairs. His arm around her shoulders, Tran too turned serious:

'Kim – I don't suppose you know, do you? It's your mother....' She looked up in concern as his voice trailed off:

'What is it? What's happened to her?'

'Oh, Kim! She fell down the stairs, yesterday....'

'Is she all right? Did she hurt herself?' The girl's expression turned to fear as he shook his head:

'She – broke her neck, Kim. She's dead.' She gazed up into his eyes for a moment, then buried her face in his chest, her shoulders heaving with her sobs. He held her close, trying to comfort her. After a few minutes, he gently raised her, held her away so that he could look into her eyes:

'Kim, listen – it's not your fault. If you'd been there, you couldn't have done anything. She stumbled, fell backwards – you couldn't even have stopped her if you'd been right beside her.'

'*But I should have been there!* She shouldn't have died all alone!'

'Oh, Kim! She never knew what happened – the moment she

fell, it was all over. We could all have been there, and it wouldn't have made any difference.'

'Oh Daddy – I suppose you're right – but I still shouldn't have run off like that, left her alone. Perhaps she wouldn't have gone upstairs, perhaps…' she looked helplessly up into his eyes, tears brimming in her own, then leant forward, burying her face in his shirt once more. This time he just held her, feeling her body trembling in his embrace until the first wave of her grief subsided. Liu slipped quietly out from beside the child, went into the kitchen to prepare a light lunch, knowing that the girl must be hungry, that she would be ready for some food before long, once her sorrow had settled from its initial storm.

Saturday, 10.15 pm.
He led the girl up the stairs, showed her into the top floor room where Hannah Buckland had died. New sheets freshened the bed, a clean cover on the duvet; the child turned to him:

'What a lovely room! I bet the view's super, as well, in the daytime.'

'It is!' he assured her 'it looks right out across the river.'

She smiled at him in silence for a moment; when she spoke again, her fondness for him was clear in her tones:

'Thank you, Uncle Mac – thank you for everything. I don't know what I'd have done today, if you hadn't been there. You saved my life!' The unconscious irony of her words wasn't lost on him, as he shrugged his shoulders in self-deprecating reply:

'You just get settled, Kim. Sleep well – I'll look in in a little while, make sure you're all right.'

The girl nodded, her big blue eyes shining. She went to undo the robe, stopped, giggling, as she remembered that she was naked underneath it. He laughed with her, turned away, pulled the door too and went downstairs to the lounge.

There, he fell into one of the soft armchairs. His mind was in complete turmoil: He had picked the child up, treated her to lunch in the pizzeria, knowing full well that his motive was entirely founded upon those old lusts, stirring, making their presence felt deep within him once again. And yet, as the day had gone on, his feelings for her had taken an unexpected turn. He found himself attracted to her, not only as a sexually-desirable victim for his urges, but as a personality. She was exerting a strange kind of power over him, that he was at a loss to explain.

Oh, for sure, she was still physically arousing, her slim body desirable in the extreme – the thought of possessing her, taking her youthful slenderness in his arms, the warmth of her nakedness against his own body, excited him to fever pitch. But at the same time, he felt constrained, held back by this strange reluctance to hurt the child who had so unselfconsciously befriended him. He thought of her cute face, her carefree smile, the way her heavy golden hair moved as she turned her head, her open, innocent eyes, such a lovely shade of denim-blue. He pictured her young, sleek body, nude, enticing in its pre-pubescent perfection, imagined what it would be like to slip into bed with her, to feel her satin-smooth skin under his hands…. But the image of those laughing blue eyes got in his way, frustrating his carnality even as he tried to wind it up further.

He got up, poured himself a stiff brandy, drank it off in one. In careful silence, he made his way up the stairs once more; easing the door open, he looked in on the child, to find her sleeping, curled innocently into a sprawling ball under the quilt. As he watched, she stirred, turning her head; he stepped into the room, reached down to brush the hair from her face where it had fallen across.

Now, he understood his problem. Yes, he still desired her, physically – but he knew he could not just force himself upon her, as he had done with Hannah, with the girls in Hastings, so long ago. Somewhere, somehow, in the course of that short day, he'd fallen in love with her. Impossible though it seemed, he was, at fifty-six years old, in love with a girl who had yet to reach her twelfth birthday. Not a love that the world would recognise, that ordinary people would accept or condone, he knew – but he knew, too, that it was true. Rather than indulge his lusts upon her, he felt a deep need to help her, to look after her, to take her under his wing and protect her.

Incredulous at this realisation, he bent close, kissed the sleeping child on her exposed cheek. He turned and left the room, with a last backward glance from the doorway.

The brandy bottle in the lounge took quite a hammering that night, before he retired to his own bed.

CHAPTER THIRTY-FOUR

A few streets away from where he had dropped the girl, George Andrews pulled in to the kerb. He stopped just long enough to put the roof of the car up again before driving on – it was still quite fresh, despite the sunshine, and he had only put it down for the trip to Cambridge to please the child. For the same reason, they had kept to back roads all the way, a fact which had probably helped them to escape unwittingly the notice of the prowling police patrols.

As he drove out towards the A14 once more, his mind returned to the turmoil of the night. His thoughts seemed split in two – one part of him was still the slave of his sexual urges, cursing himself for letting the girl go, for not satisfying his lust with her while he had the chance; the other was happy for her, pleased that she was where she wanted to be, with her father, in a position to sort out her family problems. And almost proud that he had overcome his carnal self in passing up the chance of a brief physical satisfaction for a greater goal in the child's happiness.

But he had more pressing problems. What had the newscaster meant, that the police wanted to talk to him about other matters? That had to be something to do with Hannah – but why were they wanting to interview him again, he had thought that they were happy with what he had told them already? They must know something – but what?

He drove on autopilot, pursuing possibilities in his mind.

They'd found her body over a week ago now – it couldn't be anything to do with that, surely, or they would have been to see him before now. So what? The one thought he kept coming back to was that they might have found the car – that was the only thing he could think of that might have led them to him again. Leaving it in the dealership yard had been the best idea he could come up with to make it disappear from sight, at least for a while – he'd known that he would have to remove it again sooner or later, but he'd hoped it would go unnoticed for long enough for the search for it to die down before he did so.

If that was the case, how much did they know? He realised that modern forensic science would probably be able to prove that the girl had been in the car – he had cleaned it, but he knew that wasn't likely to be good enough. Would they accept his continued insistence that he had sold the car, look for another suspect, or did they already believe he was lying about that? He'd felt the underlying doubts of the Inspector and the Sergeant when they'd been talking about it. Despair began to rise in him – they only had to fingerprint him, and they'd be pretty certain that no-one else had driven the estate!

What was he going to do? It had been madness to grab little Hannah and relieve his desires on her, he should have seen that. But he'd lost control of himself! After all these years! His sadness welled up, threatened to blind him, make him lose control of the car as well – Sheila had been the strong one, the rock, the foundation that he had been able to cling to, the one who gave *him* the strength to control his urges when they arose. With her no longer by his side, when the pretty child had got into his car so willingly, told him of the bully-boy's interfering with her, it had aroused him beyond the point of no return….

He'd had psychiatric therapy while he was in prison before – but it hadn't cured his innate desires. All it had done was to overlay them with an intense feeling of guilt, and now that guilt had returned, threatening to destroy him. He knew that he would be subject to his old recurring lust for young girls, now that Sheila wasn't there to keep him on the right track; he knew that he would give in to it again, as he had with Hannah, that he would wreck more young lives even if he didn't kill again. The only bright spot on the horizon was the miracle of Kim, the way the unconscious force of her personality had deflected his lust, turned it into – yes, it was the only word which could complete the sentence – love.

He needed to think! To go somewhere where he could be alone, focus his mind on the future, try to see his way forward. Where? He knew a spot, just off this very road – a reservoir, peacefully secluded in open countryside. A lane led to the far side, away from the road, where only a fisherman or two might be encountered at this time of year – that would serve his purpose! As long as he could get there, before the police picked him up, assuming their desire to talk to him was that urgent – but he had to assume that, didn't he?

Cruising at a steady fifty-five along the A14, doing his best to remain inconspicuous, his mind occupied with his problems, he hadn't noticed the dark Vauxhall Omega fall in some distance behind, keeping pace with him. In the following car, Sergeant Philip Ackroyd, riding shotgun, had informed his control that they had the suspect car in sight, and been told just to stay with it until they could get further instruction from Grancester. A marked Traffic car had joined them, further back still to avoid arousing the suspicion of the subject car's driver, and now the two tailed their quarry on his gentle journey back towards Northamptonshire.

* * *

In Grancester, Russell's frustration and his intense self-condemnation for leaving Andrews free to abduct another child were straining relations at the Embankment house. The forensic team were doing their usual efficient job, under the eccentric but careful direction of the Mad Professor; Rimmer had taken a full statement from Mary Parrott, covering both the incident of the incinerator and the arrival and departure of Andrews with his victim, and other teams were questioning other residents about comings and goings at the house over the previous weeks since Hannah's disappearance, leaving the Inspector little to do but fret about the whereabouts of his suspect and his own culpability.

A little after twelve-thirty, he decided to leave them to it and return to his office. He was just walking out to the Jeep, giving Rimmer some unnecessary last-minute instructions, when the call came over the radio. He reached into the car to pick up the microphone:

'Russell.'

'Sir? We've just heard that the Hsung girl has appeared at her father's house in Cambridge.'

'Yes? Is she hurt, has she been attacked?'

'Apparently not, sir. She claims she's fine, that Andrews put her up overnight, drove her there today; but she insists he did nothing to her, nothing at all.'

'What? That makes no sense, no sense at all!'

'That's what she says, sir. The officers on the spot reckon she's on the level, too.'

'Okay, I see. Where's Andrews now?'

'They don't know. He dropped the kid, drove off before anyone knew he was there. Cambridgeshire have alerted all their patrols, and a car which was at the house is combing the area to try to pick him up.'

'Damn! They've no idea where he's heading?'

'No, sir. The girl says he knows we're after him, it was mentioned in the news on the car radio.'

'Damn and Blast! He could be going anywhere, now! With his wife dead, he could try to disappear again. Make sure everyone's on their toes, will you?'

'Yes, sir.' He replaced the mike, turned to the Sergeant:

'What do you make of that?' Rimmer shrugged, as puzzled as his superior:

'Could we still be all wrong about this?'

'I don't see how. We can put him away for killing Hannah with no trouble at all, on what we've got now. So why should he pick up another kid, and treat her like royalty? Surely his intentions must have been to vent his perversion on her, like he did with Hannah – so why the sudden change of heart? It doesn't make any sense.'

'It doesn't, sir. Maybe we'll find out when we catch up with him.'

'I hope so, Doug. This case seems determined to throw back-handers at us at every opportunity. Anyway, I'm off – I'll see you in the office, later.'

'Right.' Rimmer turned back and re-entered the house; Russell got into the car and drove away.

He had got less than a mile from the house when the radio sprang into life again; he pulled over, reached out to answer it:

'Russell.'

'Sir – Cambridgeshire have just called to say they've got Andrews' car in sight. An Unmarked car is following him, on the A14, heading West.'

'West? This way?'

'That's right, sir. He could pick up the A1, mind, at Huntingdon.'

'Mm, right. Is he in a hurry?'

'Doesn't seem so, sir, they say he's doing a steady fifty-five.'

'That seems strange, if he knows we're on to him. I'm going to pick up D.S. Rimmer, and head out to meet them. We'll aim to pick them up at Thrapston – keep me informed of his movements as you get them, okay?'

'Yes, sir. I'll have traffic alert their cars, too, maybe have one of them join you.'

'Yes, that's fine. Russell out.'

He spun the car around, headed back to the house. There, he picked up the Sergeant, along with an eager P.C. Dorman for support, alerted by a call from the control room, and the three set off Eastwards out of the town. They cut across by minor roads, turning North onto the main road from Northampton to Kettering; there, they picked up the major cross-country route of the A14, and headed East. At his gesture, Rimmer picked up the radio microphone:

'Delta Control; Delta 131 – D.S. Rimmer.'

'Delta Control – what is it, Doug?'

'Hi Suzy – any news from Cambridgeshire about Andrews?'

'No – they're still following him, two cars now. Do you want them to stop him?'

Rimmer looked at his superior; Russell shook his head. The Sergeant spoke into the mike again:

'No – not yet. Just ask them to keep him in sight. We're on our way to Thrapston – keep us posted, okay?'

'Will do. Traffic have a car heading to join you at Thrapston, by the way. Delta out.'

Rimmer replaced the microphone:

'What's he doing, do you think?' Russell, his eye on the road, shook his head:

'I don't know, Doug. He doesn't seem to be running for it; I wonder if he's coming back home. Perhaps he thinks he's still in the clear, thinks he can talk his way out of trouble.'

'Yeah – I don't suppose he knows we've got the car. What are you planning to do?'

'Take my lead from him. If he carries on heading this way, we'll pick him up, follow him, see where he's going. We can stop him any time, if we think he's making a break for it. If he turns onto the A1, we'll have the Cambridgeshire boys pull him over before he gets too far, worry about what he's up to later.'

'He's on his own?' Russell glanced around, caught unawares by the question:

'I'm assuming he is, since he dropped the girl off – call in, see if the car following can see. We ought to make sure before we make our move.'

'Right.' He picked up the microphone once again:

'Delta Control – 131. Suzy, can you call Cambridgeshire for us?'

'Sure, Doug.'

'Can they see if Andrews is alone in the car?'

'I'll find out – hold on.'

A minute or so later, she came on the air again:

'They can't be sure, Doug, can't see with the car's roof up, back window's too small. And they say he's approaching the interchange at Huntingdon.'

'Can you patch them through to us direct?'

'Yeah, sure – hold on.' Another pause, then the radio crackled into life once more, Ackroyd's voice rattling from the speaker:

'Foxtrot 441 – Sergeant Rimmer?'

'Yeah, 441. What's happening over there?'

'Your man's just coming up to the interchange, sarge. We're a bit behind him, keeping our heads down. Bear with us a mo – he's – yes, he's taking the slip road, down towards Brampton and the A14 West. We're following. He could still go South on the A1, for London, of course.'

'Okay. We're close to the interchange at Burton Latimer – we can make Thrapston to pick him up if he heads this way.'

'Right – we'll let you know.'

Silence fell in the Jeep, as it continued at an easy eighty towards the East. After a lengthy pause, Russell spoke:

'If he carries on towards us, we'll pull off at Thrapston, wait for him. I want to know what he's playing at, Doug – I expect we'll be following him home, we can arrest him when he gets there. Makes it simple, doesn't it?'

'Yeah. What if he goes on, past Grancester?'

'Where's the County line, that way?'

'Just our side of Junction 19 on the M1, the M6/A14 interchange.'

'Hm. We'll stop him before he gets there, save complicating things. But I reckon he's coming home.'

The radio squawked again:

'Delta 131 – Foxtrot 441.' Rimmer grabbed the mike:

'Yeah, 441, go ahead.'

'Sarge – your man's stayed on the A14 Westbound. Do you want us to stick with him?'

'Please. Can you follow him as far as Thrapston, where we can take over?'

'Sure, no trouble. You'll be there before us?'

'Yes – let us know immediately if he speeds up, or anything, won't you?'

'Yeah, sure. 441 out.'

In the Jeep, the two detectives and their uniformed supporter rode on in silence towards their rendezvous. Fifteen miles away, Andrews cruised obliviously to meet them, still unaware of the car discretely tailing him, mildly surprised that he had seen no police cars on the motorway or elsewhere, but grateful for the fact none-the-less. He would drive to Naseby reservoir, try to clear his head, think things through in the fresh air, make his decisions about the future....

CHAPTER THIRTY-FIVE

Near the old market town of Thrapston, the major East-West highway of the A14 meets the North-bound A45. Just off the interchange itself, hidden from the main road, stood a dark green Jeep Cherokee, with a fully marked police car right behind it; a casual observer might assume that the Jeep's occupants had been stopped for some minor traffic infringement.

In fact, the two men inside were listening with rapt attention to a running commentary being relayed to them from the Cambridgeshire force's unmarked car, still cruising at a steady speed some distance behind the red Mercedes convertible which was the focus for everyone's interest. The second tailing car had already peeled off as they neared the county line. As Sergeant Ackroyd warned his listeners that the pursuit was rapidly approaching, the Jeep began to inch forward, gathering speed down the on-ramp as the Mercedes appeared on the dual carriageway alongside. It pulled into the nearside lane a hundred yards or so behind, settling to a steady speed, invited by a flash of the headlights from a dark-coloured Omega which promptly accelerated, pulling out to overtake both vehicles. A discrete wave from the uniformed sergeant in the passenger seat, and it was past.

Moments later, the radio sprang into life again:

'Delta 131 – he's all yours! I got a look as we went past – your man *is* alone in the car.'

'Thank you, 441. We'll deal with him now. Thanks for all your help.'

'Don't mention it! 441 out.'

The Cambridgeshire car disappeared into the distance, headed for the next interchange in order to be able to turn for home. Mercedes and Jeep continued their steady progress; the marked Northamptonshire patrol car travelling a further half-mile behind its unmarked compatriot in case it was needed.

To get back to Grancester, Russell anticipated that his quarry would turn from the motorway at Kettering, following the route they had taken earlier in the opposite direction. He was surprised, therefore, when Andrews ignored the junction, continuing along the A14 without so much as a change of speed. Unsure of the man's intentions now, Russell decided to continue the low-profile pursuit.

Eight miles on, he also ignored the next Southward junction, at Kelmarsh. Only the interchange with the Welford road now remained between the trio of cruising cars and the Western border of the County. After a quick discussion, Russell and his deputy agreed to go on, only stopping the Mercedes if he carried on past that point. But then, the situation was changed unexpectedly for them.

Another car of the Traffic Division, routinely patrolling this stretch of the main road, came past the tail of the convoy. Travelling at around seventy-five past a gaggle of other vehicles, its driver had failed to notice the other Traffic car in the slow lane; as it passed the Jeep, Rimmer grabbed the microphone to try to hold it back before Andrews saw it. But he was too late.

In the Mercedes, Andrews had seen the group of cars coming up behind. Suddenly realising the leading vehicle was a police car, he panicked, and accelerated away, pulling into the middle lane to pass a slow box-van in front of him. As he wound the Mercedes up to near a hundred miles an hour, the newly-arrived Traffic car set off in pursuit, leaving Russell and his back-up no option but to follow suit. A frantic exchange of radio messages at last had the second Traffic car drop back, to sit with the Jeep as a second support crew for what now had to be a stop and arrest situation.

Traffic on the road was quite light; the high-speed chase quickly covered the distance to the last interchange, its participants uninterested in the historical importance of the area as they swept along the new road between the village of Naseby and its famous civil-war battlefield. At the junction, Russell and his fellow drivers were almost caught off-guard when the Mercedes pulled to the left and took the off-ramp up to the roundabout. They were nearly fooled again when, by the exit onto the Southbound A-road, it suddenly braked hard, and turned onto an access track which led into a land-fill site beside the road.

Dust billowing from its tyres, the red convertible dropped down the track, which turned to run almost alongside the dual carriageway they had just left. It forked; rather than turn into the land-fill site, the car carried straight on, beside the fencing along the motorway. The surface of the track was pitted and uneven; the car leapt and bounded in the pot-holes, dust flying along with water from some deeper, undried puddles. The track went on, rising gradually until they were above the level of the main road alongside, easing slowly farther away from it until a narrow field separated the two. Glimpses of water flashed between the trees to their right.

Russell kept the bouncing, leaping rear of the Mercedes in sight through the dust-cloud as best he could. The Jeep was better suited to this kind of driving, but it still took all his concentration to stay safely on the track; the two Traffic cars behind were making heavy weather of the job, rearing and bucking over the ruts and pot-holes. Andrews almost caught him napping again – the track went straight on, but the Mercedes braked savagely, swung hard right through a gate, the rear sliding around so that the wing hit and crumpled against the gate-post. But he was through, onto a small patch of open ground. Swinging right again, he headed for a fence, with a steel gate set into it; beyond, the pursuers could see the glint of water again.

The Mercedes hit the gate full-on; the padlock flew into the air as it slammed back, the car's bumper taking the worst of the impact although glass sprayed from the headlights. Beyond lay the headbank of the reservoir; Andrews drove on, along the flat grassy surface, the sandstone copings at the top of the bank alongside the left-hand wheels of his car. As the Jeep hurtled through the gate in pursuit, the convertible suddenly turned slightly to the right, almost going down the dry side of the artificial bank before swinging viciously the opposite way. The rear wheels scrabbled for grip on the slick grass; then they bit. Horrified, Russell brought the Jeep to a skidding halt as the car hit the coping stones, bounced up, and launched itself into the air. The rear tyres hit the stones; carried by its momentum, the Mercedes flew in a graceful curve some forty yards over the water before gravity decided to take a hand; it dipped, front-first – spray exploded into the air as it hit, still travelling forward at some speed.

Before the Jeep had come to rest, before the Mercedes had begun to settle deeper into the water of Naseby Reservoir, Andrew Dorman had thrown open the back door and leapt out. Kicking off his boots at the same time as he cast off his uniform jacket, he ran to the water's edge and dived. Stroking hard and swiftly, he reached the car just as it sank out of sight, had to back off to avoid being drawn down in its undertow. He let it settle for a few seconds, and then dived after it.

On the bank, Rimmer had begun to throw off his own jacket, but a traffic officer from the first back-up car stopped him:

'Leave it to me – I've got medals for life-saving!' He threw his coat into the car, tore off his boots and followed the young constable into the water.

Out in the reservoir, Andrew had had to return to the surface, frustrated in his search for the sunken car. The older officer joined him, he panted:

'I can't see it – there's too much shit been stirred up!'

'Let me try!' The traffic cop dived down. As the constable had told him, the sinking car had stirred up a lot of silt from the bottom of the reservoir; he was met by thick clouds of it, swirling and twisting, obscuring his view. He too had to give up, return to the surface to breathe. He nodded to the younger man, who once again dived.

Casting around in the gloom, just before he had to give up, Andrew caught a glimpse of brightness deep down, light reflecting from the trim around the Mercedes' rear lights. He came up for air, told the other what he'd seen; they rested for a few seconds, then dived together. They found the car, made their way to it, managed between them to get the driver's door open before, their lungs about to burst, they again had to surface for air. Another quick rest, and down again – both had seen the well-dressed man, still strapped into his seatbelt in the driving seat. This time, working together, they released the belt, dragged him out and up to the surface. A quick wave to the men waiting on the bank, and they set off to get back to the shore, supporting the limp figure between them.

Many hands reached to help, dragging the unconscious body over the copings and onto the grass. Two of the traffic officers set about their resuscitation techniques as Russell congratulated Dorman and his companion on their efforts, led them to the Jeep and sat them inside, the heater going full-blast to dry them out.

'Paramedics are on their way, sir.' Rimmer had been busy on the radio; Russell nodded his thanks, too tense to reply verbally, watching the uniformed officers at work on the prone body between them.

The ambulance took some time to arrive, from the nearest town. It skated to a halt beside one of the traffic cars; the two paramedics jumped down and rushed over, the policemen standing back to let the experts take over. Inspector and Sergeant could do nothing but stand and watch as they tried to revive the man on the ground; no-one spoke. After ten minutes of intense effort, their shoulders slumped as they gave up and stood away from the body; one turned to the two detectives:

'I'm sorry – we can't do anything here. How long was he in the water?'

'Probably around five minutes, maybe longer.' Russell replied. The paramedic shook his head, looking at the traffic cops:

'I'm sure you did everything you could. He was almost certainly beyond help by the time you could start on him. We'll take him to hospital, they'll have to confirm the death – Kettering'll be quickest. Do you want to follow us?' he asked the Inspector.

'Okay.' Russell turned to the traffic policemen: 'Can you fellows get your colleague back somewhere dry and warm – and could you get my constable to Grancester, where he can dry out?' One of the men, wearing Sergeant's stripes, replied:

'Of course, sir. Price is my partner, I'll get him back to Mereway HQ – Jackman and Stevens here will take your man home.'

'Thank you. D.S. Rimmer and I will go with Andrews to Kettering. Thank you for your support.'

'You're welcome, sir – I'm sorry if we spooked your man, I didn't realise what we'd run into.' Russell sighed, shrugged:

'It's all right, Sergeant. These things happen.'

The traffic Sergeant nodded, and walked to his car, collecting his dripping colleague from the Jeep on his way. The detectives returned to the car, told Andrew Dorman that the other traffic team would take him home; he got out, turned to Russell:

'I'm sorry sir – if we'd got him out a bit sooner…'

'Don't worry, Andrew,' Russell interrupted his apology, 'you did a great job, you should be proud of yourself. Now go on home and get dried out. I'll see you tomorrow.'

'Right, sir. Thank you.' He turned away, went to the waiting car and climbed in.

The two traffic cars drove off; the paramedics had lifted

Andrews' body onto a stretcher and were loading it into the ambulance. They closed the doors; the driver spoke to Russell:

'Ready, sir?'

'When you are.'

'Okay.' He climbed into the driving seat, his companion joining him; the two detectives got into the Jeep, and followed the ambulance away from the scene.

CHAPTER THIRTY-SIX

At Kettering General Hospital, examination quickly confirmed Andrews as Dead on Arrival. His body was taken to the mortuary; Russell and his deputy strolled out into the Spring sunshine.

'What now, sir?' The Sergeant asked. Russell ran a hand through his hair:

'I'm really not sure, Doug. I haven't caught up with events yet. We can get the fingerprints, the D.N.A., prove once and for all that it was Andrews who killed Hannah. That's that case closed. But I want to know what the blazes happened since he picked up that other girl yesterday.'

'Me too. But if she really is okay, if he didn't do anything to her, that's got to be good, hasn't it?'

'Oh God, of course! I thought I was facing sackcloth and ashes for the rest of my life, leaving him free long enough to rape another kid, kill her too, maybe. I *should* have pulled him in sooner, just in case – but if she hasn't been harmed, no-one's more pleased about it than me. But – it doesn't make sense, does it? A history of sexual assaults on little girls, albeit a long time ago – then Hannah – then he grabs another girl, but he doesn't so much as touch her, takes her all the way to Cambridge, to her father…? Why?'

'Goodness knows.'

'Yeah!' He glanced at his watch: 'Good Lord – it's only half past three! Feels like it should be about six. Come on, let's go to Cambridge, talk to the kid ourselves.'

'Right you are, sir.'

* * *

A little more than an hour later, they were in Elmfield Close, Cherry Hinton. As they had left Kettering, Russell had used the Jeep's radio to arrange, through the Cambridgeshire force, for them to visit Tran Quoc Hsung and speak to his daughter. He had also conferred with Wilson – the Superintendent had agreed that they should withhold the story of Andrews' drowning from the media, while they attempted to trace any relatives; and he had offered to go to Hannah's family and bring them up to date with developments, leaving the Inspector free to try to tie up the loose ends in Cambridge.

Rimmer knocked at the door; it was opened to them by Tran:

'Hello – you must be the officers from Grancester. Please come in.' He stepped back to allow them to enter.

'Mr Hsung? I'm Detective-Inspector Russell, this is my assistant, Sergeant Rimmer.' Each shook hands with the small Oriental man who smiled his welcome.

'Come on through – Kim is in the lounge, they're waiting for us.' Russell laid a hand on the man's shoulder, delaying him:

'Before we go in, Mr Hsung – how much does your daughter know of what's been going on? Come to that, how much do you know?' The Vietnamese smiled again:

'I suspect there is much we don't know, Inspector! Two policemen came here yesterday, at lunchtime, to tell us that Kim had had a row with her mother, and had run away. And they told us that Martha had fallen down the stairs, that she was dead – they were trying to find Kim, you see. We hadn't heard from her – this kind of thing has happened before – Martha had become... difficult to live with. She used to like a drink when we were still married; after I left, that got worse and worse – I often wondered how Kim coped with her. They would row sometimes – Kim

275

would run away, go to see her friends, but she would go back home when she was ready. So you see, we didn't really think anything of it, it was only because Martha had died that we were keen to find her. It was only today, when they told us that they thought she was with that man, the one you suspected might have killed the other little girl, that we were really worried about her.'

'She knows her mother is dead, sir?'

'She does – but I haven't told her about the man she was with. She thinks of him as a friend; and she has enough to cope with, I think. She knows the police were looking for him, but not why.'

'All right. I need to talk to her; it's important that we find out what happened to her since yesterday, you understand. It's bound to make her curious, that we want to know all about him – would you object if I were to tell her what we know?'

Tran hesitated, then replied: 'I suppose she will have to know; and it would be better, perhaps, if you tell her before she hears it on the news or in the papers. But please, be gentle with her?' Russell smiled:

'I have a son her age – and a younger daughter! I'll try not to upset her too much.' The Vietnamese nodded:

'Okay – come on through, then.'

He led the way into the lounge. In the bright, airy room, he introduced the policemen to his wife, who stood up to shake their hands; Kim rose to her feet as well, stood demurely waiting until her father introduced her, then stepped forward to greet the detectives in her turn. The two boys were once again playing quietly in the dining room. Russell was impressed by the girl's quiet composure as much as by her juvenile beauty, and captivated by the warmth of her deep blue eyes. He took both of her hands in his own:

'Kim – I'm so very sorry about your mother.' The child smiled, the sorrow showing through:

'Thank you, Inspector. It's…probably for the best, really. She didn't enjoy life much – perhaps she's happier, now.' He nodded sympathetically, held her eyes for a moment. Then he asked:

'I want to talk to you about what happened since you left home yesterday – do you feel up to it?' She nodded:

'Yes, I don't mind. It's about Uncle Mac – Mr Andrews, rather – isn't it?'

'It is, Kim.'

'Okay. I know you're looking for him – what's it all about?'

'It's a long story – I'll tell you, but can you tell me all about him, first? How you came to meet him, what you did, why he drove you here?'

The girl nodded again, led him by the hand to the settee, sat beside him. Rimmer concealed his amusement – the boss had clearly scored another hit with this little girl! She began to talk, describing how she had run away after her mother's drunken outburst, made her way unwittingly to the riverside, and met the equally distressed man on the bench there. She told of their shared lunch, the shopping, the return to his house, his promise to take her to see her father the next day; of their evening together, and the drive to Cambridge in the morning sunlight. Russell listened carefully, interposing an occasional question; when she finished, he sat back in the settee:

'Thank you, Kim. That's fine – but I have to ask you some questions. They might seem…strange – I'll explain in a minute.' She nodded:

'Okay – what do you want to know?'

'While you were with Mr Andrews, he didn't ask you to do anything you didn't want to, anything you might have thought was…rude, maybe?' The girl shook her head, clearly puzzled:

'No – nothing.'

'He didn't try to touch you, in a way…you didn't like?'

'Never.' Russell nodded slowly. He felt he should explain; the curiosity on her face was almost funny in its intensity. He thought, trying to put together an explanation that wouldn't shock her too much; as he opened his mouth to speak, she put up her hand to stop him:

'I know what it's all about. It's that other little girl, isn't it? The one who was killed?' Her eyes were wide with horrified realisation: 'You were on the television, talking about her, weren't you? You're after the man who killed her, and you think it was him? You're wrong – it *can't* have been!' He looked away, not sure how to tell her of the certainty of the man's guilt. She went on:

'It couldn't have been him! He's…kind, and generous, and…he helped me, when I needed someone! He couldn't have done anything as horrible as that!'

Russell raised his eyes to meet the girl's:

'I'm so sorry, Kim. I hate having to tell you this – but I'd rather tell you myself, than have you see it on the television news later:' He drew a deep breath, plunged on: 'There isn't any doubt about it, I'm afraid. The man who looked after you, brought you here today, was the same one who attacked little Hannah just a couple of weeks ago. There is no possible doubt' he repeated. She gazed at him, her eyes round with horror, shaking her head slowly. But, just as slowly, the realisation was sinking in. This policeman seemed so certain – and maybe, just maybe – the funny gleam in Uncle Mac's eyes, once or twice, when she'd caught him looking at her, especially after her bath when she was wearing nothing but his wife's robe…. But:

'If he…did all that, to her – *why* not me, too?' Her voice was trembling as the closeness of her brush with terror began dawn upon her.

'I don't know, Kim. I can't explain it – I'm just so thankful for it, so very pleased that you're all right, that you came to no harm.' From across the room, Rimmer interjected:

'Sir? I wonder – his wife had just died; I wonder if Kim somehow reminded him of her? Was that why he couldn't hurt her?' Russell looked up:

'Possible, I suppose;' he turned back to the child: 'He asked you to call him Uncle Mac?' She smiled, shook her head:

'No! He wanted me to call him Mac, it was me that insisted on the Uncle – it seemed more proper, 'cos he's so much older than me.' Russell nodded:

'The Sergeant might be right. Mac was his wife's name for him. And she was tall and blond, like you.' It occurred to him that she still didn't know of the man's fate; he braced himself to tell her:

'Kim – there's something else I must tell you. Mr Andrews has...had an accident, after he left here....' Her smile faded, her eyes widening in anticipation of what was to come:

'Is he...?' Her voice was no more than a whisper. Russell shook his head:

'I'm sorry, Kim. He...crashed the car; he was killed in the crash.' She gazed at him for a moment, eyes round, mouth open in shocked understanding. As her face crumpled into sorrow, he gathered her into his arms, let her weep into his shoulder for the man she had known only as a friend. Tran and Liu stood arm in arm, looking down in sympathy at their daughter crying in the policeman's embrace; even the amusement that his superior's empathy with young children kindled in the Sergeant was shadowed by the girl's grief.

After a few minutes, she raised her head, smiled at the Inspector:

'I'm sorry – I've made your suit all wet.' She brushed at the dampness of his lapel with one hand.

'That's all right, Kim. I'm sorry to bring you so much sad news.' She nodded:

'It was better to hear it from you. It would have been awful to just see it on the news – thank you for coming to tell me.' She sat back; Russell put one hand over hers as they lay in her lap:

'You'll be all right?' She nodded again.

'Don't worry, Mr Russell, we'll look after her now.' Tran's voice drew their attention: 'She's where she belongs, with us, with her family. There's nothing for her to worry about, any more.'

The Inspector smiled up at the man, nodded his understanding. He stood up, beckoned to his deputy; Tran shook their hands once more, Liu led the way to the front door. Russell turned to give the girl a last smile as he left the room.

* * *

It was gone seven o'clock when Russell got home that night. As he let himself in, Daniel came bounding out of the living room to meet him:

'Hello, Dad!' The eager expression on the boy's face heralded something special in the way of news.

'Hi, Dan – how did you get on?'

'Fourth!' Russell had guessed correctly.

'In the semis?' The boy grinned from ear to ear:

'No!' His voice was scornful: 'In the *final!*'

'The final? Well done! That's as good as I'd have done, I expect. How'd you get on with the *Dragon?*'

'Fine! She was no trouble at all.'

'Ah – I can see I'm going to have to let you sail her more often. I suppose this means I'm going to have to get myself a new yacht, then?'

'Yeah! I reckon I'll do even better, next time!' Russell laughed, put his arm around his son's shoulders, led him back into the living room. As they sat down, one in each of the armchairs, Tracy got up. She bent to kiss her husband on the cheek, then asked:

'Have you eaten today, David?' He grinned, shook his head:

'Haven't had time!'

'Okay – I'll go and rustle you up something – we had dinner a while ago. Roast Beef, beans, carrots, potatoes? I'll microwave them for you, all right?'

'Fine – thanks, love. Where's Sarah?'

'Playing in her room. I think her brother's swollen head

got too much for her!'

'Huh! I've hardly said a word since we got home, Mum!'

'Yes, right!' Her voice was full of irony as she departed for the kitchen. Daniel was gazing at his father:

'What happened, Dad, after you had to leave the lakes?' Russell ran his hand through his hair, smiled at the boy:

'Things got pretty chaotic, Dan.'

'Was it…all to do with Hannah?'

'Yeah. The man who killed her – he's dead, too. We – Mr Rimmer and I – were following him, but he spotted us, made a run for it, so we had to go after him…'

'You had a real live car chase?' Daniel interrupted; his father laughed:

'I suppose we did, at that! He drove off the road, then crashed into a reservoir. His car sank; Andrew Dorman – you remember him, he was the policeman up at the quarry, last year - he got him out, but it was too late.'

'Do you think he…did it *deliberately?*' Russell sighed, forced by his son's question to face squarely a thought he'd pushed to one side ever since the event:

'I think perhaps he did, Dan. Maybe he couldn't face what he'd done, maybe…oh, I don't know!'

There was a pause, while the boy took this all in; then he looked up, understanding for his father's deflated mood in his eyes:

'I'm sorry, Dad. But – he got what he deserved, really, didn't he?'

'I guess he did, Daniel. And I suppose he's saved us all the trouble and expense of a trial; and keeping him in prison for the rest of his life!'

CHAPTER THIRTY-SEVEN

Easter fell late that year. By the beginning of Holy Week, in the middle of April, the investigation into Hannah Buckland's abduction and murder had been largely laid to rest in the police archives.

It came as no surprise to anyone involved that fingerprint and D.N.A. samples taken from the body of George Andrews confirmed both his previous identity as Malcolm Mathers, and his guilt as the child's killer. He and Sheila were cremated together after a simple ceremony at Northampton Crematorium – the small group of mourners comprised mainly people who had known them through their business. Sheila's younger sister and her husband drove up from Brighton, and Jack Mathers, a distant cousin, came all the way from Cornwall. David Russell was there; Andrew Dorman and Jimmy Price, the two officers who had fought to save the man's life by the reservoir, stood at the back of the chapel in full uniform.

Hannah Buckland herself had been laid to rest as well, in the cemetery of the old parish church in Elwood village. It seemed that the entire parish had turned out to say goodbye to the popular, lively child they had known, however distantly, together with family and friends from around the county. Most of her class from the village school were there, with their teacher and the headmistress; Detective-Superintendent Wilson made a suitably solemn representative of the police hierarchy. Russell and Rimmer also attended, with the Inspector's son – he had been surprised and touched when Daniel asked if he could come, thinking that funerals were hardly the kind of event for a twelve-year-old to want to go to. Smartly dressed in his school uniform, he waited patiently beside his father after the burial for the opportunity to offer their condolences to the family.

At last they came face to face – Russell shook hands with Brian and Harriet, expressing his sympathy for their sorrow, and introduced his son. Daniel looked up at the couple, noting Brian's drawn features, the dullness of his blue eyes, and the tear-stains on Harriet's cheeks – in his simple, direct manner he told them how sad he felt for them. As Brian thanked him for coming, he nodded, and turned to the boy standing encircled in his father's arm:

'Josh?' The boy nodded. Daniel went on:

'I've got a little sister, too. I know…how I'd feel, if this had happened to her. I'm so sorry….'

The dark grey eyes blinked rapidly, fighting back tears, as he replied in a constricted whisper:

'Thank you, Daniel – it's kind of you to be here.' Awkwardly, he put out his hand; the other boy grasped it, held it, smiling in sympathy and encouragement. Josh smiled back; the two parted, Russell slipping his own arm around his son's shoulders and guiding him towards their car.

Next to approach the Bucklands were Len and Rachel Halifax, with their daughters. While her parents and older sister spoke quietly with Brian and Harriet, Annabel smiled sadly at the twelve-year-old. Neither spoke at first; then Annabel asked:

'Josh? Would you like to come and visit us, sometime?'

'At your farm, you mean?'

'That's right.' The boy smiled:

'I'd like that. It'd be nice to…get away – you know?' The girl's pleasure at his acceptance of her offer was evident:

'Good! We'll fix it with our parents, right?'

'Yeah – thanks.' A slightly awkward silence fell for a moment; then Annabel began:

'Josh – I'm so sorry, about Hannah – I…' she paused, knowing what she wanted to say but finding it difficult to put into words. She drew a breath, plunged on: 'I can never be your sister – but I'd like to be your friend, if I can…' she trailed off, seeing the tears welling up in the boy's expressive eyes, spilling down his cheeks. He suddenly smiled through his sorrow:

'I've got this far today without starting to cry – now look what you've done!' He laughed: 'Oh well – I've cried for Hannah lots of times; I guess once more won't hurt.'

Annabel reached out to him with both hands; he took them in his, and the next thing either of them new they were holding each other, each crying into the other's shoulder.

* * *

On Maundy Thursday, David Russell sat in his office entering a report onto the computer. A tentative knock sounded at the door; he looked up as P.C. Andrew Dorman looked in:

'Come in, Andrew – what can I do for you?'

'Have you got a moment, sir?'

'Sure! I could do with a rest from this damned paperwork. Sit down – what's on your mind?'

'Well – first, I wanted to thank you for putting me up for the commendation, sir – I mean, I only did what was necessary, it wasn't anything really special.'

'Nonsense! You risked your own life, diving into that reservoir. You deserve recognition for that. I hope they approve it.'

'Thank you, sir. Sir?'

'Yes?'

'I've been thinking – about asking to transfer into C.I.D. Do you think I should – or should I wait a bit longer?'

Russell sat back, smiling at the younger man opposite, stretching his arms and linking his hands behind his head. He thought for a while, then replied:

'If that's what you want to do, where you want to be within the force, then it won't hurt to let that be known. If you apply now, I think they'll probably turn you down – you've hardly been in the job a year, after all, they'll probably say you need a bit more experience yet, as a regular constable. But applying will register your future intentions, so to speak, even if they do.'

'You think I should, then, sir? Would I be suited for C.I.D., do you think?'

'I'm sure of it!' Russell laughed: 'If you get in, I'd like you on my team. You're keen, and you think on your feet. Picking up on those kids when we were going over Olsen's house showed that. Yes, I think you'll be a good detective.'

'Thank you, sir!' The blue eyes lit up with pleasure.

'One thing, Andrew:'

'Yes, sir?'

'If you get an interview, don't make an issue of your brother's death. I wouldn't even mention it – if they get the idea that you might be pursuing some kind of personal vendetta against criminals, it'll go against you.'

'Yes – I understand. Thank you, sir.'

'And for what it's worth, I'll back your application, if you do decide to go ahead, now or in the future.'

'Thanks again, sir!' The young man got to his feet: 'Thank you for your advice.'

'Any time! Now go and do something useful.' Russell's grin dismissed the constable, who departed, grinning all over his own face.

A minute or so later, D.S. Rimmer looked around the office door:

'What's young Dorman looking so chuffed about, boss?' Russell laughed:

'He's talking about applying for C.I.D.'

'Good! He's a bright kid, he'll do well.'

'Kid? How old are *you*, Doug?'

'Thirty Three, sir.' The Sergeant sounded agrieved.

'Hnh! Go on, bugger off, let me finish this bloody report!'

EPILOGUE

It was the Thursday after Easter. Two youngsters rode across the fields, away from Pury Home farm, in the brightness of a Spring afternoon: Josh Buckland sat with growing confidence in the saddle on the back of Annabel's docile black pony, Marmaduke – the girl was mounted proudly upon her sister's elegant bay.

Energetic persuasion by both children had achieved its goal when Brian and Harriet and accepted the invitation to visit the Halifax home on Easter Monday – it had taken a further effort, on the day, to get them to agree to their son staying over for a few days. His parents hadn't had that choice available to them, even though the offer had been made – as the new sole proprietor of Barfield Antiques, Brian had had to return home to run his business.

The two children crested a rise in the ground, found themselves faced with a wide panoramic view of the rolling, open countryside of South Northamptonshire, the fields softly green, the woodland darkly shaded in the warm sunshine, the distant horizon hazily blue as it stretched away, seemingly forever. Time, too, seemed to stretch endlessly before them, a future holding who knew what kind of thrills and adventures; the past, with its sorrows, lay behind them, not forgotten, but at least sinking into a kind of perspective as life carried them ever onward, leaving tragedy in their wake.

Annabel Halifax glanced around at her companion:

'Do you think – would Hannah have liked it, out here?' the

boy looked around, smiling sadly, turned his eyes back to the far horizon, murmured:

'Oh, yes!' After a brief silence, he went on, still gazing into the distance, almost talking to himself:

'She's here, Annie – can't you tell? She's here with me – with us. She always will be.' He looked round; their hands reached out, clasped. They smiled at each other, turned back to the view before them, sat silently happy in each other's company, hand in hand, for an eternity.